Sins of the Night

Sins of the Night

DEVYN QUINN

APHRODISIA

KENSINGTON BOOKS

http://www.kensingtonbooks.com

APHRODISIA are published by

Kensington Publishing Corp.
850 Third Avenue
New York, NY 10022

Copyright © 2008 by Devyn Quinn

All Kensington Titles, Imprints, and Distributed Lines are avaliable at special quantity discounts for bulk purchases for sales promotions, premiums, fund-raising, and educational or institutional use.

Special book excerpts or customized printings can also be created to fit specific needs. For details, write or phone the office of the Kensington special sales manager: Kensington Publishing Corp., 850 Third Avenue, New York, NY 10022, attn: Special Sales Department, Phone: 1-800-221-2647.

Aphrodisia and the A logo U.S, Pat. & TM Off.

ISBN-13: 978-0-7582-2018-9
ISBN-10: 0-7582-2018-9

First Kensington Trade Paperback Printing: April 2008

10 9 8 7 6 5 4 3 2 1

Printed in the United States of America

To Kate Douglas, who continually keeps me amazed by (and in awe of) her wonderful talent. I am so very lucky to have such a dear friend to inspire me—and to kick my tail when I get lazy.

Acknowledgments

This book wouldn't have come about without the support of the two wonderful ladies who've helped build my career: Roberta Brown, my agent, and Hilary Sares, my editor. Without these two behind me, there would be no Devyn Quinn.

A lot of hugs and kisses also go to my Wild & Wicked cohorts. You girls are my support system and I thank all of you for being such terrific friends.

Visit the Wild & Wicked ladies online—www.wildauthors.com

Prologue

Warwickshire, England—1906

Adrien Roth wasn't sure what awakened him. Perhaps it was the sinking of the sun, the gradual darkening of the chamber already shrouded in shadows by heavy velvet drapes drawn across the windows.

Or perhaps it was dread rousing him from his restless sleep, causing him to twist his wrists against the ropes binding them to the headboard. He cursed the unyielding restraints. No matter how much he writhed, he simply could not free his arms. The skin under the ropes was badly chafed and raw. Struggling only delivered more pain. He ignored it, his hands balling into tight fists to fight the ropes anew.

Helplessness consumed him. A wild-voiced cry echoed through his head.

They're coming. . . .

His eyes slipped shut. Silence hung, the lack of sound even more disturbing than a scream or the sound of ominous footfalls on the hardwood floors. His heart hammered in his chest, beating against his ribs with a fury threatening to steal his breath away. He gasped, running his parched tongue over dry, cracked lips.

Opening his eyes, he focused on the dim light behind the drapes as though it were a beacon, the only source of illumination in the world. He silently prayed to God without ceasing. Without allowing himself to think of what was to come, or of how it would end, he vehemently cursed the source of his misery. When more thoughts of torture invaded his mind, his gaze clouded over and his lower jaw trembled. The wait was excruciating.

Minutes dragged like hours. All hope faded with the last precious rays of day. As the wing of night spread over the land, misery and horror were given fresh birth. Fear became more intense.

He did not *hear* them, but *felt* them, the way one would become aware of a spider crawling across one's skin.

His eyes widened when the door swung open and two figures, a man and a woman, entered silently. He knew them both. The man was Devon, Lord Carnavorn, seventh Earl of Hammerston. Tall, well over six feet, his features were strong and commanding; piercing gray eyes, sensual but cruel mouth, tousled brown hair. The outfit of dove gray trousers, white silk shirt, and silk vest of a lighter gray well fitted his muscular frame.

The woman . . . Oh, blessed virgin and tainted whore. She was his angel and his demon, savior and tormentor; appropriately named, for she would consent to lie beneath no man.
Lilith.

Her name was a whisper on the lips of pious men, the screech of a night owl, the shimmering frost on the accursed north wind. In one slender hand she carried a gold-gilt candelabrum. The flame guttered as she walked. She was a lovely creature to behold through the wavering light. Clad in a white silk dressing gown, the sheer material whispered around her legs. Open at the neck, a glimpse of her sumptuous breasts hinted of untold delights. Black hair cascaded around her shoulders, falling nearly to her waist. Silver-flecked crystal blue eyes, a pert nose, and a pouting little bow of a mouth decorated her oval face. Beyond her beauty was a strange hardness—a hatred lingering in the depths of her eyes and the cruel set of her mouth.

Devon Carnavorn's probing stare raked Adrien's naked form. "I hope you're ready for the coming evening. We have something special in store for you this night." His accented voice was smooth, untroubled, as if all his guests were usually trussed up like a Christmas turkey ready for roasting.

Adrien gave a final feeble tug, wishing the ties would magically dissolve. There was, however, no hope of rescue, and he knew it.

He was afraid, but not for his life. Life was temporary, something he'd been prepared from childhood to sacrifice in the name of the hunt for the creatures inhabiting the night, stalking the weaker human prey. Life was fleeting, easier lost than kept. But what of his immortal soul? No amount of preparation or prayer could sustain a man when eternal damnation beckoned. All he had left was his faith in God and the church. Through the days, he'd prayed when conscious, dreamt that he prayed when unconscious, his time spent in restless sleep refusing to let him find solace or peace.

The beginning of a prayer slipped from his lips. "Our Father, who art in heaven, hallowed be thy name," he said, attempting to wrap himself in the words as if they were a shield. "Thy kingdom come. Thy will be done, on earth as it is in heaven—"

Carnavorn angrily recoiled from the words. A look of scorn colored his face. "Your prayers will not be answered! Your God does not exist here!" Hands fisted in anger, Carnavorn temporarily silenced Adrien with the venom in his voice. "I know the old prayers as well as you do. They are meaningless. Nothing."

"You mock the words of my faith, demon!" Adrien spat back.

Dark brows dropped into a frown. "They say the devil can quote scripture for his own purposes," Carnavorn countered icily. "That itself is true enough. I certainly have one that perfectly fits our, ah, situation. Something you may recognize, about an eye for an eye and a tooth for a tooth."

A shiver clawed its way up Adrien's spine. His guts turned to liquid. "If you're going to kill me, do it. I've no fear of death." How many days had he been held captive? He wasn't sure. He only knew that he was growing weaker, resistance fading each and every time the demonic pair descended.

Carnavorn laughed, mouth curling up in a half smile of disdain. "Kill you? Death is too good for you, *Amhais*. As the shadow-stalkers have hunted us, so must we of the Kynn return the favor." He turned to the woman. "Are you ready, my dear?"

An eager smile crossed Lilith's red lips, showing a flash of white teeth. "I have a special surprise for you." Her voice was a combination of warm honey on sharp gravel, throaty and sensuous. She set the candelabra aside.

Adrien shook his head. Hunger, exhaustion, and his weakening body were all making a play on his senses. The faces of those he'd slain drifted to the front of his mind. Their corpses rose to grasp at his legs, tug him down into the depths of an unhallowed grave.

He wanted to cry out, deny this evil in the name of all that was holy. Instead, only feeble words escaped his lips. "No . . . please . . . not again . . ." To beg was demeaning, but he had no more to give.

Carnavorn stepped behind Lilith. Hands on her slender

hips, he maneuvered her to the bed. Reaching in front of her, he untied the sash of her gown and slid it off her shoulders. Underneath, she was completely naked. Her figure was well arranged: full breasts, slender waist, flat belly, and legs that went on endlessly. Beautiful and feminine, hers was a body made to entice, tease, and please. A thin silver chain hung around her neck; a pendant nestled in the hollow between her breasts. Of Celtic origins, the design was that of a circle interwoven with three sharp-edged eyelets that formed a triangle around the circle.

Carnavorn's hands lifted, his fingertips grazing her temples. "Beautiful, is she not?" His fingers continued their trek, tracing the contours of her high cheekbones, the lines of her jaw, down her neck to the hollow of her throat. Eyelids lowering, she tipped her head to one side.

"We have a gift to share with you, Adrien." Carnavorn's head dipped, nuzzling the soft curve of Lilith's neck. His hands found her breasts, cupping their weight. She made a soft sound; half gasp, half moan.

"I don't want your damnation." Adrien's sputtered words were strained.

Devon Carnavorn's gray eyes narrowed, hard and flinty. "I don't recall that you were given a choice. Did you show Ariel any mercy when you put that stake through her heart? She was everything to me, and you took her away with the darkness of your hate and prejudice against our kind. There are truly more things in heaven and on earth than humankind will ever be able to understand. Your mind is too small to comprehend that. But your eyes will be opened, and then you shall see all."

Adrien fought his bonds. "I sent her back to the devil that spawned her. Just as I will send you to hell right after her if I ever have that chance!"

Carnavorn only laughed. His hands found and teased Lilith's nipples, giving them renewed erectness. "I won't let you go, Adrien. You're going to pay for what you did, not once, but again and again and again. You've only gotten a glimpse of what we really are."

He ran his palms over Lilith's hips, then her belly. A low moan escaped her throat. She hovered in a state of sexual arousal, the air around her scented from the sizzling heat of raw desire. His hand found the tender slit between her legs, that velvet treasure every woman possessed. Delving past the soft curls of her Venus mound, he stroked her clit.

Carnavorn dipped one finger inside her depths. He brought it to Lilith's mouth, tracing her lips with honeyed nectar. Her moist tongue snaked out to savor her juices. "You want to taste her." He grinned, feral and unpleasant. "Admit you are as weak as the next man and that lust is ablaze in your heart."

"No—"

Lilith looked at him from under a fall of long lashes. "But it is, my darling." Her gaze traced his nude body, settling on his flaccid penis. "How well I know." Smiling, she began to finger her silver charm. The edges of the triangle were sharpened and could slide through flesh like a razor. The charm had meted out a lot of pain and would deliver still more. The agony itself was not nearly as great as the apprehension of pain to be inflicted. "You belong to me now, beloved."

Adrien winced, his eyes drifting downward. A series of cuts crisscrossed his chest and abdomen, his skin red and swollen, part of the bondage and bloodletting ritual his captors had inflicted.

Devon gave her a gentle push. "Take him."

Lilith flicked her hair off her shoulders and stretched out on the bed. The feather mattress was thick and soft, covered with a warm down comforter.

By day, Adrien was chained in a damp, windowless cellar. When night neared its fall, two silent male servants would bring him to her bedchamber. He was too weak to protest or try to fight his way to freedom. Through his long captivity he'd been given no food and very little water.

Propping herself on an elbow, Lilith trailed her palm over his chest, tracing his dusky male nipples. Her nails were long and sharp. Her touch was chilly, as if no blood flowed through her veins. Her skin had a strange opalescent opaqueness, reminding him more of stone than of living flesh.

Sexual hunger exuded from her like an exotic perfume. Lust pummeled him in a series of gut-wrenching kicks. Adrien caught a quick breath. When she was so close, every breath he took sent his need soaring. He ached to touch her.

Lilith's hand moved to one of the small cuts marring his abdomen. Her fingers felt like silk against his skin. "Don't you like what I do to you?" The wounds were deep and wide enough to draw blood, but do no serious damage. They seemed to mark him as hers and hers alone. Dipping her head, she circled one of his nipples with her liquid-silver tongue, flicking the little nub until it grew as hard as a bead. Her breath caressed his chilled skin as her searching hand rubbed over his bare chest in sensuous circles.

Adrien closed his eyes, trying to fight her alluring touch. A growl rumbled deep in his throat, but he was barely aware of it. "Please—don't—" His voice was hoarse, wavering with desperation. As if to betray his words, sweet inertia washed over him.

Devon sneered. "Words Ariel said. Words your men ignored."

Lilith jerked off her necklace, snapping the thin chain. "Tonight, I will close those mortal eyes of yours." She drew the sharp edge of the charm across his skin, just below his navel. Crimson welled to the surface, and her head lowered. She soothed away the brief sting with her tongue, licking hungrily. Low snarls escaped from her throat as she drank, the way an animal would growl when its food was in danger of being snatched. She made two more cuts, going lower with each, licking and suckling his skin.

Adrien shivered when she wrapped her fingers around his growing erection. His thick, jutting cock pulsed, alive under her touch. A drop of semen leaked from its head, glistening in the candlelight. What she was doing appalled him. It was against his will, but it also fascinated him on a deeper, more primeval level.

"You will pay for murdering my sister in cold blood," Lilith murmured. "As you took Ariel from the collective, you'll replace her."

Adrien's senses spun away when Lilith spread her long hair across his torso. Eyes alight with anticipation, she flicked out her adept tongue. Wetness swirled over the tip of his penis. She suckled in long, deep strokes that stole away his breath and tightened his balls.

Anticipation ran riot through Adrien's veins. Lilith's teeth scraped, a bit more pain to feed his deep-seated erotic desires.

He wasn't willing, but he could be persuaded.

Appalled by his excitement, Adrien was also secretly intrigued by this strange world of sexual vampirism. Fantasies he'd never believed would be fulfilled were bursting into a painfully carnal kaleidoscope of sights, sounds, and sensations. Sex was suddenly not just something to have or have done. It was sustaining nourishment drawing from the very core of energy that could create life itself.

Still, he desired it even as he despised it. The conflicting ideas were plunging him deeper into confusion. Sanity was slowly turning to madness as the carnal desires harbored in his heart took seed and sprouted. The devil had laid a feast before him, and even though he should turn away and embrace the famine, he was a man of desires unfulfilled.

He hungered.

And he ate.

Watching from the edge of the bed, Devon Carnavorn grasped the bedpost, leaning closer. "Show him no mercy, Lilith. Take him in the most painful way."

The malicious words drew Adrien from his enjoyable apathy. "I was sworn of an oath to erase your kind from this earth," he replied. "I will not stop, no matter the hell you send me into."

Despite his words, he was completely under the domination of these foul beasts. The ache to possess Lilith completely worsened. Fiercer than his own disgust at his weakening will was the unquenchable desire to dominate her the way she was controlling him.

Devon chuckled. "Heaven is just a sin away, my friend. Your lips say no, but your body betrays your piety. You can't resist the needs of the flesh, so give in and have the benefit of what is so generously offered."

The shackles of repression were easily cast aside.

I'm too weak, Adrien thought.

Pleasure took control.

Bracing his head on the pillow, Adrien moved his hips, savoring the way Lilith flicked her tongue over the tip before taking him deeply. His mouth felt incredibly arid, his lips tender from his hot breath rolling over them. He longed to be kissing her, holding her; he needed to be inside that tight, velvety cunt, feeling her smooth belly against his as she writhed under his body.

Just as he was about to explode, Lilith drew back. She shifted and moved onto her knees, straddling his body. She lowered her hips to his in a smooth motion, guiding his erection into her welcoming depths. He could feel her thighs tightening against his hips. Her sex clenched his cock, soft as rose petals and strong as steel bands.

Lilith dug her nails into his shoulders, bringing a fresh pain of the most exquisite kind. Leaning forward, her mouth captured his in a long, suckling kiss. He tasted his blood on her lips, a sample both forbidden and thrilling. Even as she kissed him, he could feel the strange ripples drawing away his sexual essences the way her lips had drawn in his life's essences. She quivered violently when orgasm ripped through her.

Adrien's own arousal was simmering at a heat threatening to boil over like a volcano disgorging molten lava. Straining against the ropes tying his wrists, he thrust his hips upward, driving deeper into her slick, silken channel.

Face framed with a tumble of dark hair, white teeth sinking into her lower lip, Lilith slammed back, grinding down on his cock. Bracing her hands on his shoulders, she rose a little, then back down, meeting his upcoming thrust with perfect synchronicity. The power of their joining was more erotic than anything he'd ever experienced.

Adrien lost control.

Lust searing his senses, he speared deep in one long thrust. Clenching his teeth, unable to hold back any longer, he felt the pull of his loins releasing. The muscles across his abdomen ridged, then rippled. His brain short-circuited as a quake of pleasure thundered through him. Hot semen jetted. Lilith's inner muscles rippled around his cock in long, blissful waves.

Adrien moaned, struggling to master his breathing. He was woozy, dizzy, feeling as though his very soul had been drained away.

Sleep would be welcome. Food even more.

The offering he was to receive for nourishment wasn't what he anticipated.

Bodies still joined, Lilith retrieved her charm. Lifting her hand, she slashed through her palm.

Warm blood dripped onto Adrien's chest, the droplets falling like shards of ice in a winter storm.

Lilith reached out and grasped his face. Her nails dug into

his skin, the pressure at his jaws forcing his mouth open. Fierceness blazed behind her gaze. "Drink." She positioned her bleeding hand over his mouth. "Drink of me, and shed your mortal shell." Foul blood dribbled past his lips.

Gagging, Adrien twisted his face to one side. "No . . ." Stomach lurching, he spat her blood back at her.

With a little laugh, Lilith righted his head. Digging her fingers into his mouth and wrenching down his jaw, she fed him more of her blood.

Adrien renewed his efforts to refuse her offering, gagging and gurgling sickly through his efforts not to swallow even as his lungs burned from lack of air. He had to breathe to live.

He had to swallow.

Gasping, he reluctantly swallowed. The strange, sweet taste coated his tongue, sliding like cold lead down his throat. When the chill hit his stomach, he could feel the exotic organism enter his veins, slithering through his body like an evil snake.

Adrien's vision dimmed alarmingly as an unfamiliar euphoria overtook him. An unearthly and wholly incredible energy was burgeoning inside him, spawning outward like a child fighting to be birthed. He could not speak, he could not move. His flesh tingled as though consumed by an inner fire, feeling dry and papery. He could feel the energy pulsing, conquering, consuming. . . .

His soul was being swallowed by the black entity stealing his mortality away.

Darkness rose.

Helpless, a mist shrouded his brain, spreading a strange numbness over his senses. Then unconsciousness claimed him, and he knew no more.

1

Broadview, New Mexico
Present day

Mind trapped in the manacles of a nightmare, Adrien fought to drag his sleeping soul away from the dreadful abyss unconsciousness had plunged him into. The devils of his dreamscape world were unmerciful, digging steel-tipped claws of fear and oppression deep into his psyche.

He fought harder, thrashing to escape a realm existing only when he closed his eyes. Eyes blazing with flames, the twin demons smacked their lips. The sound of obscene laughter shredded his soul as surely as their nails ripped his naked flesh asunder. Parting his rib cage, they gazed upon his heart and then lifted it from his chest. Blood drizzled from the pulsing organ even as awareness that he was dying filtered into his dim brain. A final desperate scream burbled from his lips, the agonized wail of the damned soul. . . .

Finding and seizing consciousness, Adrien's eyes snapped

open. Through a long moment he found himself looking at . . . nothing. His vision was blurry, disturbingly blank.

Comprehending that some sort of a white veil covered his face he instinctively lashed out, half expecting his arm to remain immobile. Sweeping the sheet away from his head, he caught sight of a shadowy figure. Leaping to his feet, his muscles coiled in anticipation of the coming attack.

No intruder lurked. Instead, he was confronted with his own reflection in the nearby mirror: a huge man thrashing like a chicken in convulsions. Relief flooded his body, a merciful release from the tension. He was safe. It was only a nightmare.

A thin smile warped his lips. Drawing a shallow breath, Adrien visually checked every corner. His hands trembled slightly until he clenched his fists. *Just to be sure.*

Shaking his head, he dropped back onto the mattress. He pushed damp strands of hair away from his face. Jesus, he practically dripped sweat. And no wonder. Elusive wisps of his dream continued to linger. He could see the images floating like ghosts over open graves in the back of his mind. He shook his head slightly to chase them away.

Hard to do, even in the privacy of his own bedroom. A chill insisted on skittering down his spine, settling into tight cold knots in the pit of his stomach.

Brow furrowing, he frowned and cursed softly. "Christ. That can stop." Pressing his palms to his face, he took several deep breaths. The act of drawing air into his lungs, then slowly exhaling, helped calm him.

He relaxed ever so slightly. Tension eased to a more manageable level. Fear was the formidable beast haunting his dreams, a nasty imp visiting him time and time again. He hated feeling overwhelmed and out of control. It frightened him more than he cared to admit.

His nightmare was not the ruminations of a mentally disturbed psyche. What he dreamt had actually taken place. Images of his former captors were seared onto the walls inside his skull. If he closed his eyes he could easily slip back into the mental, physical, and sexual bondage they'd inflicted.

An unbidden tremor scratched its way up his spine. He doubted he'd ever be able to successfully vanquish the memories of his appalling kidnap and rape. The memories never failed to come when he tried to sleep, seeping from the cemetery of bones littering his brain. He glanced down at his wrists. Both were scarred by rope burns. Though he was presently a free man, he'd been tied down for so many years that he was almost unfamiliar with the concept of uninhibited movement.

It's over now. He swallowed down bitter acid. *My life is again my own.*

Still, fear lingered. Part of the reason he continued to have trouble resting, even in the daytime. His gaze jumped to his wrists. Vision blurring, anxiety knotted through him all over again. Torture wasn't easy to forget. And he certainly hadn't forgiven.

Adrien rubbed his eyes. "Why do I even bother?" Shrouded in shadows, his room was dim and cool. Heavy blinds were drawn against the bright light of the afternoon.

The digital at his bedside gave the time. Three thirty in the afternoon; much too early to get up. The sun wouldn't be going down for at least another hour and a half. That's what he liked about winter. The days were shorter, the nights much longer. Maybe he could doze a bit, then get up in an hour or so.

Adrien punched his pillow into shape, then rolled over onto his side. A slight smile crossed his lips when he saw a spill of black across the pillow beside his. Gisele still slept in her place, undisturbed by his thrashing. Glad he hadn't disturbed her, he stroked her soft, silky hair. The most beautiful shade of smoke he'd ever seen, her hair was her crowning glory.

At his touch Gisele rolled over and stretched, giving a big

yawn. Wide, almond-shaped eyes revealed startlingly green orbs flecked with gold. She stared up at him, a question mark on her face.

Adrien quirked an apologetic grin in her direction. "I know it's too early to get up, Gizzy." He sighed, then added with resignation, "I just can't sleep."

Gisele looked at him with a look guaranteed to melt pure stone. Then she turned up her cute pug nose and meowed.

Fingers flexing around her head, Adrien gave her a series of scratches behind her ears. Persian cats were his weakness, and he loved owning them. He and Gisele had been together five years, and hers had been the only warm body to share his bed in a long time. She never questioned his odd hours and the fact that he only went out at night. She was always there, calming him when he was upset and offering a love that was unconditional.

A wet nose touched his fingertips, hinting for more pats.

Adrien stroked the cat's soft fur, calmed by her trilling purr, so peaceful and content. This was how he wished he felt inside, but peace and contentment eluded him. The paths he insisted on treading took him toward unhallowed ground that was his mental hell. He ruthlessly dug up the old graves again and again, examining the rotted corpses.

More than his human life been taken away by the demonic beasts masquerading in human guise; he'd been robbed of his soul. The thing inside looked like him, acted like him. Deep down inside, though, the man known as Adrien Roth had died when Lilith's tainted blood invaded his body.

Sleep wouldn't come.

Adrien sighed and tossed aside the bedcovers, throwing his legs over the edge of the bed to stand up. Urging Gisele off her pillow, he quickly straightened the sheets and tucked the bedspread into place. By the time he finished, the bed was perfectly made. Disorder disturbed him. He needed to have everything in its place. More than a part of a compulsive personality, such care was necessary. He had to maintain a façade of normalcy. He could only live with what had happened and try to go on. He called it staying sane.

If nothing else, he was a survivor.

Adrien headed toward the adjoining bathroom to take a quick shower. Lathering up, he could not help but notice the multitude of tiny scars marring his neck and abdomen. Lilith had used him well to sate her many hungers—for blood, for sex. More than her scars marred his skin. Her demonic brand was burned into his left shoulder. The "slave" collar he'd been forced to wear still cast its thin scores around his neck.

He didn't want to think about Lilith. Not today. Face twisting into a scowl, he redoubled his scrubbing efforts, as if by adding more soap and rubbing harder he could wash away the hateful marks. He couldn't, but the act of cleansing his body made him feel a little less tainted. Rinsing the soap off, he turned off the water and snagged a towel.

Fingering his chin, he decided yesterday's stubble was acceptable; it added to the bad boy outlaw biker look he'd cultivated lately. He could use a haircut, though. Thick brown hair tumbled around his shoulders. He looked like a shaggy dog, all scruffy and unkempt. He skipped a shave and pulled his hair back with a band, then dressed in jeans, a sleeveless T-shirt, and black biker boots.

Gisele waited for him in the kitchen. She wove between his legs, demanding attention. Getting up meant it was time to eat, and she wanted her food. *Now.*

Adrien laughed, retrieving a bowl and can of food from the cabinet. "Yes, my lady. Always at your service."

He popped the top, spooned out tender flakes, then filled a second bowl with fresh, cool water. Gisele ate only the finest money could buy. Cheap and off brand wasn't good enough for this finicky feline. She knew what she was—a pedigree—and she knew that she deserved it, too. Her owner wouldn't have it any other way.

As Gisele munched, Adrien made a cup of instant coffee, heating water in the microwave. Sugar and a liberal dash of bourbon made it palatable. Sipping the hot liquid, he leaned against the counter. The rush of caffeine gave him an instant boost. He wasn't hungry. Later, he would fix something to eat. Who could face eating first thing after getting up? At this point food was a thing he consumed to live, not the other way around.

Glancing around, he mentally assessed the place that could barely be classified as a dump. The little post-WW2 cracker box didn't come close to the Taj Mahal. It didn't qualify as bohemian chic, or even decent. Out in the middle of nowhere, electricity and water service were negligible. You were lucky to have one, blessed to have both.

Still, it served its purpose. This place wasn't for putting down roots. Just a temporary roost. He wouldn't even be staying that much longer. A week, maybe two, before he had to get moving again. Personally, he owned nothing more than his clothes, cat, and motorcycle. Gisele had a kitty carry that she rode in, though she was happier when stuffed in his backpack, furry head sticking out so she could watch the landscape go by.

Finishing his first cup, he fixed a second, pouring in extra booze. There. That would do just fine for breakfast.

Retrieving yesterday's paper, he sat down at the kitchen table to read. The table wobbled alarmingly, one leg shorter than the other. He'd solved the problem by pushing it against the wall and shoving a Reader's Digest condensed book under the short side. Nobody really read those things anyway. The paper didn't succeed in keeping his attention. Instead, his gaze drifted to his wallet and keys.

He reached out and picked up the folded leather case. Opening it revealed the usual items: driver's license, Social Security card, fifty dollars in small bills. No pictures, though, or any other items that would mark it as a truly personal possession—anyone finding it would take the cash and toss it. The address was a local post office box, not a physical address. He'd deliberately chosen a small rural farming area where there was no home mail delivery. All mail had to be picked up at the post office the next town over.

Sliding the wallet in his back pocket, his tongue worried the inside of his cheek. Adrien Roth did not exist anymore, hadn't existed for a long time. He was presently A. J. Bremmer, and the life he was living did not belong to him. The day and age he was born to was now one hundred and forty-one years in the past.

He'd gotten used to borrowing other people's names. All part of surviving in the modern world, when one's life had overrun its natural span.

Another sigh. The cash layout for a new identity hadn't come cheap. His funds were running short. He had only a few thousand dollars, hardly enough to keep body and soul together long.

It's enough to see me through this.

Adrien flexed his fingers. His were hands that had taken many lives. His avowed mission was to kill the beasts haunting the night in search of victims. There was no turning his back on his own true birthright.

Amhais.

Shadow-stalker.

Another sip, but this time his coffee tasted bitter. He swallowed, fighting a rush of nausea. His stomach curdled, churning acid. As a human being, he'd never imagined viewing the world through other eyes. As a Kynn, he not only saw, but perceived the veiled realms existing beyond mortal boundaries and limitations.

He'd always expected to lose his life in the hunt, never anticipating that he would one day join their ranks. He had all the gifts of the incubi, and their curse. He didn't choose or covet the ways of such misbegotten beasts. The appetites of his "kith" were insatiable, forbidden, and unholy. He continually cursed his own fall to his need to survive even as he secretly anticipated the hunt for fresh conquests.

As much as I might despise what I am, I am one of them.

His penance for his own crimes against humanity must be—and always would be—total isolation. He would never walk with a mate, or sire another like himself. Until the day he died, he would be alone.

Adrien sighed, lips pressing together in distaste. His coffee was cold, the cup more than half full. He didn't want any more. There was a sinking sensation in the pit of his stomach, and he knew too well that that meant.

Two weeks since he'd last fed.

He was pushing the edge, keeping himself hungry in some sort of self-imposed penance he didn't entirely understand. He didn't like what he was, didn't relish what he had to do to survive. But he had accepted it because the alternative—not existing at all—was even more frightening. Becoming part of the clan had changed him in more ways than one. The man he'd been before his capture and torture was a person he could never aspire to be again. He had never considered himself an innocent. He knew the ways of the world.

He thought about the dream again. It never left his mind, lurking at the edge of his consciousness, just waiting for his eyelids to fall, for the walls of mental defense to crumble in his sleep.

Why did he still fear her? Lilith was decades in her grave, but her memory lingered in the vaults of his mind, rising up like a demonic angel from a sealed tomb. When she'd sired him, he'd become one of *them.*

Fallen from grace.

Cast into hell.

Eternally.

There was no redemption.

But there was revenge.

"Not just Devon." His hands closed into fists, fingernails digging into his palms. The pain was welcome, reaffirming the direction he'd chosen to take. "Far from it."

Carnavorn had a wife now, a very pregnant wife. Normally the Kynn did not reproduce but recruited from the ranks of human beings. Somehow some deviant force had brought together two unique souls who were able to procreate. Devon's present wife, Rachel, was six months pregnant.

Adrien had often questioned his destiny, wondering what perverse god of justice maneuvered to drop him into the center of his enemy's camp. Now there was no more wondering. Recent events led him to believe that he'd been chosen for a holy mission.

"Three months before hell's spawn is delivered into this world," he growled, not caring that no human ears listened. "Just enough time left to put Carnavorn and his kith in their graves."

Like a hound on the scent of possum, Adrien felt his calling as an Amhais more strongly than ever before. He was anointed, the lone man who could prevent the birthing of a new race.

An unbidden smile turned up one corner of his mouth. Devon Carnavorn was soon going to be in for one hell of a surprise.

Draining the last of his coffee, Adrien pushed away from the table. "I hope you enjoy the gift, my friend." A vicious chuckle escaped. "It's only the beginning."

2

Warren, California
Hammerston Manor, present day

One hand resting on her protruding stomach, Rachel Carnavorn struggled to lower her awkward body into a chair. Feeling her rear connect with the cushion, she smiled in relief. "Whew, for a minute I was afraid my butt was bigger than the seat."

Devon Carnavorn hovered anxiously at his wife's side, ready to offer assistance. "Are you sure you should be up, darling?"

Rachel tilted her head back, treating him to a flash of her dazzling blue eyes. Black hair a tousle around her face, she smiled. "I know the doctor ordered me to rest, but I'm so tired of being stuck in bed, looking at the same four walls."

Her gaze turned longingly toward the back gardens. Outside the bay windows the darkening horizon was a mixture of pinks and deepening navy hues. In another few minutes the sun would disappear into the west and night would spread its velvet cloak over the sleepy sky. "It seems like forever since I've been outside the house."

Devon caught her hint. "Maybe you'll be up to sitting in the garden a little this evening."

"I'd like that." As if caught unaware, she suddenly gasped and shifted uncomfortably. Her grip on his hand tightened subtly. She hesitated a beat. "Oh, good one."

Devon frowned, concerned. "You sure you're all right, darling?"

Stifling a groan, Rachel forced a laugh. "I'm fine, I think." She patted the voluminous tummy protruding from her robe. "I swear I'll soon be giving birth to football players."

Throat aching with happiness, Devon offered another light peck, this time finding her soft lips. "As long as the babies are healthy," he whispered, "I don't care what they grow up to be."

He bent, placing a light kiss on her forehead. Even hugely pregnant and perspiring, Rachel still looked desirable. Her flawless skin was fair, almost translucent, her cheeks lightly flushed with a pink tint. Her slender body had filled out, breasts and hips offering lush and feminine curves. He felt blessed that this incredible woman had consented to join his world and become his life mate. "Just don't tire yourself."

"Easy for you to say," she groused good-naturedly.

A female voice behind them interrupted. "Are you ready for breakfast, sir?" Nocturnal, the Kynn reversed normal habits, living night to day, rather than day to night. Though able to function during daylight hours, their energies waned. The coming of darkness returned their strength and renewed their many hungers.

Devon straightened up, nodding toward one of the kitchen maids. "Yes, Anne. Thank you." He looked to Rachel. "What would you like, darling?"

At the mention of food, Rachel blanched. "Just a cup of tea, please."

Devon felt his guts twist. "Nothing to eat? Some crackers, or maybe a little fruit?"

Rachel wanly shook her head. "I'm a little nauseous," she admitted. "If I eat anything, I'd just be sick. Tea will be enough."

Devon quickly seconded the order. "Just tea for me, too, Anne. Don't make it too strong." He would eat later. Why force Rachel to watch him perform the simple function she could no longer manage? He knew her inability to keep solid food down had become a torture. Instead of enjoying all the strange cravings a pregnant woman would normally and delightfully indulge in, his wife couldn't eat without vomiting a few minutes later.

"Yes, Lord Carnavorn." Dropping a quick curtsy, Anne hurried off.

Trying not to show his concern, Devon took the chair opposite Rachel's. Something was wrong, very wrong, with her. Looking at her, he couldn't fail to notice how much worry had taken a toll on her mental and physical state. This in turn vexed him. These last months had been difficult, with unforeseen events slowly turning their joy into dread.

Less than a month into her pregnancy, Rachel's hungers had deviated strangely. She no longer seemed to need the sexual energies of a victim to recharge her waning energies. Her rapidly diminishing appetite had become stripped down to a single element.

Blood.

Her thirst was insatiable. There were no clear answers as to why her cravings had taken such a turn. Unlike *sangre* vampires, the Kynn did not subsist wholly on blood; the act of taking blood was a very small part of the ritual allowing them to feed off human sexual energies. To meet Rachel's need for constant feedings, Devon was liberally bribing a blood bank attendant.

The look on Rachel's face said she wasn't pleased with this strange turn of events. "I wish I understood why this is happening to me." A tear slipped down her cheek, the beginning of a torrent driven by frustration and fear.

Devon hated to see his wife cry. It made him feel weak, helpless. Her emotions were strung tighter than a harp. He feared that she was going to have a complete mental breakdown.

He laid a hand on hers. "Pregnancy is unknown among our kind. The doctors have said they're sure it's only temporary, your body's way of nourishing the fetuses." Rachel was being treated by the finest physicians within the collective. Doctors who understood the physical characteristics of the Kynn. Still, even the experts were baffled by the changes her body was undergoing—they could only wait and hope for the best.

His explanation failed to placate her. "Not that any man would find big, fat me in the least bit attractive."

He made a *tsk*ing sound. "Fat or thin, you're beautiful. As soon as the children are born, you will go back to normal."

Rachel sniffed, looking at him through a tear-jeweled gaze. "But what if I don't?"

Leaning forward, Devon cupped her chin with one hand, wiping away her tears with the other. Just touching her caused his body to heat up in an unsettling way. Their sex life had waned recently, and he hungered for his wife's intimate touch. "You will."

A whisper of a smile touched her lips. "You think so?"

"Oh, I know it." He kept his hand in place, his gaze steady. Soft and smooth, her skin still felt like silk to his touch. Enjoying her, he brushed his thumb over her lips. "Once the children are born, you'll go back to your old self." He arched a suggestive brow. "Remember her? That sexy vixen who captured my heart?"

Amused, Rachel sniffed and shook her head. "I barely remember being thin," she groused good-naturedly. "Much less sexy." A grin caught hold despite her negative thoughts.

Devon cocked his head to one side. "Oh, trust me. You are one very sexy woman." He found her hand, lifting it to his lips. "And you're the love of my life."

"At least I mean something to you." Not the first time she'd hinted of her unhappiness.

To spare Rachel's feelings, he'd settled on a course of discretion by keeping his victims away from his home. Just as a man had to separate work and play, he now had to separate his craving for raw sex from that of his desire to make love to his wife. A very thin line to walk, but he was determined to make a success of it.

He placed a hand over his heart. "You're everything to me."

Gaze sharpening, Rachel looked at her husband. A small frown marred her forehead. There was a pause while she digested his words. She didn't look entirely convinced.

"Am I?" She shivered as if a chill wind had swept through the room. Devon knew doubt lingered behind her acceptance of the Kynn's open sexuality. She still had trouble believing he loved her even as he fucked other women. Burning up with curiosity, she'd never questioned him even though she knew the late hours he kept weren't always due to work.

Clearing his throat, Devon reached for her hand. "Absolutely and undoubtedly." He said it so firmly he thought that maybe he was trying to convince himself as well.

Truth be told, he hadn't relished the idea of his wife making love to other men during her pregnancy. She carried *his* children, a joy he didn't want to share with any other man. This change, however unsettling, meant that he would have her to himself just a little while longer. Later he'd have to let her go, knowing she must physically embrace other men. She would be a predator, her chosen lovers the prey. It was inevitable.

And hurt like hell.

She closes her eyes and pretends I make no indiscretions, he thought. He felt no bitterness, only resignation. Embracing the cultic realm always exacted a price. *Just as I will have to pretend she'll make none.*

A burden they would always bear, but together.

Rachel glanced down at their linked fingers and exhaled. "You always were a smooth talker. No wonder I couldn't resist your seduction."

Tucking away his own melancholy mood, Devon gave her hand a light squeeze. "I did my damndest to get you," he said. "And I intend to keep you."

She laughed. "Flattery will get you everywhere."

Feet back on solid ground, Devon relaxed. "Feel better?"

She winced, patting her tummy. "Fine. If only our twins would stop punting my kidneys."

Anne arrived with tea just as Simpson, their majordomo, arrived bearing a large box. "This parcel has just arrived via private courier, Lord Carnavorn."

Devon eyed the package, wrapped in plain brown paper and neatly addressed. "I wasn't expecting anything." Most anything he received was usually delivered to the nightclub.

Simpson set the parcel in front of Rachel. "It's addressed to Lady Carnavorn."

"Ah, that makes sense." Since word of her pregnancy reached the Kynn collective, presents of all sorts had been flooding in for his wife. All were eagerly anticipating the successful birth of the first-born Kynn.

Rachel rolled her eyes. "It's been nothing but Christmas every day for months. My God, I've gotten so many baby things I could open my own store."

Such adulation pleased Devon to no end. "You are their queen, darling." He sipped his tea, piping hot Earl Grey with an extra helping of sugar. "Get used to the spoiling."

Rachel stood up so she could better handle the size of the box, about a foot high and a foot wide in circumference.

"Spoiled rotten already." She tore away the first layer of

paper, revealing an elegant hatbox. "How lovely." Using her butter knife to cut the ribbons, she lifted off the lid and peered inside. A look of dawning horror crept onto her face. The scream that followed was as sharp and fractured as shards of glass.

Face paling alarmingly, Rachel gagged. "Oh, God. I think I'm going to vomit." Pushing the box away, she clamped a hand across her mouth and squeezed her eyes shut.

Devon rushed to his wife's side. Glancing into the box, he slammed the lid down. Fear bit with the force of an arctic front. He ignored it. He had to be strong.

"Get Lady Carnavorn back to her room," he ordered Simpson in a tight voice. To the hovering Anne, he barked, "Call Rachel's doctor. Get him here. Immediately."

"Yes, sir." Confused and upset, Anne hurried off to make the call.

Panting, Rachel didn't want to go. "Devon, what is—"

He cut her off. "It's nothing, darling. A cruel prank. Let Simpson take you to your room.

Rachel shook off Simpson's hands. She swayed slightly, gripping the edge of the table to retain her balance. "I—I'm all right." She regarded him narrowly, her grimace frozen across her lips. She was trying to be brave, and failing.

Devon insisted, his voice sharpening with authority, "Please, Rachel. You've had a bad shock. The doctor is coming. He'll want to check you out," he told her flatly. "Think of our children."

His words seemed to convince her. She flinched, jaw clenching in a spasm, but made no protest. "All right," she said quietly, and reluctantly let Simpson take her upstairs.

Alone, Devon returned to the box. It sat on the table, a specter bearing unspeakable evil. His senses reeled, but his mind remained amazingly clear.

Inhaling a steadying breath, he let it out, slowly and shakily. A grim expression settled on his face. "What fresh hell is this?"

Though he didn't want to, he lifted the lid. The sight had the impact of a hundred pound anvil. Inside was a mummified skull with a few hanging wisps of black hair. The identifier was in the silver charm cleaving the center of the forehead.

Devon's entire body went weightless, his vision tunneling toward the single spinning view. His chin trembled slightly until he clenched his teeth. He fought to keep his nerve, too well aware that he was close to failing. "Oh, shit. This isn't good." He drew a shuddering breath, wanting, needing, to deny it all. He couldn't.

The charm had belonged to Lilith. The head, too, had been hers.

Seeing the charm, a million conflicting feelings poured through him. She'd had several of them made, had even given him one in an earlier time. The gruesome part of his mind led him to wonder if the charm had been introduced before or after her death. Either way, the vision wasn't pleasant.

Tucked beside the head, a plain white envelope beckoned. Hand shaking, Devon retrieved it. A bold hand had incised a message across its smooth white face: PAYBACK IS HELL.

A thin smile warped his lips as conscience prodded with a sharp barb. Guilt shredded his soul into tiny little pieces. He gasped in bitter misery; the past had just circled around and bit him squarely on the ass.

The avenger was now being pursued by the man he'd punished. The realization struck the wind from his lungs and the hope from his heart. For a moment he couldn't think. The scars of old memories were ripped open, again becoming as fresh as the day they were inflicted.

He didn't open the letter. He already knew what it would say. Just as he knew who it was from.

Adrien Roth. The man who'd brutally slain Ariel Van Sandt, Devon's sire.

Tucking the envelope back into the box, Devon closed its

lid. Temples throbbing with tension, he sat down and passed his hands over his numb face. A man he'd thought long dead and buried had just crawled out of the grave.

"Apparently I've been mistaken." An understatement.

Mistake or not, he realized his wife and unborn children were in very real danger. Adrien had made sure that Rachel would open the box.

Fear banged in Devon's chest, not for himself but for his wife and the babies she carried. Despite the warmth of the evening, he was suddenly freezing, chilled to the bone.

"He's not just after me," Devon murmured. The shock alone could have caused Rachel to miscarry the babies; they were far too premature to survive at this vulnerable stage.

That wasn't going to happen. Not by a long shot.

He needed help. No, he couldn't call on the collective. He'd helped turn Adrien against his will. The Kynn were not about force. That in itself was a crime by occult justice.

Kill an avowed enemy. That was fine. Fair.

Make Adrien what he despised.

That was a crime punishable by death. Only it would be Devon's execution the collective would seek. Not Adrien Roth's.

Anxiety knotting through him, Devon pushed the fatalistic thought out of his mind. He had no intention of meeting his maker if it could be at all avoided. Because Adrien had never become a member of the collective, formally he wasn't recognized as Kynn. That was good. It might give him a chance to clean up this mess without facing a tribunal.

Devon swallowed the panic lodged in his throat, and a curse slipped out under his breath. "Lilith promised she would control him. I shouldn't have let her have him." He swiped his tongue over his parched lips. "I should have killed him myself and sent his miserable soul straight to hell."

Hands clenching into fists, Devon glanced at the hatbox. Undoubtedly Adrien was thinking the same thing.

Regret. Remorse. No. He refused to feel either. The only thing he'd done wrong was trusting Lilith to keep Adrien. Somehow she'd lost her hold over Adrien and had paid dearly.

He wouldn't make the same mistake.

Urgency nudged him hard. Plans crowding his mind, Devon already knew he had to meet this threat head on, but quickly and quietly—and without further involving his wife. He couldn't afford another mistake like that. Gut-level aggressiveness kicked in. He needed someone outside the Kynn collective, but within the occultic realm.

He knew just who to contact, too. Everything could be accomplished with no fuss, no muss, and without getting his own hands dirty.

To catch a slayer, you send a slayer.

3

Adrien liked the adrenaline rush of riding a motorcycle, the perfect fusion of man, machine, and asphalt all performing in absolute sync. He gunned the engine, increasing the speed from fifty-five to sixty. He had no fear of the velocity. Anything could go wrong at any second: a tire could blow, a jackrabbit could run into his path, an oncoming vehicle could drift into his lane. All of these things could be lethal, but he was willing to throw his dice and take the gamble.

He had nothing to lose.

The open highway stretched endlessly ahead, a black snake slithering across the desert's face. The sun was only a sliver on the faraway horizon, sky shifting from shimmering hues of pinks and blues into the concentrated shade of evening's purple veil. The night was his world, the moon the only orb he could safely bask beneath.

The Kynn possessed various strengths, but there were a few things they could not fight. Sunlight presented a definite problem. Spend ten minutes in direct light and he felt as though a serious case of the flu was setting in. Twenty minutes of exposure and he'd be on the ground, gasping and writhing in agony, frying like an egg on the sidewalk in hundred-degree heat. An hour, and all that would be left of him would be bones and the ashes that used to be flesh. It was a terrible way to die. If there was anything more destructive, he hadn't encountered it. Yet. In that respect, he considered himself to be fortunate.

Cracks in the asphalt made the ride uncomfortable. The state wasn't very interested in spending a lot of money maintaining its back-area roads. Out in the middle of nowhere, it was the deadest, damnedest piece of Godforsaken land to be found on the face of this earth.

A ranching community no bigger than a blink in the road, Broadview was the kind of place that could sink into the vast flat land and never be missed.

Adrien chose this wasted hole in the wall because living was cheap, the winters were mild, and it was easy to settle in without a lot of questions. Migrant workers from Mexico walking the endless stretches of highway were commonplace, and drug traffickers running methamphetamine labs had free rein of the desolate tracts throughout the area.

There was a certain sense of peace to be found in such overwhelming isolation. It had been a long time since he'd felt so comfortable. Were he to choose a location to settle down in for the rest of his life, he believed it would be this one. He was getting to know the area well and liking it. The spaces were wide and open, a far cry from the damp, fog-shrouded streets of London. He no longer belonged in England, hadn't for many years. He'd never go back. The paths bringing him to this crossroads in his life were ones he had no desire to tread again. England was Lilith, and he didn't like thinking about his imprisonment.

She took her pound of flesh from me, determined to make my eternity a living hell.

His speed increased to seventy-five, then eighty, eighty-five.

The miles whizzed by, a dark, dangerous blur. If he lost control of the bike, he'd total it, and there would be no walking away.

Realizing that he was going into that bad place in his head, he eased up and let the motorcycle drop back to a comfortable cruising speed, a more legal sixty-five.

Setting his sights on the road ahead, Adrien stuffed the sinister memories back into the shadowy velvet box of his consciousness and locked the lid. The demons might escape unbidden during sleep, but he did not have to let them haunt his every waking moment. He wanted to simply enjoy the ride, savor the peaceful desert scenery and its freedom.

Thirty minutes later, the city limits of Cimarron came into sight. With a population of thirty thousand plus, it was the kind of location to be born in, but rarely one that people chose to die in if they didn't have to. Like every city, it was sectioned off between the business and residential districts, one side of town being upper class and prosperous, the other being on the low end of the poverty scale.

Literally across the railroad tracks, the bar, convenience, and junk store trade flourished, positioned haphazardly in a neighborhood where many of the houses were barely above the ranking of falling-down shacks. Living on this side of town put people in fear for their lives, and it was not uncommon to pass rows of houses with bars in the doors and windows. Sad but true, residents locked themselves in at dusk to feel safe.

A strip called the "ho strut" ran straight down the middle, part of the train underpass leading to the seedier side. Ladies of the evening worked there, mainly because it offered shelter from the elements. It also gave the girls a quick place to hide when the cops were on patrol. On weekends, the strip was crawling with people, both on foot and on wheels. The biker bars had sawdust on the floor and signs at the door demanding all guns and knives be surrendered before entry would be permitted.

Adrien felt right at home among the dregs and outcasts of society. It might not have been the lower class east end of London, but the sleazy atmosphere reeking of poverty and desperation came damn close. Technology might have advanced in the century since he'd crossed over, but the basest, most depraved desires of mankind had not. Drinking, fighting, cruising loose ladies for a quick blowjob—it was all business as usual.

He spent about a half hour dragging the strip. He'd picked up prostitutes here before, used them to feed. It helped assuage his guilt a bit to know that these were working girls, women who knew the score and were willing to sell their bodies to men. They were used to being treated badly, roughed up, and slapped around. He tried to treat them with respect and always made sure he paid extra.

Though he hated the Kynn curse, he'd never managed to quell the thrill of the hunt that set his heart to pounding. Conquest of the weaker species was now a part of his nature. He knew of others like himself, other Kynn who walked among mortals as though they were gods, but that was not his way. He only took what he needed, never more or less. He tried to be discreet about his unnatural needs. Better that way, to be a lone wolf and not run with the pack.

Rolling up to the curb, Adrien eyed the ladies. Clad in short skirts and stiletto heels, faces garish masks of heavy layers of makeup, they primped, waved, and smiled.

"Hey, honey, take a look at this," one black woman called in a sassy voice, turning around and lifting her skirt to show the thong nestled like a piece of floss between her firm, round ass cheeks. She was stacked like a brick shithouse, too: rack front and center, a sheer defiance of the natural laws of gravity. They were also very fake. She probably made enough to easily afford that big set of tits. The trade in this market was not lacking for customers.

Most of the women working the streets were of various origins—Latinas, blacks, and Caucasians of all shapes and sizes—and huddled together sharing a cigarette when they weren't hitting the curbs. The night was beginning to cool, but the women were hot, sexually primed, the dry desert air mingling with the scent of heavy perfumes. It was heady and enticing.

Adrien knew the one he wanted. It didn't take long to find her.

Leaning against the wall, smoking a cigarette, she wore a tight, faux leather mini-dress zipped down the front, gartered hose, and open-toed sandals. Her long cinnamon-shaded hair was parted down the middle, hanging straight to her shoulders.

Recognizing him, she waved.

Adrien motioned for her to come over.

Tossing aside her smoke, she sauntered with the attitude of a woman who had plenty of time, visually sizing him up. She clearly liked what she saw. She smiled, showing a row of crooked white teeth. "I wasn't expecting you tonight." She spoke in the flat drawling tones that revealed her to be a native of the area.

"I need a little action, Trisha." His own voice held only a trace of an accent. He'd almost managed to completely erase his English origins. Anyone who picked up on it, and few did, usually mistook him for an Aussie. He didn't bother to correct them.

She nodded. "Fridays usually aren't this slow. I was just about to cut out and go home." She reached out, giving his bicep a brief squeeze. "All the way tonight?"

"Always." He didn't bother with the smooth-talking phrases she most likely heard. He wasn't here to flatter her. He needed to feed. Soon.

"My place, around the corner." She tilted her head toward the end of the block. "Give me ten minutes."

He nodded tersely. "Okay."

Knowing the score, she turned and walked away. Confident in her abilities, she didn't glance back. If he didn't show, that was his problem. She'd be back out on the streets hustling another john. It was nothing more than business, pure and simple.

Adrien smashed the gearshift down into first and eased back into traffic.

Hunger gnawed.

Time to feed the beast.

4

Friday night. Mystique was jammed wall to wall.

Multicolor strobe lights whooshed to the thudding beat of a Marilyn Manson remix. Faux fog crept across the dance floor, rising to mingle with the thick haze of cigarette smoke. The theme was an eclectic mix of occult and medieval, pandering to people who believed in magick, people wishing to escape the drudgery of everyday life by immersing themselves in vampire-themed fantasies. Scantily clad waitresses wove through the sea of bodies, intent on delivering food and drinks.

Devon Carnavorn stood in front of his two-way wall of mirrors, gazing down onto the dance floor. The Goth crowd was out in full force. Anyone not having a selection of tattoos, piercings, and spiky jewelry was ridiculed as a freak. In any other place but Mystique, the patrons would be considered ready for the state mental hospital. Faces pale, eyes lined with kohl, lips a slash of crimson, they mutilated themselves in ways that indicated emotional illness. These people drank and drugged, viewing the world through dilated pupils as large and empty as black holes and wishing they weren't a part of it.

As he watched sweating bodies thrash, a slight smile played around the corners of his mouth. He understood his patrons, those lost souls who fit into normal life like square pegs in round holes. They were searching for something beyond themselves, something that would give meaning to their tiny lives. He understood because he'd once been a young man searching for a greater meaning beyond life, beyond death. But whereas he'd found the answers to his many questions, these deluded souls never would. Many were called to join the true ranks of predators of the night. Few were chosen as worthy enough to cross over from human to immortal.

Devon felt he was blessed to be chosen, and for that he would always be most grateful. A hundred and thirteen years had passed since his initiation into the clan.

Memories of Ariel Van Sandt were tucked away in a box in the back of his mind, a box rarely opened nowadays. He was distressed that her image had begun to fade of late; her death had occurred over a century ago. In that time he had found and sired Rachel, the woman who was his own destined *she-shaey*, his blood-mate. Was it because of his happiness with her and the pending delivery of their twins that he was beginning to forget Ariel?

Tension knotted his shoulders. *Maybe it is better to let her memory go. . . .*

Devon shook his head, frowning at the unwelcome thought. There was still a piece of his past unresolved. Following the hatbox, a series of letters had arrived from Adrien. Obviously the letters had been written through several years, then bundled together and sent. They contained more threats, terrible threats. The kind that would make a man's blood run cold, whether he be mortal or immortal.

And Devon's blood had chilled. Enough that he knew he had to take care of this situation fast. Yesterday wouldn't have been soon enough.

He checked his watch. Ten after twelve. The night was just gearing up, and so were the patrons.

His restless gaze flitted back over the crowd, toward the entrance. As if on cue, the doors opened and a lone figure entered.

A brief smile crossed Devon's lips followed by an absent nod. *Holy shit. He actually came.*

Nothing was extreme or unusually out of place about the stranger's appearance. He was outfitted entirely in black: jeans, shirt, boots, all covered by a calf-length denim duster. He wore sunglasses—black, impenetrable, and totally audacious. And unreservedly eye catching. The stranger looked like he might belong, but that was far from the truth. He had the hardcore look that appealed and intimidated. But he didn't run with the Goth crowd. People felt it, too. All heads immediately swiveled, taking him in. They acted as though a god had walked into their presence.

"Morgan Saint-Evanston." Devon mentally and physically held his breath. He'd taken a chance in getting in touch with his old acquaintance, a meeting he both anticipated and dreaded. There was no turning back. He'd placed the call and an answer had arrived. He could not very well say he'd changed his mind.

Devon watched as Saint-Evanston paid the cover charge, fifteen dollars. When paying with cash, he never handed over anything less than crisp hundred-dollar-bills. He never took the change, a quirk most enjoyed. Two bouncers trained to look for trouble immediately intercepted him. No weapons were allowed in the bar, and it was clear to their eyes that more than the average patron had arrived.

Devon winced. This could get nasty. Morgan was never unarmed. Ever. To his relief, no violence ensued. Morgan's hand rose up like a cobra coming to attention, a single finger extended as a warning. He said something—tersely, quickly—and the bouncers moved aside, all grace and smiles. Devon had no doubt about the tone and content of Morgan's words. He'd heard a few of Morgan's threats in earlier times. What that man could say—and do—would put the fear of God into the most depraved heart. Morgan demanded and received respect.

The drama continued. Saint-Evanston briefly surveyed the layout of the bar, noting all strategic areas, entrance and all exits, then dipped back his head. You could almost hear the gears in his head ticking as he deigned to remove his sunglasses. Morgan knew exactly who was standing behind that second-story wall of mirrors. He wasn't the kind of man who'd take a chance on getting trapped in a place he didn't want to be. Always on the lookout for the enemy, he trusted no one. If things did not fall into place his way, he'd vanish—never to be seen again.

When Morgan decided to walk through the bar, the crowd rippled aside until not a single person impeded his path. The minutes seemed to tick by in slow motion. A buzz filled the smoky atmosphere, not of music or of voices in conversation. It was silence. Dead. Awed. Silence. His ominously clad figure vanished from view a minute later.

Devon did not find it odd or unusual that people should part like the Red Sea to admit the stranger into the belly of the beast; even mortals knew when death walked among them. He did find it absolutely fascinating. Morgan clearly exuded an aura of power, a silent signal that said, "look, but don't touch." Saint-Evanston could intimidate with just the arch of an eyebrow, and heaven forbid that he turn his laser-beam stare your way.

That was true power. An enviable power.

It was not a power Devon would ever seek for himself, though. That kind of power came with enemies. It was danger-ous to seek out such a being; the entity he had summoned was of a different kind within the fabric of the occult.

When you are dealing with the devil, show no fear.

Devon was prepared when the door to his office swung open.

Without so much as a by-your-leave, Saint-Evanston swept

in as though he owned the place. Rosalie Dayton, Devon's manager, followed in his wake. She was moving as fast as a lady her age could. In her case, it was pretty damn speedy.

"I'm sorry," he heard Rosalie saying. "But I don't believe you have an appointment to see Mr. Carnavorn." Tenacious as a bulldog on crack, Rosalie was hard to get past. His visitor had apparently slipped through the lower floor offices with the ease of a chameleon.

"You can't go in there," she insisted.

"Then stop me," Saint-Evanston growled over his shoulder. Passing under the threshold, a flick of his fingers shut the door firmly in the face of his pursuer—even though he'd not touched it.

Nice trick, but unimpressive. Devon could do it, too.

Without lingering, Saint-Evanston made a complete transit of the office, visually examining everything, missing nothing. Satisfied with what he found, he paused before the wall of mirrors, briefly glancing down over the people partying away their night.

"I see you have made quite a success for yourself in this world, Carnavorn." No beating around the bush. The greeting was short and to the point.

Hands in his trouser pockets, Devon also looked down on the establishment that had made his name a household word. Instead of hiding in quiet obscurity, as many nocturnal beings did, he'd brilliantly exploited the Gothic subculture, bringing it into the public eye through a successful chain of nightclubs. Mystique had made him a fortune.

"Nice view, by the way. Very controlling." Tinged with just a hint of a brogue, Morgan's voice was akin to a whiskey sotto: deep and touched with gravel.

"Then you know I couldn't fail to miss your entrance." Devon nodded to indicate the people below. "Still showing off, I see."

Pleased that his show among the masses hadn't gone unnoticed, Saint-Evanston smirked. "I love the way they all back off."

Drawing a deep breath, Devon had to forcibly stop himself from rolling his eyes. "You just like scaring the hell out of them."

A shrug. "If you have the power, use it."

"Not your usual philosophy," Devon countered dryly. "I wasn't sure I believed it when I heard you'd returned to the occult."

Another shrug. "Exile bored me."

Devon shot him a look that said he didn't quite agree. "I think you missed the power," he prodded.

Morgan cocked his head, flashing a devious smile. His pale complexion, mane of unruly black hair, and piercing dark eyes added up to an exotic, almost stunning look. "That and the benefits of being a demigod were too damn hard to resist." He spread his arms. "I am multidimensional again."

Devon snorted, not sure the words were entirely in jest. An entity of indeterminate age, Morgan was rumored to be well over a thousand years old, though a true number was impossible to pin down. "It's frightening to think you were born into such power."

Morgan's grin manifested a cast that wasn't completely reassuring. "More frightening is the thought that I lost my mind centuries ago, and there is nothing anyone can do about it." A mischievous brow lifted. "Imagine that. Power coupled with absolute insanity. Quite a brilliant combination, don't you think?"

Knowing Morgan, Devon wasn't entirely sure he was joking. He tsked, offering his best bored look as he pretended not to take the bait. "You always were an ass."

Ignoring the slight, Morgan's hand dropped. He dipped into a pocket and extracted a slim gold case. Flipping it open and selecting a cigarette, he planted it in one corner of his mouth. "But an entertaining one."

Devon's friend seemed to be in a decent mood. Good. Catch him hungover and in a bad mood, and Morgan might be inclined to turn him into a toad.

Seeing the cigarette, Devon wrinkled his nose in distaste. "Still hooked on those coffin nails, I see. I'd prefer it if you didn't smoke in my office, please."

The remark engendered a look of extreme annoyance. The tip of the cigarette burst into flame without benefit of a lighter. The strong scent of cloves emanated from the rich tobacco.

Morgan took a deep drag. "What are you going to do, Carnavorn?" His taunting smile was followed by the exhalation of smoke through his nostrils. "Throw me out of your fucking bar for smoking?"

Some things never changed.

Brow wrinkling, Devon drew back his shoulders. The little bastard only stood five foot eleven to his own six four. In theory, he should be able to nail this pipsqueak into the ground. Still, he wouldn't dare insist the cigarette be extinguished. No reason to rile the beast unnecessarily. When welcoming a snake, take care to mind its fangs.

In truth, the cigarettes weren't half as offensive as some other brands; they were much more akin to incense, which he could tolerate after a fashion. The scent of those strange cigarettes, too, ushered a rush of images to the forefront of his mind. He could easily recall the time when he'd first encountered Morgan. Every second of that surreal night was etched in his mind.

The year was 1895. . . .

Devon and Ariel had been lovers for less than two weeks, but already she was enticing him into exploring her world. Each night she would take him to a new place, leading him further and further astray from the life of a moral, upstanding young lord.

In truth, he was none of those things to begin with. At that time in his life he regarded all women as prostitutes, good for little more than giving a man pleasure. Not even a married woman held any esteem in his eyes, for what was a wife but a whore, bought and paid for. That Ariel was a lady of the night was true enough. But where other women had failed to capture his intellect, as well as his body, Ariel had succeeded brilliantly.

A willing convert, Devon had eagerly trailed her as she introduced him to life in the slums. He was not surprised when one of her stops had been one of London's most notorious opium dens, a place where one could buy oblivion, where the memory of old sins could be destroyed by the madness of sins that were new. The degradations seemed to speak to her on a deeper level. He was soon to understand why.

He entered the hideaway in her wake. A haze of smoke hung in the air; opium easily overwhelmed his senses, making him light headed. As if in a dream, they'd waded through an ocean of prone bodies, Ariel leading him to a private chamber, one she seemed to know. Inside was a couple already in the throes of a strange ritual of lovemaking. Devon remembered thinking there was a whiff of decay under the lavishness of the decadence.

Cigarette in hand, Morgan Saint-Evanston had lounged on a bed. His topcoat was discarded on a nearby chair, and his white dress shirt was unbuttoned to the waist. Lilith lay naked beside him: beautiful, sensuous, and leonine. He was murmuring in a strange tongue as she made small cuts in his flesh with a strange sharp-edged silver charm. Stroking his inner thigh through his tight trousers, she lapped up his blood like a cat taking cream. Fingers tangled in her thick hair, he was clearly enjoying her assault on his flesh. Devon was mesmerized by the sensuality of lovers sharing more than their bodies as they engaged in a crimson-stained kiss.

Guiding him to a chaise lounge, Ariel had undressed, shedding her clothes as a butterfly sheds its chrysalis. Naked, she settled on the floor between his legs. The words she'd next spoken were compelling ones.

"We take of our men," she'd murmured with a smile. "But we give pleasure in return. Much pleasure, as you will see."

Indeed he had, watching Morgan and Lilith engage in violent sexual intercourse. At the same time, Ariel had set to arousing him in the most carnal of ways. Her cuts into his flesh had sent a delicious shiver straight into the very core of his soul. He knew then and there that he had found the place where he belonged.

I wanted to cross over. I had no hesitation when I was given the chance. . . .

An abrupt movement brought Devon back to the present. He reluctantly packed away the cherished memories of a past he could no longer reach out and touch. His life was in a different place, and his priorities had changed. Rachel had rescued him from the oblivion Ariel's shadow had too long cast. What he had now was precious. He would make every effort to preserve it at any cost, even sell his soul if he must.

Bored watching the patrons below, Morgan shifted, losing patience. He turned away from the wall of mirrors. "I have not got all night to waste admiring the view." Smoke curled in the air, drifting easily toward the ceiling before dissipating. "I only came because your message mentioned some fine old times. Drinking. Fucking. How could I resist?"

Devon slanted a sideways look at his friend. "You haven't changed a bit."

The impish gleam returned. "Why mess with perfection?" Morgan nodded toward the bar. "Pour me a drink and I will hear you out." He commandeered the nearest chair, not just sitting, but sprawling. One leg hooked over the armrest, the other stretched out in front, he looked comfortable and in command.

Ashes fluttered, but he didn't seem to notice them or care. "I admit your message was intriguing. Lilith was one of my more . . ." His brow wrinkled with remembrance. "Captivating affairs."

Devon felt butterflies take flight in his gut. His gaze skimmed the man sitting before him. Manic-depressive, alcoholic, and an absolute hedonist who pumped every poison known to mankind into his body, Morgan had a taste for beautiful women and carnal sex. He liked the intense pain and utterly erotic pleasures inflicted during the act of being taken by a Kynn woman.

However it wasn't that side of the man Devon was currently seeking. When Morgan bothered to snap out of his haze of booze, drugs, and sex, he was the best damn mercenary walking the face of the earth. Killing was his art, and he the master composer. Logical, lethal, and absolutely ruthless, the assassin had never failed to bring down his prey.

"I'm glad you remember her so fondly." Devon stared. "It's because of her that I need your help."

"Oh?" More ashes were flicked. "I doubt she has inquired after my health and well being." A pause. "We broke up rather unpleasantly. You know that viper's mouth of hers."

"She's dead," Devon informed him flatly.

"And you think I did it?" Morgan thought a minute. "Though if I had, it would have been entirely justified. The woman was barking mad—crazier than I am."

Devon refused to go near that outrageous comment. "I know you didn't kill her. But I know who did."

5

Adrien turned into the parking lot. Killing the engine, he lowered the kickstand, letting the bike lean over to one side. He doubted anyone would bother it. The worn leather saddlebags didn't contain anything worth stealing, and if thieves wanted the bike badly enough, they'd simply roll it away. Also, it was not a particularly new or enticing vehicle, just an older Harley, scratched and dented, reliable enough to get from point A to point B.

An invigorating breeze pulled his hair with invisible fingers. He paused for a moment, inhaling the night air. Boots crunching over bits of broken glass, he walked to the door and went in without knocking.

The place Trisha called home was decorated in nondescript colors: browns and greens. There was a bed, bureau, table, and chair. A television was tucked into one corner.

Trisha sat on the bed, legs crossed, swinging one sandaled foot. She drank diet Coke laced with bourbon out of a jelly glass. "Hi, honey," she greeted.

Adrien's eyes skimmed over her. "Hey, babe." He'd known her about five months. She was one of the first he'd taken.

At twenty-six years of age, Trisha had been ridden hard and put away wet, appearing much older than her physical years. Despite her time on the streets peddling her pussy to strangers, there was still a sense of innocence lingering in the depths of her fawn-brown eyes. She actually believed the fairy tale that someday a rich man would fall in love with her and sweep her off her feet. Finishing her drink, Trisha set her glass aside. "The usual?"

"Yes."

Reaching up, she caught the zipper dangling between her full breasts and yanked it down, peeling away the faux leather. Cupped in a lacy red bra, her breasts were real; small, but firm. Her waist was tiny, the soft curve of her belly disappearing under a pair of matching silk panties.

A wave of lust immediately rolled through him. His gaze traced her throat down to the gentle vee between her legs.

Adrien's cock twitched, pressing against the confines of his tight jeans, eager to break free and slide into that hot cunt of hers. The Kynn were highly sexual creatures—needing sex, craving sex, as surely as other men craved air in their lungs. When he wasn't having intercourse with some willing female, he was thinking about having sex.

Sanity and sense were going fast when he cupped her left breast, teasing the taut tip of her nipple under the silky material of her bra. Trisha pressed herself closer.

Adrien lifted his hands, taking the straps of her bra and easing them down her slender arms. Spiraling warmth took hold in his belly, working its way to his balls, making them tingle and tighten. His hands found and teased the little nubs, giving them refreshed hardness. Trisha made a soft sound, a half gasp, a half laugh. When she looked up at him, her eyes were full of desire. A shudder of longing shadowed her face.

"I wish that you'd take your time with me," she whispered. "Don't just use my body for sex, but make love to it."

Adrien laughed. "No time, babe." He felt the unmistakable

urgency of sexual need radiating from her body. He wanted to screw her until she wept with pleasure. He kept circling the pink aureoles with his fingers.

She gasped. "Don't stop, babe. Oh, please . . ."

Adrien caught her around the waist and bent her back. His head dipped, his mouth sucking at a tender peak. He teased her nipples one after the other, swirling in soft circles, gently biting then massaging away the ache. Trisha squeezed her eyes tight, her breathing ragged from the sensual motion of his mouth. "God, that feels so good." The vulnerable expression in her eyes was quickly replaced with a look of wanton desire.

"Good." Adrien rubbed one breast with his palm, until she released a soft gasp. His cock was throbbing, a thing alive. The flutter in his stomach was not nerves. It was need.

Trisha slid her hand toward his crotch, finding the hard bulge.

"Why don't we do it a different way tonight? I think we'd be so good together." She offered her mouth, moistening her lips with the tip of her pink tongue. "One kiss."

Jaw tightening, Adrien turned his head. He never kissed the women he fed from. That was an intimacy he could not bring himself to share with a common whore. A true, heartfelt kiss was reserved for a woman he desired. Loved. It was the part of himself he held aside, a thing sacrosanct and sacred.

"It's just business, honey," he told her. "You know that." The rule was to always keep it brisk and impersonal. Don't get involved, don't put heart or emotions on the line.

Her expression saddened. "Yeah, I know. You don't want to get tangled up with a whore."

His answer was terse. "That's right. I don't need a woman for anything but sex."

"Then that's what you'll get." Her voice was resigned, but not hurt. She was pro enough not to push a customer. He paid well and demanded very little for the evening's work.

With Adrien, she knew she'd be taking the rest of the night off. It was a necessary thing, something she didn't mind at all.

Breaking away, she walked over to the chair. Back to him, she grasped it for support. She flexed her taut ass cheeks and cast a glance over one shoulder. "Come and get it, babe."

Adrien positioned his body behind hers. His hands went to her shoulders, brushing her long hair away from her nape. A series of small scars covered her neck. She'd recently washed her hair, and the clean scent of fresh peaches tickled his nostrils. She wore no other perfumes. He inhaled her scent, memorizing it, savoring it—part of the connection he needed to make with his victim. He ran the pad of his index finger over one of the scars, causing her to shiver. Goose pimples rose on her skin.

He nipped lightly at her pale flesh, nuzzling the crux between shoulder and neck as his hands moved downward. He grasped her hips and pulled her back against the bulging erection straining against the front of his jeans, moving his hips in a slow rhythm. Through that simple touch he could feel the pulse of blood in her veins, feel the forces of life coursing through her body. The heat was rising, the energy was building, just waiting to be tapped and drained away.

Trisha moaned when he slid one hand across her belly, pushing under the waistband of her panties to find the soft bud between her legs. Her mound was shaved bare, the lips slick with creamy juices. She eased her legs apart, letting his hand perform magic.

He easily found her tender clit. He moved his index finger in a stroking motion against the tender nubbin, beginning a sensual tease, then dipped one finger inside her, swirling it. Her vaginal muscles spasmed around his finger. Her sex was slick, warm, and ready. He slid a second finger inside. He was none too gentle, using her as he pleased. She met the thrust with increasing fervor, her wild needs increasing the pulling motions deep within.

His free hand slid into his pocket. He drew out a small

pocketknife. He slashed with a quick motion. Crimson rose from the wound, rich and red against her porcelain skin.

Trisha cried out, but made no protest. She accepted it as part of the sex games her customer wanted to play, the kink he couldn't fulfill with any woman but a whore.

Adrien lapped at the cut, enjoying the texture and taste filling his mouth. Needing more, he pressed his lips against her skin, swallowing. The union had been made. Now he could draw from her, recharge his body with her essences.

Trembling with pent-up desire, Adrien slid her panties down. He squeezed her rear cheeks, fondling them. Somehow he worked open the zipper on his jeans, freeing his jutting cock. His own desires were blazing when he bent her over the chair. He entered her sex with a single thrust. Silky inner muscles rippled around his cock.

"You're so tight, Trisha." Adrien thrust harder, frantic to feed the furious hunger threatening to consume him. Each plunge went deeper than the last. The air around them crackled and sizzled. A thin trickle of sweat traced her spine before disappearing down the crack of her ass. Her moans and his growls echoed off the thin walls.

An irate neighbor beat the wall, shouting for quiet. Adrien was too far gone to notice or care. He couldn't have stopped now if he'd wanted to.

"Come on, baby," Trisha gasped. "You're close. Let yourself go." Her own arousal was simmering at a level that threatened to boil over like a volcano disgorging molten lava.

"I'm coming—" Clenching his teeth and digging his fingers into the soft flesh of her thighs, Adrien's hips smacked against her buttocks a final time. Cock thrust as deep as physically possible, he felt the pull of his loins releasing from the very tips of his toes.

Pale and trembling, Trisha collapsed in a limp heap. She would have fallen to the floor had he not caught her.

Sweeping her up, Adrien walked over to the bed and deposited her on its lumpy mattress covered by a stained flower-print bedspread. Tucking his penis into his jeans, he zipped up and sat down.

Trisha was barely coherent, drifting in and out of consciousness.

Adrien brushed strands of hair off her pale forehead. A fresh pang of guilt stabbed at his conscience. He'd gone too long without taking sustenance and had almost drained too much.

He rolled her over onto her side. Her hair was tangled around her neck. He burrowed through the thick mass to check the wound. He swore softly under his breath. The cut was worse than he'd intended. What had he been thinking? He always tried to be careful, inflict as little damage as possible. He traced the cut with his tongue. The taste was not unpleasant, but rich, with a cloying sweetness. The rush of energy felt as though he'd walked right into a hot-wire fence. He felt stronger, more alive than ever before. He could understand the need some vampires felt to take more.

Trisha stammered, "W-what's g-going . . ."

"I'm just making sure you're okay, honey." Tasting her again, Adrien whispered a few words, old words, ancient ones that he'd learned during his captivity as Lilith's pet. When he lifted his lips away from the cut, it had healed, leaving only a small white scar. She would forget, too, that he'd cut and drunk of her. It was too dangerous for her to remember everything.

Her eyelids fluttered, gaze focusing on his face. "You always take it out of me."

A fatalistic grimace bent his features, lips turning down in a frown. Guilt stabbed again, wielding all ten of its razor sharp talons.

"I want to make sure you get a good rest." Adrien drew out his wallet, fishing out two crisp bills, a hundred and a fifty. He folded the money and tucked it into her hand, closing her fingers over it. "Here's a little extra. Stay in tomorrow, okay?"

"Sure," she mumbled before sinking down into a leaden slumber. A soft snore escaped her parted lips. When she woke up, she'd feel like she'd been on a week's bender and kicked in the head by a mule.

He spread a blanket over her. "Sleep well, babe."

6

The door to Devon's office opened just as he was about to launch into his speech. Rosalie stuck her head inside. By the look on her face, she was expecting to find him spread out on the floor in a pool of blood. Relief was written on her wrinkled face when all that met her eyes was two men talking quite amicably. Devon didn't fail to notice that it'd taken her ten minutes to decide whether or not to open the door.

Rosalie's suspicious gaze raked over the stranger. "Is everything all right, sir?" Just in case he was being held hostage against his will—like there was anything she could do.

"Everything's fine," Devon said, then hurried to fill in. "My friend here was expected. I simply forgot to mention he would be arriving late."

Rosalie's pursed lips said that his friend was quite rude in announcing his intentions. "Shall I get you and your guest something to drink? A cup of tea, perhaps?" She was giving him one last chance to scream for his life before she sent security in with guns blazing.

"That will be fine."

Morgan winced, lighting a second cigarette off his first, but saying nothing detrimental.

Devon threw him a look, begging him to be kind. Saint-Evanston was rarely polite or kind to most humans. As with children, he tolerated their presence, believing that they should be seen but not heard.

Trotting into the office, Rosalie busied herself with the business of preparing a tray. She set out delicate cups and saucers, spoons, cream and sugar, making hardly a sound against the silver platter.

The Earl Grey tea she poured was strong, hot, and black as tar. She was a terrific manager—gave no slack to lazy employees—but her skills as a beverage hostess left a lot to be desired. Age hadn't slowed her down one whit, nor had her diabetes. At seventy plus, she was still blowing and going. In fact, Rachel almost hadn't gotten past Rosalie's screening. Needing a job, though, his future wife had worn the old woman down with her own immovable will. He treasured both the women who were the backbone of his life: one guarding his business interests, the other his personal ones.

Tray balanced regally, you would have thought that she was serving the queen of England. Attempting her smile, prickly though it was, Rosalie grandly handed Devon's guest a cup.

Morgan had the good grace to take it. "Thank you, darlin'," he said, thickening his brogue and putting on the Irish charm that could lure birds from the trees. He waved off an offer of further enhancements.

Devon accepted his own cup, taking it as he normally would—loaded with cream, but no sugar—but did not drink it. "Thank you, Rosalie. That will be all. Please see that I am not disturbed for the rest of the evening."

"You're quite sure?" It was apparent she expected to be asked to stay.

Devon made it clear that he wanted her to go, giving a dismissive wave of his hand. "Yes," he stated firmly, then hammered in: "I will call you if need be."

Rosalie reluctantly headed toward the door. "I'll be just outside, Devon." She shut the door behind her.

Morgan made a violent twisting motion with his hand. The lock on the door snapped shut. Balancing the cup on its saucer, he remarked, "Charming woman." To be polite, he sniffed the tea but didn't drink it, instead unceremoniously dumping it into the ivy plant sitting on the table beside his chair. He held out the cup. "As I have said, Devon, I will have a drink."

Devon headed toward the small wet bar. His private offices offered every convenience, testament to the many late nights he'd put in. There was even an adjoining bedroom and bathroom suite. He spared himself no comfort.

Cracking open a bottle of good scotch, he filled two glasses and delivered one to his guest. He ignored his own, holding the glass but not drinking.

Morgan knocked his drink back in a single swallow. "You always were tightfisted with the booze." He held out the glass. "Pour."

Devon refilled. "I'm not paying you to sit here and suck up my good scotch." His words were only half in jest.

"Who says you have enough money to afford me anyway?" Morgan shifted in his chair and lit a third cigarette. White tendrils of smoke played around his head, forming a strange, opaque halo. "Besides, I have yet to hear your story."

Devon grimaced, his instinctive reflex at the approaching subject. "I guess you've figured out why I contacted you, then."

A snort. "Of course I know. You did not summon me to talk over old times. You need my expertise." Morgan settled back, obviously preparing to listen. "Death never delivers without a reason. Give me a reason."

Devon's hand tightened around his own glass. Time to spill

his guts. "I'll give you two reasons: my wife and children. They are the ones I need to protect, not myself."

Morgan's left eyebrow shot skyward. The news registered on his face like a 9.0 earthquake. "You? Married with children? That is truly frightening, considering you were once known to fuck a tree if it had a knothole."

Ouch.

Devon took the words with good grace. Once, they would have been true. "I, too, would've believed it impossible. I never thought I'd find a woman I wanted to settle down with."

Morgan's eyes narrowed. "You mentioned children. I thought your kind did not reproduce."

Devon explained. "That is what makes my union with Rachel so wonderful. She is my true she-shaey, my bloodmate. She even bears a mark that completes mine. What has happened between us is a rare and wonderful thing—a new way to continue our species. I am sure I don't have to tell you the Kynn are few and far between. The children we have could mean that our race is beginning to evolve."

"By your earlier words, I take it there is someone who wishes to prevent the birth of your children."

Devon swallowed his drink. The sting on the back of his throat helped center his nerves. Time to confess. "I have an enemy. One who could cause me a lot of grief. I want that grief to end."

Morgan merely shrugged in response. "We all have enemies, Devon. It is part of the package that goes with long life and success."

Devon's gaze raked his visitor. "Please. You mock me by telling me something I am well aware of. This threat doesn't come from mortal ranks. If it were just that, it could be easily handled." He glared for a moment to let the gravity of his words sink in.

Morgan put his glass aside, all attention now. "I am not exactly following you. Are you telling me the trouble is on *our* side?"

"Yes." Devon pressed his lips tightly together. Time to spill the truth, however unpleasant. "It comes from within the Kynn dominion."

"Someone not pleased your wife is pregnant?"

"Exactly. His name is Adrien Roth."

Another look of surprise from Morgan. "I remember Adrien Roth as being one of the Amhais. I used to hunt with his group when the fancy took me."

Devon shot his friend a narrow look. "Yes, I am well aware that you straddle both sides of the fence when it comes to questionable moral practices regarding human and occult justice. One of these days you're going to be called to judgment for that."

Unholy amusement lit Morgan's gaze. He laughed, but without humor. "That day is yet to arrive." He scowled defiantly at the thought, then dismissed it. "But let us get back to your narrative. From what I gather, Roth, who was a slayer, is now Kynn?"

Exhaling with the frustration of trying to lay out his case, Devon poured another round of drinks. He was going to need some liquid fortification to explain. His insides quivered with fear. Nothing was coming out the way he'd planned.

Clearing his throat, he said, "The story gets a little complicated here, but it must be told anyway. Adrien Roth was the man who slaughtered Ariel."

That one grabbed Morgan's attention. "Ariel was slain? When did this occur?" His eyes narrowed, taking on a distinctly feline cast.

"It was after the scattering—" Devon lifted a single brow. "If you were sober enough to recall any of it. Roth's people were the ones who burned the dens."

Morgan grimaced. "Ah, I remember. It was best to get out of London then. Distasteful business."

"Distasteful. Yes. Quite," Devon agreed. "Anyway, after you left, the hunt became more intense. Ariel was taken soon after. Her death—" He choked up, unable to go on. The pain and anger he believed that he'd mastered a long time ago welled up inside him, a rancid acid threatening to eat right through the walls of his very heart.

Attempting to regain composure, Devon cleared his throat. "They took her and held her captive, tying her down and keeping her from the things she, ah, needed to survive."

Again, he had to stop his narrative.

Because he and Ariel had still been mates, they had still been psychically linked. Everything the men did to her, he saw in his mind's screen. Disarming her supernatural strengths with a sigil of etched silver, Adrien's men had tied her to a bed, naked and defenseless. Through a week they'd treated her as little better than an animal, a freak of nature, keeping her in a heightened state of arousal—without giving her the relief of the feed.

Morgan held up a hand. "Keep the details to yourself." His eyes were dark, intense, as he turned Devon's words over in his mind. "Knowing you, I get the feeling you went after him."

Devon tightened his grip on his glass, tracing the smooth edges of its rim. "How could I not try to avenge my sire?" he admitted. "Roth was human when he took Ariel's life. To even the score, Lilith and I devised the plan to bring him across. By making him a part of the collective, we had hoped—perhaps foolishly—that he would see that the Kynn were not such dreadful creatures."

"And he did not quite see it that way?" Cigarette clenched between his teeth, Morgan began to clap, albeit sarcastically. "Quite brilliant, my friend. Make him the thing he hates and hunts, plus give him all the abilities of a Kynn minion." More clapping. "That is akin to handing him the keys to your house and asking him not to rob you."

Devon accepted the admonition. "A huge mistake, I admit. Perhaps in my grief I was not thinking right."

Morgan rose and refilled his glass. "Not all are as eager to embrace the occult life as you were. It is true most fear what they do not understand, hate what they think is hell-spawned evil. That evil is us."

Devon's anger rose. "So is it fair that even as they hate and destroy us that we must preserve them? They *are* the lesser species."

Morgan considered the depth of his glass. "At my age, I have often questioned that wisdom. But we are not here to debate the old philosophies or the sides we have chosen. You asked me to come here for a reason. Roth—you want me to kill him?" He said the last words matter-of-factly, as if Devon were asking nothing more than the time of day.

Wearily, Devon set his glass aside and ran his fingers through his hair. The hour was late, and the pressure behind his eyes was tremendous. This problem had harried him too long. He was ready for resolution. At any cost.

"Yes." Then, as if to justify why he was putting out an order of execution, he hurried to explain. "I don't intend for my children to live in fear of what may come from the shadows of my past into their futures. They have the right to survive, to grow and thrive, if they can." He drew a sharp breath. "Adrien has made threats on our lives, threats I do not intend to let him carry out."

"I see." Morgan nodded thoughtfully. "He can threaten all day. Question is: do you think he will follow through?"

"I know he's serious. Dead serious."

Abandoning the bar, Devon walked to his desk. He opened the bottom drawer, setting out a stack of letters, along with a rather large hatbox. "He's sent these vile things outlining what he intends to do to my wife and children. Going to the police is not an option, of course. Roth's letters reveal too much about the Kynn and the underworld we exist in. Even if Adrien were deemed a lunatic and captured, the truth would too soon come out."

"He obviously knows that," Morgan commented. "But letters cannot do any harm."

"No?" Devon indicated the box on his desk. "Then what about this?" He pushed it to the edge. "Go ahead. Look inside."

Morgan sauntered over. Drink in one hand, he lifted the lid with the other. He cut a quick glance to Devon, who nodded, then back to the box. Shock did not register on his face. Surprise, yes. Letting the lid drop, he cleared his throat. "Lilith?"

"Yes. What's left of her." There wasn't much.

Morgan sent a meaningful look over the box. "Got her comeuppance, I see."

Devon sat down in his chair. Elbows on his desk, he cupped his forehead in one hand. "He must have escaped her, somehow freed himself from imprisonment."

"No doubt."

"It was a mistake to let Lilith keep him—but how could I refuse her?" He moaned. "I thought she could control him."

His words seemed to annoy.

"I think you had better do some explaining about the *control* part," Morgan said. "Your story is taking on unexpected elements."

Devon leaned back in his chair. "Lilith kept him like a pet of sorts, for her own amusement."

"I recall well Lilith's idea of pleasure." Morgan peeked into the box again. "She had a, ah, perverse sense of amusement. Even I found her trying at times."

Another long groan. "I know. Everything she did to him is in those pages. I was ashamed to read them." Devon raised his head. "I swear that I didn't mean for things to go that far—tormenting another being to the point of madness."

Morgan opened a few of the letters. He paced slowly as he read, going through each with care. The only motion that gave away his personal thoughts was a thinning of his lips as he silently absorbed the long saga of abuse Adrien Roth had carefully and completely documented. Morgan clearly was not happy either; the letters cast Devon and Lilith as the villains. He checked the envelopes.

"They were hand delivered," Devon informed him. "Some

vagabond he paid." He already knew Roth was very mobile and hard to pin down. Like smoke in the fog, his enemy was invisible in the mass population.

"These go back almost half a century," Morgan noted. "He's been holding his grudge a very long time."

"Just waiting for the right moment to destroy me," Devon said angrily. He knew the letters forward and backward. The words were imprinted on his brain. There was nothing good to be found in them; only the ranting of anger and the lust for revenge.

"Death would have been fairer. Giving him the chance to die with honor, and me the chance to avenge Ariel as a gentleman." Devon lifted his chin. "I'm not a heartless monster or a man of violence. I didn't mean for this to happen."

Morgan tossed the pages back on the desk. It appears Adrien has every right and then some to kick your ass to Hell and back. I would."

Devon crumbled. "I know, I know. That is why I want him found and stopped in his tracks. Were I on my own, I'd not give a damn and take my chances. But a man must become more cautious when his kith are concerned. They are my weakness, but also my blessing. I do realize now the preciousness in this life when I didn't see it beforehand. I knew only anger when Ariel was taken. With Rachel, I've learned to understand the value of real love. For her sake, I want Roth out of our lives forever. That's where you come in."

Morgan's gaze grew thoughtful. "I can understand the need to protect your interests."

Clenching his jaw, Devon forced himself to swallow against the acid rising in his gut. "I want Roth brought to me, and I want to see him die." He slammed his hand down. "Whatever the cost, I swear I will pay it. Money is no object. Name your price."

Dark eyes grew devious. "Please. Spare me the dramatics. I know exactly how this needs to be handled."

Relief was instant. At last, an end was in sight. "Then you'll take the job?"

"After we discuss my fee." Saint-Evanston smiled and lit another cigarette. "I no longer work for money." He exhaled a stream of smoke. "That is useless to me."

Very few people had the nerve to call money useless in this world. Morgan was, perhaps, the only one who would.

Regaining his composure, Devon sat up straight, lacing his fingers together and looking the hunter in the eye. He made his own gaze as unwavering as the assassin's laser-beam stare.

"What is your price?" he asked, not daring to blink. Inside his skull, the wheels were turning furiously. Was he about to go in over his head? He knew Morgan . . . but did he trust him? He wasn't sure. No time to second-guess his decision, however.

The tip of the cigarette grew brighter, burning away. "My price is a favor."

His answer caught Devon off guard.

Devon shook his head. "Did I hear you correctly? Did you say you wanted a favor?"

A brief silence. A nod. "Anything I might want, anytime, anywhere. If I call on you, you must fulfill the obligation."

Devon considered the deal. "That's all? One simple favor?"

Morgan answered with authority, with presence, with the security and power benefiting his position. "Held in reserve until I need it. Whatever I ask, you must grant. Unconditionally."

Ouch. A steep edict.

Like the sword of Damocles, it would hang over his head until fulfilled. How long would it take for Morgan to put in his request? A week? A decade? A century? More? The businessman in him said not to make a deal; never walk away from the table owing anyone anything. It was supposed to be the other way around. In fact, most of his life it had worked exactly that way. He always worked things to his own advantage. He had the money to make things happen, to make people miserable, bend to his will. Such was not the case at this moment.

Checked and mated, there was no other option in his arsenal. *I've got to agree, or he'll walk out.*

There was no point in trying to bargain, ask for a secondary choice. The price had been set, and the ball was in his court. Refuse and he was back to square one. Accept and the solution would be set into motion, soon to conclude.

He wanted that conclusion before Rachel gave birth. Thoughts of his wife spurred him on. "I accept."

"Good." Morgan snuffed out his cigarette on the palm of one hand. He flicked the butt toward the nearby trash can—and missed. "I will start immediately."

"How long will it take?"

As if amused by the question, Morgan smirked and pressed his lips together. "You will have him when I am ready to turn him over." Without saying another word, he headed toward the door.

Devon couldn't help asking a final question. "This favor. What if you never need it?"

Saint-Evanston halted. He turned slowly on his heel, long coat whispering ominously around his legs. "Then you would owe me nothing, Devon."

The sunglasses perched on the top of his head came down, hiding his eyes behind an impenetrable shield. The meeting was clearly over. And then he vanished. Not bothering with a conventional exit, he slipped through the invisible veils parting the dimensions; a wraith fading from sight with the ease of a shadow.

The damned door was still closed and locked.

Alone, Devon sagged back in his chair. "Whatever you ask in return, Morgan, I shall grant."

His eyes drifted to the stack of letters, then to the box holding Lilith's head. Guilt began to fade a bit, replaced with a sense of relief.

My family will survive.

7

The aftermath of the feast was the hardest time to face alone.

Adrien's entire body surged with the energies absorbed from his victim. More than ever, he became aware of faraway voices on the night winds crying out to him.

Walk with us, they whispered from afar.

At first he listened to the siren song, unable to resist. The blood coursing through his veins was the blood of the collective. Embrace their gifts and he would be welcomed—forgiven.

Adrien felt he had nothing to be forgiven for. He had not chosen their ways. Memories of Lilith were too clear, too strong. He would not accept becoming one of them, would not join their pack for the hunt. It was the only way he could continue to hang on to his humanity, to the remnants of the soul stolen away. It was in tatters, the threads precious and few, but he clutched at them like a drowning man going under for the last time. Let them go, and he would be lost in the darkness of eternal damnation.

"You tempt me, devil," he snarled back. "I won't listen to the words of demons."

The voices faded into mocking laughter. He could banish them only temporarily. The next time he fed, they would return.

Unable to stand the thought of four walls confining him, he decided he couldn't go home. Even the city streets seemed too narrow, the traffic bumper to bumper. There was too much angst inside his brain to give him any rest or respite. He'd long ago escaped Lilith's bonds, yet he still felt trapped. Hate kept him more shackled than any chain ever could. He walked in two worlds, yet fit in neither. He no longer belonged to the human world, yet he wouldn't allow himself to fully embrace that of the Kynn.

Grinding his teeth in agitation, Adrien gunned the motorcycle's engine. He pulled into the city park thirty minutes later with half a dozen bottles of beer in his saddlebags. Brilliantly, someone had decided it would be better located about eight miles north of town, a small oasis in the desert. He followed the meandering drive, heading for the denser cul-de-sac of towering old oaks shading a large, rambling picnic area. The tables were broken up by a series of smaller pine trees and hedges that offered a sense of privacy. Adrien chose the table nearest the pond. During the day, ducks and other waterfowl would descend like locusts, eager to get a handout of stale bread and other goodies.

The city didn't pour a lot of money into upkeep, and the park bordered on shabby: broken swing chains, rickety slides, and glass-strewn playgrounds. It wasn't the safest place to be at night, but neither was it the most dangerous. Like anyplace else, you drew your lot and took your chances. He doubted anyone would bother him.

Butt planted on the tabletop, boots resting on the bench, Adrien twisted the top off his first beer and took a long quaff of the lukewarm ale. He didn't really care for the malted brew, but it was strong and might help fuzz his mind a bit. Normally he wasn't a drinker, but he needed to wash Trisha's blood out of his mouth. Maybe the alcohol would help chase away the impression that he'd enjoyed the taste.

No such luck.

Elbows resting on his knees, he fingered the smooth glass. He stared out over the still pond. Only the barest whisper of a breeze rippled the water.

Since killing Lilith, he'd centered his mind on the goal of getting even with Devon Carnavorn. He'd written all that needed to be said. He'd believed that the writing could purge the bile blackening his heart. Instead of helping to cool the heat of his anger, the letters had reignited it. The point, he supposed, was to let Devon know he was still alive—and hell-bent on revenge. Sending Lilith's head—well, that was his coup de grâce, a warning to Devon that he was on his way.

Swirling the liquid in the bottle around, he took another drink, wincing when it hit his empty stomach. Blood was not a full meal. He needed to eat. He'd been neglecting that need, eating only when necessary and then not very much. He'd centered everything around his plans for revenge, to the exclusion of everything else. He wasn't thinking about life, he was focusing on death, and that wasn't good.

Adrien took another sip of beer and grimaced. Did he truly have the right to pursue such a devastating act of revenge? Taking the stand of the Amhais, he'd never felt any guilt as a slayer.

So why was doubt plaguing his thoughts, eating at his conscience like a dog gnawed a bone? He'd been taught to believe that the Kynn possessed no souls. Or did they? Now he was not so sure. He was Kynn, yet he felt that he still had his soul. He'd died . . . that must mean his soul was forever lost to him. But what if he still had a soul? If that were so, then he would surely be condemned by God for killing the Kynn. The notion that mortals and Kynn might have originated from the same core of creation disturbed him.

Dipping back his head, he cast an unsparing stare toward the sky. The full moon was beginning to wane, bathing a dark earth in its cold illumination. Stars sparkled across the endless void like dust sprinkled by pixies. The planet Earth was just a tiny speck in the gaping maw of the universe. It was awe inspiring. He felt tiny, insignificant. At this moment there was only the darkness, stretching out into eternity. Where did the true war for lives and souls really rage? Out there in that endless void, or in the hearts and minds of men?

The night didn't last forever. He knew that. Time would pass and the Earth would revolve on its axis. In a few hours the sun would peek over the horizon. The day would arrive, illumination burning away the shadowy wraiths of darkness.

I live as one of them even as I plan to kill more of the collective. If I deny their right to survive, where is my own?

In the back of his mind was the vague notion that he would stay right here, waiting for daybreak. He didn't have to be strong, worry about the failure to pull the trigger or slide a razor through vulnerable flesh. He would look the sun in the eye and then he would know the real truth.

The sound of an engine and the glare of headlights cut into his internal conversation. Shading his eyes, Adrien watched a car wend its way into the park. Apparently he wasn't the only one seeking seclusion. Seemingly unaware of his presence, the car pulled into the neighboring picnic area. The park was a well-known lovers' lane. The pond, the grass, trees, it was a perfect romantic setting after dusk.

He sighed and tipped the bottle up, swallowing more beer. Finishing it, he tossed the bottle toward the nearby trash bin. His aim was on the mark. Score two points. Shrugging, he opened a second beer. One more and he would go. Two beers wouldn't make him too drunk to drive.

The driver killed the engine, but left the headlights on. The muffled sounds of conversation emanated from the car. He could make out the voices of a man and a woman, raised in argument. He rolled his eyes. Sheesh. A fine night, and these two wanted to duke it out. A car door opened and the woman sprang out.

"I told you I didn't want to!" She slammed the door to punctuate her point. Clearly upset, she started to hurry away.

The man also got out. Arms spread wide, he yelled in her wake, "What's your problem?"

The woman stopped and spun on her heel. Her mistake. She should have kept going. "You," she shrilled. "You're the problem, Kevin. You don't see a woman when you look at me; all you see is a bank account." She threw her hands up. "Jesus. Couldn't you have at least fucked me before asking for a loan?"

Adrien's eyebrows rose. Whoa! Quite a fight these two were having. Perhaps now would be a good time to get up and leave, to at least let them know they were not the only ones in the park tonight. Something, call it instinct or curiosity, kept him rooted. He remained still, peering through the hedges, head cocked to hear every word.

The fight escalated. Time seemed to accelerate into a blur, and a burst of violence occurred in the blink of an eye.

Rushing after the woman's departing figure, her date grabbed her arm. Spinning her around, he delivered a sound slap.

"Goddamned bitch," he snarled, dragging her back toward the car. "What's the matter? Think you're too good for me, Cassie? All that Wilson money made you rich, but it doesn't make you better than me, and it doesn't stop you from being a slut. Everyone in town knows you'll fuck any man who looks your way."

The woman screeched, twisting every which way. Her efforts earned her a second slap and a violent shove. She crumpled to the ground, whimpering in pain.

The man dropped to the ground on top of her, pinning her down with his knees. Ripping her blouse open, he exposed her breasts. "Just like you . . ." he panted. "Not even wearing a bra. You're wanting it tonight, Cassie. I bet that pussy of yours is wet, just waiting for a cock to open it up." He started to unbuckle his belt, then unzipped his slacks.

"No, Kevin," she whimpered. "Not like this . . . I'm sorry . . . please . . . don't."

He slapped her into silence. "I'll show you what the hell you're throwing away, bitch," came the nasty retort. Pushing her skirt up, he worked her panties down around her legs.

Adrien had heard quite enough. Tearing around the bushy hedges at full speed, he bounded toward the man. He hated to see the weak exploited by the strong. It ignited an unquenchable anger in him. The lady was clearly not consenting.

He grabbed the man by the scruff of his neck, hoisting him high. With a grunt, the man broke free, whirling and attacking Adrien with a full body blow. The sheer desperate power of hands closing around Adrien's neck startled him. The man was strong, damned strong. No wonder that poor woman wasn't physically able to resist him.

The two men tumbled to the ground together, a mass of arms and legs. The man was as big as Adrien was and almost as bulky. A sound punch was delivered to Adrien's jaw, followed by a second, and then a third that split his lip. He tasted his own blood, salty and warm.

Blind, shocked paralysis quickly passed as Adrien's own fighting instincts kicked into high gear. There was only a single thought in his mind: to pound the living shit out of this son of a bitch.

Determined that he wasn't going to take the worst of this ass kicking, Adrien bucked his body and dislodged his attacker. Quickly on his feet, he lashed out with all the power of his right foot and tripped the man as he attempted to get up, taking him down and then delivering a devastating kick to his rib cage.

When the man tried to roll away and scrabble off on hands

and knees, Adrien came down with a knee squarely in the man's back, putting him facedown in the dirt. Capturing one of the man's arms, he wrenched it up, none too gentle in his grip. "How does it feel to be on the other end?"

The man howled. "You're breaking my arm, you bastard!"

Adrien gave another hard twist. "Give me a reason, punk, and I will," he breathed. The man cried out a second time with more intensity.

The woman still sat on the ground, arms wrapped around her half-naked body. Sniffling through her tears, she slowly dragged herself to her feet. She'd lost one of her high heels in the scuffle, which caused her to walk with an odd limp.

Adrien caught her movements out of the corner of his eye. "Are you all right?"

The woman wiped at her dripping nose and nodded. "Yes, I think so." Her voice was shaky, but clear.

Her date started to squirm. "Tell this goddamned lug to get off me, Cassie."

Adrien looked to the lady. "You want me to let him go or break his fucking neck?" He was dead serious. "It's your call. I can snap his little spine like a matchstick." To make his point clear, he delivered his words by inflicting just a bit more pain for emphasis.

His words brought a vague smile to her face. "Just let the creep go."

"You're sure?"

She nodded. Her reply was unintelligible, but it sounded like a whimpering, "Yes."

Adrien stood up, relieving the man of his weight. He gave her date a prod with his heavy boot. "The lady says to get up, asshole."

Livid with anger, Kevin climbed to his feet. "You did the wrong thing." He straightened his clothes, apparently having more concern for his wardrobe than he did his date. "You'll be hearing from my attorney, Cassie. I swear to God I will sue you for every dime you have and then some."

"Forget the fucking lawyer," Adrien barked back, giving a hard jab to Kevin's chest. "When I get through with your ass, you'll need a priest to administer last rites."

When the man didn't take the hint and move fast enough, Adrien gave him a helpful shove toward the car. "You heard me. Get in your car and hit the road, or I'm going to stomp a mud hole right in the center of you."

Backing away, Kevin lifted his hands. "Okay, okay. Give it a rest." He hurried toward the car and slid inside. The engine roared to life. The window buzzed down. "You're going to regret this, Cassie. Don't turn your back, bitch. I will be waiting." He threw the car into reverse. Tires peeled into the ground, sending a spray of gravel into the air.

The woman seemed to lose all strength. She crumpled into the grass.

Adrien hurried over and knelt down, gingerly putting a hand on her shoulder. "You okay?"

She nodded, touched her swollen cheek and grimaced. When she shifted, she seemed to forget her torn blouse. She wore no bra and her breasts were clearly exposed. The tips of her nipples were enticingly taut.

"Yeah, I think so." Her trembling hand belied her words.

Adrien quickly averted his gaze. He took off his heavy leather jacket and put it around her shoulders. "He really knocked you around."

"So much for that relationship." She gave him a grateful smile and drew the jacket closer around her body. "Thanks." She shivered. "I'm so cold."

Adrien shrugged, unexpectedly feeling like a schoolboy. "No problem."

He looked at her. By the light of the nearby lamppost, he could see she was a beauty, with blond hair done up in a braided chignon. Stray strands of gold curled around her face and shoulders, giving her the vulnerable guise of a little girl. Her features were classic and Nordic: forehead high, eyes widely spaced, sharp cheekbones, chin gently cleft.

She looked around the deserted park. "What a way to end the evening. Stuck out in the middle of nowhere with a busted lip." Tears prickling her eyes, she laughed. There was an edge of hysteria in the sound. Shock was beginning to wear off. "How pathetic is that?"

"I'll take you to the police station," Adrien stammered, trying damn hard to put those enticing breasts out of his mind. Now was not the time to be thinking that he'd like to ravish this woman himself, albeit in a gentler, more loving manner. "You can file a report and see a doctor."

His words seemed to snap her back to reality. She immediately shook her head. "No." She touched her swelling cheek. A bruise was beginning to darken her pale skin. "No doctors. I'm fine. Just take me home, please."

"Okay." He helped her stand, then retrieved her stray shoe. She flashed a timid smile and held his arm for balance when she bent to slip it on, giving him a flash of thigh and a sexy, lacy garter. He inwardly groaned, immediately squelching his attraction.

Taking her elbow, he led her around the hedge to where he'd parked. "My motorcycle's right over here." A pause as sudden shyness overtook him. No woman had ever turned him into a nervous wreck. This one did. "You don't mind, do you?"

The woman smiled. "As long as I don't have to walk all the way back to town in these heels, a three-wheeled wagon would do."

Adrien laughed and straddled the hog. He flipped out the kick-starter and smashed it down with a heavy boot. The great machine roared to life, thrumming with an animation entirely its own. He turned around, reaching out to help her climb on, almost aching for another look of those sexy legs when she scrambled on. He didn't mind a bit when her body brushed his, her thighs spread when she settled into the passenger's seat behind him.

"Hang on." He pulled in the clutch, downshifting into first gear. The massive machine went into immediate motion when he released the clutch and gave it the gas.

"Oh, God," she laughed, half in fear, half in delight, as they exited the park and picked up speed on the open highway. "It's been a long time since I was on one of these things!" She automatically wrapped her arms around his waist. Then, as if all strength had deserted her, she rested her head on his shoulder. Her hands locked around his chest and she hugged him close, as if to silently say she never wanted to let him go.

Adrien felt a thousand-watt jolt zing through his body. A hitch rose in the back of his throat. Damn. That felt so right, almost like she belonged there behind him—and would always be there. In his time, he'd taken a lot of women, but he'd never encountered one affecting him so deeply with just a simple touch. She was a stranger, someone in need of help. Once he delivered her to her destination, he'd never see her again. It was just as well. He was a man with no immediate future. He had nothing to offer a woman, less to give.

Still, some other force took control of his tongue. "You'll be just fine," he called back, words vanishing in the roar of the engine and billowing wind. "I promise I'll take care of you."

8

Devon arrived home at four in the morning. In an earlier time, he would have remained downstairs, drinking wine and making love to any attractive woman he'd happened to entice for the evening. Since meeting and then marrying Rachel, those days were over. No longer did he play host to endless orgies for his brethren kith. The home he shared with Rachel had become their sanctuary.

He hurried to the second floor bedroom suite he shared with his wife. A thin line of illumination crept out under the double doors, indicating she still waited. She always did, refusing to sleep until he came home.

Slipping through one door, he found her as she usually was, propped up in bed. Seeing him, she smiled. "You're so late." She put the book she was reading aside. Worry was etched on her brow. "Work again?"

He pasted on a fake smile and lied. "Of course. Isn't it always?"

Knowing her husband, Rachel tipped her head, gaze searching his face. She cut in before he could speak again. "You're sure it's just work?"

Devon sighed. She was obviously picking up on his tension. *I must not burden her any further.* Sliding out of his coat, he hung it up, answering, "Just work, darling."

Suspicion creased her features. "Promise me it's just that."

He put up a hand. "Scout's honor, I swear."

Discarding his vest, he walked over and sat down on the bed, gazing at her calm figure. She was dressed in a soft pink negligee, just transparent enough to give a hint of the ripe breasts and belly beneath. He'd fallen in love with her the moment she'd come into his office asking for work. Love at first sight was an old cliché, but a true one. Her feisty attitude and refusal to back down in the face of adversity had impressed him.

Rachel pursed her lips. It was clear what was on her mind, a shadow that could not be easily cast away. "No more packages from that crazy man?"

"Nothing more—or less—than the business of making money." Leaning forward, he kissed her pregnant belly. "These two are going to be spoiled rotten with all that money can buy."

She giggled and lifted his head, planting a quick kiss on his lips. "Who'd have thought the notorious Lord Carnavorn would settle down into fatherhood?"

"Before I met you, I never would have thought it possible." In truth, Devon was the first to say that it'd taken some time to get used to a feminine presence in his all-male domain. The first thing she'd done was redecorate the suite, throwing out all the heavy dark furniture and replacing it with lighter, more modern pieces. She'd had the good sense not to bury him under pinks and whites, instead choosing rich spring tones to bring a sense of warmth and peace to their private haven.

The soft strains of a Bach concerto issued from the stereo. Piled on the table at her elbow was the usual array of needlepoint that she regularly worked on. She was sketching and designing a complete fantasy trilogy based on the Mother Goose fairytales. Under her creative hands, most of the old fables had come to brilliant life in thread. She was presently working on the lovely blond Rapunzel in her high tower.

Once in a lifetime, two perfect souls found each other. He and Rachel were much more than husband and wife. They were eternal mates. She had taken his loneliness and banished it, taken his hate and tempered it with mercy.

Receiving the murdered woman's head had horrified her. Instead of crumbling, she'd held her ground, drawing on her inner core of strength. She was an iron butterfly, a tigress. Nothing was going to stop her from birthing her babies.

She lifted his head, staring into his eyes. "You've not done anything . . . foolish . . . have you?"

Devon couldn't lie to her. She'd know in a moment any untruth he tried to slip past her. And he didn't consider hiring an assassin to take Adrien Roth out foolish at all. Still, she didn't need yet another upset. Her health was precarious as it was.

"I have taken care of the problem in a civil gentleman's manner. He won't bother us again." He looked at her again, noticing how cool her touch was. The tips of her fingers were blue, as if she were not getting enough oxygen. "You look so tired, darling. You didn't have to wait up."

She sighed, laying a hand on her belly. "I can't sleep when I'm so hungry, Devon. It's as if these two are draining me. I can't seem to get enough to keep them—or myself—fed."

His heart sank. It wasn't enough that trouble from the past was brewing. Trouble also continued to loom in their future, a future becoming more and more uncertain with each passing day.

He stood up. "Let me get you something."

She smiled. "Thanks. I was just about to." She patted her tummy again.

The master suite was luxuriously outfitted. Tucked away behind sliding cabinet doors was a small bar/kitchenette area. Opening the dorm fridge, he sighed. There was no edible food inside, only row after row of neatly stacked packets.

Taking one out, he cut the corner and poured its contents into a glass. He delivered the glass to his waiting wife.

Her own face twisted into a scowl of displeasure when she took a sip. "God, how I hate it cold," she exclaimed. "It's so much better body temperature."

"It's getting harder and harder to find volunteers, darling," he cautioned as she drank. "We have to be careful how often we draw from live victims."

Tears rose in her eyes. She blinked them back, trying to put on a brave front. "I know, I know," she burbled angrily, more at herself then at him. Nuzzling her cheek, he gave her a quick kiss.

She pulled back. "No funny stuff, mister," she admonished. "Not until I get rid of this disgusting blood breath." With a little help, she hefted her ungainly body out of bed and headed toward the bathroom. She returned minutes later, teeth freshly brushed. She stopped before a full-length mirror, cupping her belly. "God, I'm so fat," she lamented. "I'm as big as a house."

"You are not," he soothed.

Walking up, Devon folded his arms around her. Rachel sighed and put her head back on his shoulder. For a few blessed minutes, the outside world seemed to disappear.

The last months were a jumble in his mind. Examining each memory as if it were a piece of a larger puzzle, he laid them out in sequence to form a clearer picture.

The first piece was how shocked he'd been when Rachel had revealed her secret. She was not completely sure, but she believed she'd become pregnant the night she'd shed her mortal coil and crossed over into the Kynn realm. That wasn't the first time he'd dared to have full intercourse with her, but it was, perhaps, the single and last moment she could have been impregnated.

After the delight had faded, there were many questions to be addressed. The first and foremost in their minds was whether or not their children would be wholly human, as he and Rachel once were, or something else. They believed the former. It only made sense that the children would be born as normal human beings—*mortal* human beings.

As the months began to pass, Rachel's needs had changed drastically. Unable to keep down even the lightest and gentlest of foods, the only thing she could stomach was blood. Was the conception and carrying of two babies the root of her peculiar craving? Or was her surprise pregnancy the genesis of an entirely new race?

In truth, there were no answers.

There was one solution that Devon had cautiously broached while Rachel was still in her first trimester. Abort the fetuses.

Rachel's answer was an emphatic, "No!" Eyes blazing anger, hands protectively covering her belly, she'd refused to consider the idea. She was determined to carry and deliver, even if it meant she might die.

Devon had no choice but to comply. On one hand he was overjoyed at the prospect of fathering a new race. On the other, he was terrified of losing Rachel. If she died in delivery, he doubted he would long survive, especially if the children were lost, too.

He nuzzled the back of her neck. "Have I told you that you're perfect, the most gorgeous woman in the world?" He tightened his hold, hugging her harder. He could feel Rachel's body trembling against his. It was real—he was real, and yet she didn't feel like she was truly there. She slowly leaned back her head, looking up at him. A bit of the old playfulness glimmered in her gaze.

"You're just saying that to be nice."

Devon shook his head, looking into her eyes. He loved getting lost in them. She was the first woman whose eyes he could look into as he made love to her. When he was pleasuring her, he wanted to see every reaction, enjoy the sight of her soft body writhing beneath his.

"It's true." He bent down and kissed her, lips lingering on hers before he pulled back. His hands moved to her breasts, savoring their ripeness, soon to be full of the milk that would someday suckle two new lives. "I would never lie to you about that."

She batted her lashes coyly. "You always were a silver-tongued devil."

He laughed and kissed her again. This kiss was nothing like the one he had given her a moment earlier. This one was heated with delight as his hands moved up and down over her full abdomen. He could feel that familiar tightening in his groin.

"I am not lying when I say how much I need you tonight," he groaned in her ear. Pulling her hips to his, he ground his growing erection against her firm ass. Each day his physical ache for his wife grew stronger. She aroused him beyond words.

Rachel stepped away. "Then your wish is my command, master."

Licking her upper lip, a mischievous grin lit her features as she slipped her gown off her shoulders. It dropped to the floor, a soft pool of pink. Stretching her arms over her head, she brought her hands back down, running her palms over her shoulders, breasts, belly, and hips. It was a totally erotic and unselfconscious gesture.

Devon was delighted. Rachel hadn't shown much interest in intercourse these last few months. He might have to take other women to survive on this earth, but he preferred the loving arms of his wife around him in bed each night. In his mind, there was a very clear line between sex to replenish one's energies, and sex given and taken through the love of another soul.

"Are you sure?" he breathed, almost unsteady with need.

For an answer, she ran her tongue over his top lip before nipping the lower one. "Oh, yes."

Their kiss grew hotter, tongues meeting to liberally explore each other's mouths. She pulled at the front of his shirt until it was out of his slacks. Giggling, she slipped her hands up his abdomen.

Devon needed no more urging. He bent, easily sweeping her up in his arms. His desire was to throw her on the bed and ravish her until she screamed in pleasure. Since that was neither wise nor possible in her present condition, he'd have to be gentle, take his time. That idea pleased him even more as he settled her on the soft mattress. He couldn't get out of his own clothes fast enough.

Naked, he stretched out beside her. To accommodate her bulging belly, he lay on one side, propping himself up on an elbow. She lay on her back, hooking one leg over his hips. The position allowed him access to her body without discomfort or stress. His cock strained, a mere inch away from her creamy slit. It was hell not to enter her right then and there.

Eager to feast after the famine, he gazed at her, visually tracing her every feature. Stroking her cheek, he let his fingers trail down her slender neck. He could feel her pulse under his fingers, the beat of her heart strong and sure. His gaze fell on the birthmark on her thigh, one that strangely mirrored one on his own chest. Together the two marks completed a symbol sacred to the Kynn. Ariel had chosen him because of his strange birthmark. He, in turn, had chosen Rachel. Together, they were fulfilling an ancient prophecy among their kith. Rachel's stunning pregnancy certainly seemed to indicate truth of the prophecy.

"I've missed making love to you," he whispered, hardly recognizing his own voice. He began to tease one firm peak with tweaking fingers.

"I'm sorry I've been such a grouchy bitch," Rachel whispered. "Let me show you much I love—and need—you."

Tangling her fingers in his thick hair, she guided his lips to her pink nipple. He nipped at the hard little bead, pulling and twisting the other. Her response was instant. His wife loved her nipple play to verge on painful. With enough of it, she would easily climax.

Rachel's body trembled against his. He could smell her excitement, which caused his penis to surge with an electrifying intensity. Taking his hand, she guided it down between her legs. She briefly squeezed her thighs together when he drew her nipple in deeper.

"Oh, God," she panted. "I think I'm on fire."

"Mmm, good." He gently stroked the soft petals of her labia. She was moist and eager, her body fertile ground. Already planted with his seed, he could still reap the pleasurable fruits of her ripeness. Resting the heel of his hand on her Venus mound, he slipped his middle digit through her softness. Using the tip of his finger, he slowly stroked the sensitive little nubbin.

Rachel writhed in pleasure, pale skin flushing. "God," she moaned, pushing her hips against his fingers. "I need you inside me. It's been too damn long since I felt this way. . . ."

"Not yet, love." Devon slid an exploring finger inside. He smiled as her narrow channel clenched; soft, warm, and silky. He pulled out, and then slid two fingers in. He felt her body responding in a way that could only mean one thing. He twisted his fingers and rammed harder. He knew hc needed to take her soon, or he was going to lose control and climax without entering her.

"Let me see you come, Rachel."

Hands twisting the sheets, she moaned and shoved her hips up, growling as the waves of orgasm consumed her. She climaxed hard against his hand, and seconds after she dropped back to the bed, he could feel her creamy juices drenching his skin.

She released her grip, panting as he gently positioned the head of his cock at her luscious slit. Using only the slowest of motions, he eased into her honeyed depths. They both moaned. He held his hips still, waiting to see if he was hurting her in any way.

Rachel was the one who couldn't wait. "Don't be too gentle," she grated in a husky voice. Strong vaginal muscles rippled around his shaft.

Spurred by the need in her words, Devon thrust deeper. He'd been hovering at the edge of tension too long, and it was sheer hell to hold on to his control. Rachel wasn't helping. Eyes half closed, lips slightly parted, she caught hold of the headboard and arched her back, slamming into his groin, meeting him stroke for stroke. The air around them sizzled, redolent with the scent of two perspiring bodies locked together in unadulterated desire.

Unable to hold back, Devon pulled out, then rammed back in. After that, he was lost in the wonder and beauty of the simple sexual act, awesome and wrenching at the same time. Gritting his teeth against the rush, his orgasm overcame him with the force of a sun going nova.

He collapsed onto his pillow, panting to catch his breath. Bodies locked together, neither had the desire to move.

Skin beaded with sweat, Rachel wasn't half as exhausted. She snuggled against him and sighed softly. "That was wonderful." She beamed at him and touched his cheek. "Do you think we could do it again, in the shower?"

Giving a mock groan, he countered playfully, "Woman, you'll be the death of me yet."

She shook her head. "Oh, no," she laughed, patting her belly. "You're going to hang around and help me handle these two hellcats."

Devon drew her closer, giving her shoulder a playful nip. "Gladly, my love," he whispered, swallowing to quell the lump rising in his throat. "I will cherish you and our children until the end of time."

9

Silence hovered over the earth, poised between dusk and dawn, between waking and sleeping. Cool but not unpleasantly chilly, the early morning hours should have been still, touched only by the gentle flow of the earth's breath. Even the night birds were at rest, heads tucked securely under their wings.

So it was, until a subtle change came into the air. Trouble had arrived, creeping in on silent feet. Where before an atmosphere of peaceful tranquility had reigned, the breeze all of a sudden kicked up, growing stronger as a small orb of light appeared. Hovering mere inches above the ground, the orb grew wider and rounder. Lightninglike tendrils of vapor churned in its core, fighting to break out.

Without warning, the four winds merged. The orb disintegrated, freeing the strange mist. The fog spread out in undulating waves that seemed to devour the earth. It gave the impression of flow and ebb, radiant bursts of illumination and purple shadow dancing together in a strange synchronicity. An all but invisible pulsation of power surged, parting the veils between the dimensions.

A single figure from a more ominous side of existence materialized.

Morgan Saint-Evanston emerged from the veils. Vapors around him shimmered like frost, but the odd, filtered light cast no shadows. Centering his mind, he lifted a hand, palm out, as though pushing away an invisible force. The strange fog instantly dispersed, leaving not a trace. He quickly glanced around, just to be sure no other eyes watched. As he expected, the park was deserted, and he was alone.

The sky above was a luminescent haze of mixed purples and grays. Magenta shadows formed, rimmed with just a hint of gold. The breeze that sent the clouds skipping across the sky gently ruffled feathery fingers through his hair, hardly doing damage to its untamed style.

Closing his eyes, Morgan cocked his head to listen to the night, to the sounds of the distant city yet to awaken. Obscurity was his world, disbelief his cloak. To walk among mortals was to wander a blossoming orchard brimming with fruit. Lives and souls were there for the taking, the tasting. Many creatures haunted the darker side of the dimensions, each fall of darkness luring them out in search of weaker animals to dominate and destroy. Some hunted for the thrill of the chase. Others hunted for blood, flesh, or bones to feed the unnatural desires driving them into the herd of mankind.

Humans were the prey, and many joined the uncounted souls who were food for the insatiable legions of the damned.

The weak succumbed.

The strong postponed the inevitable.

It was the law of an unnatural nature.

As an entity, Morgan had walked the earth for over twelve hundred years, prowling among the human flock. But he was hardly a wolf in sheep's clothing. No, he was much more. He was *the* gatekeeper between natural and supernatural.

Opening his eyes, he readjusted the strap of the heavy crossbow slung across his back. The medieval weapon was loaded with deadly bolts, the serrated tips hard to remove from flesh. That wasn't his only armament. He was prepared to take down any beast, be it two-legged, four-legged, or more. A Beretta 92 handgun rode in a shoulder holster concealed by his long coat, along with three sheathed daggers. Death was his profession, and he delivered it with a ruthless and emotionless efficiency.

He slipped a hand into his pocket. Out came his gold case. He opened it and selected a cigarette, lighting it with a gold-plated lighter. True, he didn't need the lighter, but he also knew when to rein in his psi-kinetic energies and not act like a damn show-off. Immortal did not mean utterly invulnerable. He fought burnout as much as any other of his kind. He needed to center his concentration on tracking Adrien Roth.

Cigarette clenched between his teeth, Morgan strolled toward the picnic area. This was the place where Adrien Roth's vibrations were the strongest. He paused, briefly putting out a hand. Every living thing exuded a unique spiritual aura, in much the same way that a body radiated heat. Each person's "psychic imprint" was exclusive, belonging only to that individual, just like a fingerprint. Morgan possessed the clairvoyance to sense those energies. He only needed to touch an object that person had handled to pick up the lingering impressions. With just a touch, he knew a person's whole life forward and backward. It was not an ability he relished; he used it rarely. He'd picked up Adrien's trail from the latter's letters.

Roth's presence was definitely very strong. Morgan felt the thrumming of energy, the straining of suppressed frustration, anger, and strength. Roth was going to be an easy one to track.

"I feel you, Adrien. You are close, very close."

Adrien Roth was a very angry man. His letters had made

that more than crystal clear. His calling was that of watcher and protector. He didn't know how to deal with being the victim.

Having an ability to read people through psychic impression, Morgan had been able to detect more from the pages than what the man had written.

Past Adrien's words of rage was the great confusion he was suffering. He was finding it difficult to reconcile his past with his present existence. He was repulsed by his new life even as he was fascinated by the world he was attempting to shun.

Adrien wants to explore the life further, but the ties of training and belief have kept him bound.

Following the psychic currents, Morgan walked around a high hedge. His probing gaze immediately settled on the ground. He paced the area, making a wide, slow circle. Once, twice, three times; clockwise, then counterclockwise. By the last turn, he'd gathered a complete picture of the events that occurred there earlier. He frowned, brow wrinkling in consternation. Other unexpected impressions were muddying the psychic atmosphere; one definitely very strongly female. The woman's were mingling and mixing with Adrien's, the two seeming to become one for a moment.

Taking a long drag off his cigarette, he flicked aside the ashes. "Something happened here," he muttered, pacing the area. Damn! Usually two auras didn't fuse like this, unless . . .

Definitely something he hadn't anticipated. He frowned, snuffing out his cigarette in the palm of one hand. The brief burn didn't even register on his senses.

Surely this can't be . . .

He glided, unconscious of the movements of his physical self as he slipped between the veils to get a closer look.

Morgan lifted his eyes, searching the endless void. Rather than adding his own impressions, he chose to keep the currents in their natural state. Around him the dimensions were still, unusually so, allowing him undisturbed access to intangible realms existing beyond reality. Had he thought of it in physical terms, he might have been strolling an endless path colored by light and shadow. Impressions were sometimes very bright and brilliant, other times dim and gray.

The astral realms were usually teeming with other entities seeking answers. Sometimes minds would meet, chat a bit, and move on. No one came near him.

Well, being a Reaper did have its advantages. The smart ones left him alone. The stupid ones . . . well, they usually never bothered him a second time. He had a particularly nasty talent for being able to make conscious thought manifest as action.

A long shiver rippled down his spine, and he felt a chill curl in his guts. Too damn bad that power usually gave him a nasty migraine and pushed him one step closer toward his own mental burnout. Use his psi-abilities to manifest in the physical world and he'd pay in the long run.

Time ticked away, unnoticed. It felt as though he were moving rapidly, when in reality he hadn't taken a single step.

He studied the impressions again, carefully sorting through the remnants of each person's psychic aura. Their psi-level tracks were beginning to fade as time passed. Soon there wouldn't be a trace that either had ever been present. Here, he picked up a look. There, he picked up a touch. And every time Adrien and the female physically met, the auras merged.

Adrien was Kynn. His should have been the stronger impression. Oddly, it was not.

The woman's was. Strange. He searched through her lifeline, going back to the day of her conception. Just in case she had any occultic forebearers in her family tree. She did not. An utterly normal human. Still, some force in her pulsed strongly, as if she not only clung to life, but was determined to suck in every last drop. Her passion for life flowed through him like a thick boiling cloud. As for Adrien's aura, it was understandably black, curiously shaped, and slashing as if to destroy all around it.

Fortunately, it didn't succeed.

Strangely, when the two auras met, they merged so completely that they looked—and felt—like a single. Adrien's lightened a bit, hers darkened. Perfect synchronicity, like two cells meeting to form an entirely new organism.

"Hmm, this is getting interesting." Had Morgan not had the experience of a millennium behind him, he could have easily confused one for the other.

Groaning, he smacked his forehead. "I am so blind," he muttered. "How long has it been since I have seen such a perfect blending of souls?"

Adrien had a soul mate.

Definitely something to think about.

Morgan lit a fresh cigarette. Drawing in a lungful, he exhaled, watching the smoke drift into the air, grow opaque, then vanish completely.

The sun peeked over the edge of the earth, reminding him dawn was near.

He sighed. The night never lasted long enough. He reached up, pulling the shades perched on his head back down over his eyes. He was definitely not a worshipper of the sun.

Better get going. Best not to be seen by any humans. It would be hard to explain the gun. Harder still to explain the crossbow to any authority figures who might happen along. As a courtesy to humans he didn't use his supernatural abilities— unless there was no other way to get out of an uncomfortable situation. He had to live in this world, too. No reason to make trouble for himself with the human population.

Morgan departed as he'd arrived.

Where the winds could go, a skilled conjurer could as well, for it was easy to merge with the air currents. He slipped to the silvery embrace of nothingness, melting into the cool breeze like a soft haunting sigh as his search continued.

The wheels in his mind turned as he harnessed and rode the night's zephyr like an eagle at wing.

He'd visited with Devon.

Now it was time to pay a little visit to another old friend.

10

Closing the door behind her, Cassie Wilson slid the deadbolt into place. Looking out the window, she couldn't help smiling when she eased the curtain over to take a peek.

The man who'd rescued her sat in the driveway, watching to make sure she'd made it safely inside. Only when he was confident that she was secure did he put his motorcycle into gear and depart. She'd come to believe there were no more knights in shining armor to rescue a damsel in distress.

I was mistaken. Her smile widened. Her knight hadn't ridden a white horse, rather a battered Harley Davidson that had eaten up a lot of asphalt. It was nice to be proven wrong. *He's awfully nice. Wonder if he's available . . .*

A frown replaced her smile, mouth turning down. She rested her forehead on the door and closed her eyes. Her face still stung from the blows Kevin had delivered. A raging headache was building behind her eyes. Neither was a good sign that the evening was going to get any better.

Her mind drifted back to the man who'd so gallantly and unhesitatingly arrived to rescue her. He was undeniably good looking: a lean, serious face; clear brown eyes; long dark hair tied back. God, how'd she love to see it down and flowing free. He was sexy, too. She certainly hadn't failed to notice the way his T-shirt hugged his broad shoulders or the way the material of his tight jeans stretched across his crotch. Tall, lanky, with muscles in all the right places, he was packing quite a cock. She'd relish taking a bite out of that apple.

A fierce heat crept into her cheeks even as the flutter of desire took delicious flight. Men who truly set her mind and body aflame were few and far between.

"I didn't even get his name." A thought flitted through her mind. *I'd like to see him again.* Like a hummingbird it hesitated to land, instead hovering in perpetual flight, ready to dart out of sight.

Drawing herself up, she squared her shoulders. "When will you learn, Cassie? Men aren't any good for you."

Leaving the foyer, her eyes roamed over the romantic little dessert that her housekeeper had earlier arranged in the living room. Set out Japanese-style was a low table brimming with fresh fruit, dark chocolate warming in a fondue pot, and a nice bottle of chilled wine. Soft silk pillows and a thick romantic comforter scattered with fresh rose petals were all arranged before an unlit fireplace. She'd planned a romantic evening for two. Or so she'd believed. That was until Kevin hit her up for a personal loan right in the middle of her shrimp cocktail. He might as well have dashed ice water in her face.

Cassie fumed. "I'm not stupid. Men use me because I have a lot of money."

She bent over and popped a piece of pineapple into her mouth. "Bastard." She winced when the sweet juice made contact with her tender lips. "Fucking leech."

Cassie ate a few more pieces of fruit, dipping some strawberries in chocolate, savoring the rich sweetness. Later, she'd come back downstairs and stuff herself like a pig. Presently, she needed time to unwind and relax. A hot shower would help.

Grabbing the wine and a single glass before kicking off her high heels, she climbed the stairs to her second-floor bedroom. The house really was too big for one person to be rattling around in.

She laughed to herself, remembering the awe her rescuer had shown when she'd directed him to her home. She lived in what was, literally, the mansion on the hill, a three-story behemoth that her grandfather had built. The house was a white elephant. No one wanted it because it had too much of a history behind it. She didn't blame them. If she had her druthers, she'd drop a match on it. She'd always thought that would be a glorious way to walk out—with a bang.

Going up the stairs, she passed portraits of her family, almost a layout of their entire family history in paintings and photographs. She paused to look at her great-great-grandfather's black-and-white ghostly image.

Everyone knew who H. B. Wilson was in the scheme of the business world. Officially, he'd founded a small company making paper products in 1879. Then, in 1896, the Wilson Paper Co. marketed the first rolls of toilet paper. Success was practically guaranteed. People needed to wipe their butts, preferably with something besides the Sears and Roebuck catalog.

And that's how Cassie's family made its fortune, because people were full of shit.

She'd grown up an only child, shuttled between nannies and boarding schools. She had no real ties to any place, no real friends she could call close. At twenty-one, she'd inherited full access to her trust fund. Always a young woman of privilege, she then became a young woman of incredible means. She had a finishing school education, which meant a degree in some branch of the arts she couldn't even remember—but she did still recall how to match her tea cozies with the sofa cushions! As a debutante she seemed to have a life most would envy: a semirespectable pedigree, beauty, and wealth. The world should have been her oyster.

It wasn't.

Money couldn't buy happiness. Or love. Or health.

It can only buy stuff, she thought.

Heading into her bedroom, Cassie punched a few buttons on the console by her bed. Her room was outfitted with the latest entertainment technology: giant flat-panel television, DVD and CD player—all remote and all easily controlled without having to get out of bed. Hardly in the mood for the romantic classics she'd programmed in, she decided on something more kick-ass to listen to. The steady beat of Don Henley's "Dirty Laundry" began to play. She liked that song. It was practically her theme.

Mood set, wine in hand, she made a beeline for the bathroom. There was every convenience at her disposal, including a full walk-in glass-walled shower and a bathtub big enough to swim laps in. She decided that a long soak in a tub full of hot water would be just the ticket. Flipping on the taps, she decadently dumped in a handful of expensive bath beads. The scent of lilacs rose in the steam.

Waiting for the tub to fill, she sat down at her vanity table. She groaned when she saw the damage. Both her eyes were blackened, her cheeks swollen, and her bottom lip three times normal size, with a nice split right down the center.

She leaned in closer, gingerly touching her swollen cheek with the pads of her fingers. Her skin felt thicker, harder. *Forget the Botox, baby. All you need to rid yourself of those ugly age lines is to have a boyfriend slap you around a bit. Works every time.*

She giggled, but it was hardly a sound of amusement. It was more like a whimper in the back of her throat. It wasn't the first time a man had smacked her around, though the others usually had the decency to wait until she'd married them to start the heavy-handed abuse. Given her choices of husbands, people speculated that Cassie Wilson didn't have a brain in her head.

Well, she did have a brain.

She also had a tumor growing in it.

After a series of headaches that had long been misdiagnosed as stress migraines and flights of fancy that went from grandeur to depression in a matter of seconds, the doctors had finally arrived at the true diagnosis.

Glioblastoma multiforme was the official name of the cancerous mass growing in her brain. It was highly malignant, as infiltrating as an undercover CIA operative. She already knew that few patients with GBM survived longer than three years and only a handful survived more than five.

Cassie was almost two years into her cancer. For her, surgery was not an option; the tumor was too deeply embedded for surgeons to reach. Chance it, and she'd surely die on the operating table or, worse, be left a total vegetable. That was not an option, either.

Radiation and chemotherapy were unsuccessful treatments. Learning her cancer was going to be most likely fatal even if she underwent further treatment, she'd ignored the advice of her too-numerous doctors and made her final decision. Before her symptoms worsened and the disease conquered her body, she'd live her life to the fullest. She had money enough to keep herself comfortable right through to the end. The specter of death might be hanging over her head, but what the hell! Everybody in this world died. It was just a matter of how, where, and when. She already had one answer.

The Reaper, however, wasn't laying hands on her tonight. Life was way too short to be wasted pining over useless pricks like Kevin. There were still a few days yet to be enjoyed, and she intended to seize every moment. She didn't care if people thought she was crazy or a whore or whatever. She literally did not have the time to worry about what other people thought of her.

Head swimming from the wine, which at least helped dull her headache, she stood up and began to undress. She realized she was still wearing the biker's leather jacket. She pulled in a breath to clear her woozy head. It was so comfortable and well worn she'd forgotten she had it on.

She held out her arms, examining it. It was extra large, enveloping her tiny frame like a sleeping bag. It wasn't a fancy style. The black leather was faded and scuffed, collar and sleeves frayed by years spent out on the elements. Her rescuer obviously wore it as a regular part of his wardrobe.

Gathering the leather in her hands, she lifted it to her nose. The odor of musk mingled with the smell of the dusty desert and male sweat, not at all unpleasant. Like a junkie sniffing coke, she drew in another deep whiff. God, how she loved the scent of him. It reminded her of his strength.

She wondered if he were missing the jacket. He did know where she lived. Perhaps he'd return for it.

Her heart began to beat a mile a minute. Everything about the man was solid, from the body that made her go weak in the knees to the concentrated gaze that had eaten her up without blinking. She felt herself shift from hot and bothered to downright blazing.

Cassie closed her eyes, remembering the solidity of his flesh. He was all male and all muscle, moving with the ease of a wild coyote across the desert plains. She let her mind wander through a wonderful fantasy. He was her hero come to life, and she wanted a taste. A soft moan escaped her lips. It was easy to imagine meshing her fingers in his thick dark hair as he went down on her, pleasuring her . . .

"I've got to see him again."

Curious to learn more about her mystery man, Cassie dug through the outside pockets. To her disappointment, she found nothing more than a pack of mints, some loose change, and a couple of gas receipts.

She gave the jacket a shake, turning it inward. There were a couple of inner pockets. She delved eagerly into the first, bringing up a switchblade knife.

Ah, it was a beauty, just the thing a bad-boy biker would have on hand. She pushed the button, and the blade flicked open with a smooth *shooshing* sound, eight solid inches of hard icy steel. Holding it sent a shiver of excitement up her spine. She wondered if he'd ever pulled it on anyone.

She grinned and set the blade aside. What a useful thing to have. Too bad she hadn't had it in hand when Kevin slapped her. She wouldn't have minded him having a flash of this. Might have been nice to cut that turkey-neck he called a dick clean off.

The image of that one brought a guffaw of laughter. "Oh, wicked me." She giggled. She dug into the last pocket. Pay dirt! She pulled out a small sack. Inside was a small bottle. Reading the label, she could see it was a vet's prescription for Mitacin, an ear mite treatment for a cat. The owner's last name was on the bottle, along with that of his pet.

"Gisele," she read. "How pretty." But what was her mystery man's first name? There was one more thing in the white bag, rattling against the paper. She fished out a brand-new tag for a collar—not a common rabies tag, but a custom design.

She squinted to see the tiny print. Between her contact lenses clocking eight-plus hours in overtime and the wine, her vision was a little hazy. Her heart hammering in her chest, she shook so hard that she could barely hold the tag still enough to read the inscription: the name of the cat, her owner, and the number she'd been assigned when given a rabies shot.

"A. J. Bremmer," she mouthed. All she had to do was call

the vet listed on the prescription and pretend she'd found the cat. If she could wheedle the owner's phone number, that would be great. An address would be even better.

Now she had a name to go with the face of her sexy biker. Was it crazy to feel such an attraction, such a connection, to a man she'd spent less than an hour with? She wasn't a believer in love at first sight or happy endings. She was a strong believer in the power of fate. This man had come into her life and left an impression she couldn't let go of quickly or easily.

I intend to pay Mister Bremmer a visit. Her fingers closed around the tag. *Just to thank him.*

She didn't know why he was so important to her or even how he'd figure into her future.

But she wanted to find out.

11

The door to his house hung wide open.

"Damn," Adrien swore, furiously killing the engine on his bike. Light bathed the entire house, every window in his house lit up like a Christmas tree. Someone had broken in. He'd left the place locked tight before leaving.

Hackles rising, a surge of anger shot through his chest. Oh, swell. Just what he needed. His few possessions plundered by the desert rats roaming the area. Those assholes would steal anything that wasn't nailed down. Not that he had anything worth taking. If the thieves were looking for drugs, they'd be shit out of luck. The medicine cabinet contained little more than a toothbrush, razor, and comb.

Hopping off his motorcycle, Adrien reached for the Buck knife holstered at his hip. He doubted anyone was inside, but better to be safe than sorry. Testosterone raging from his recent feed, he felt full of piss and vinegar. After his brief tangle with Cassie Wilson's boyfriend, he ached for a good old-fashioned fight.

He grinned. "I'd love to take names and kick some ass."

He approached the open door. The closer he got to the house the more he felt the strange energy in the air—dangerously still, almost leaden. An invisible current pulsed like static, crackling across his skin. The sensation snaked around him, as if to draw him into a vortex of endless depth.

A hiss of surprise escaped his lips. The strange electric atmosphere contracted his chest, sending a jolt of pure adrenaline though his limbs.

Something was inside.

Heart beating double time, he bared his teeth. At the same time a savage growl broke from deep within his throat. Yes, he felt it all too clearly. It was something very definitely *not* human.

He wasn't surprised. He'd suspected Devon might try to get to him first. You didn't send out threats without expecting retaliation. Good. That meant Devon was taking him absolutely seriously. One or the other was going to have to die.

Adrien wasn't planning to be the victim. Not by a long shot. The idea of running, of tucking his tail between his legs and beating a hasty retreat, didn't occur to him. No way he'd just run off and leave.

Gisele was still inside.

Adrien wanted his cat. And woe be to the intruder if any harm had befallen a single whisker.

Knife gripped tight, he charged over the threshold. The sight meeting his eyes could hardly be believed. Guts lurching, he stopped dead in his tracks.

Clothed in black from head to foot, a familiar figure lay stretched out on the couch. The reason for his nap was abundantly clear. A multitude of empty beer bottles littered the floor. Like Goldilocks, this visitor had obviously made himself quite at home.

As for Gisele, she'd not been in the least disturbed. She perched on the back of the couch, little pug nose upturned, and looked thoroughly regal. Apparently she liked her visitor. Unusual. Gisele definitely didn't take to strangers.

Adrien blinked in absolute jaw-dropping shock. The floor could have crumbled under his feet, and he wouldn't have noticed. "I don't believe this."

He blinked again. The sight remained the same. Recognition instantly kicked in. *Oh shit.*

The Grim Reaper had come to pay him a visit. In the flesh. And he'd come prepared. A crossbow leaned against the wall beside the couch. Well out of reach. Not so the other weapon he carried. One arm covering his eyes, the other rested on his stomach, fingers just inches away from the butt of the gun that protruded from his duster.

Adrien's mouth quirked down. *I see the son-of-a-bitch has kept up with the ways of modern killing.* He sheathed his knife. No comparison. He was definitely out armed.

Not that there appeared to be any immediate threat. Morgan Saint-Evanston seemed to have drunk all his beer and passed out.

Adrien eyed the gun. Might be better to get the damn thing off him. For safety's sake. Best not disturb his visitor. He'd just ease on in, get the gun, then ease on out.

A simple plan.

Safety was what it was all about, right? Not to mention he might be saving himself a painful and ugly death. Not to mention that he'd feel a hell of a lot better having the gun in *his* hands.

Going into stealth mode, he crept closer. The smell of stale cigarette smoke, barley, and dusty denim assailed his nostrils.

Gisele stirred from her nap. Kneading the fabric beneath her paws, she turned on a motor-loud purr.

No!

Adrien mentally warned his pet to be still and stay silent. Another second and he'd be home free. His hand went out, carefully, oh so slowly.

Except that Morgan's hand suddenly moved, much faster. Gun snatched, the barrel of a 9 mm pointed at Adrien's forehead. A forefinger ominously curled around the trigger.

The gun was aimed right between Adrien's eyes.

Fear slid like razors over his skin. "Shit." He'd blown it. Big time. He swallowed. Hot saliva slithered like lead down his throat. His bowels went alarmingly molten. He couldn't believe he'd let Gisele distract him. Cursing himself repeatedly, he considered his limited options.

Please don't splatter my brains all over the room.

Morgan's left arm still covered his eyes. No matter. He could easily pull that trigger and be assured he wouldn't miss. "You should know better than to sneak up on me when I am hung over, lad."

Careful not to move an inch, Adrien breathed out. "Guess I forgot." Ho-kay. Plan A had failed. Time to go to plan B. Except there was no plan B.

He licked dry lips. A sheen of sweat prickled his skin. "I hope the safety's on."

"Never use it." That sounded exactly like a threat.

Adrien was toast. He easily imagined the bullet tearing through bone and brain tissue with a sickening rush. He wondered what it would sound like to hear his own head explode. Probably not wonderful. Not that he'd get a second chance to ever hear it again.

"Oh." His pulse rate kicked up a notch. Icy fingers wrapped around his heart with surprising strength. As tough as he wanted to appear, visiting with a gun so up close and personal rattled him.

Morgan uncovered his eyes. His hawkish gaze raked and assessed within seconds. A nasty smile curled the corners of his mouth. "Only an idiot would bring a knife to a gunfight."

For ten, maybe twenty seconds, Adrien couldn't move.

Then he pulled nerve and courage back together and straightened to his full height to meet that lethal gaze head on. "Go ahead. If you've come to kill me, get it over with."

The silence between them telegraphed how very seriously deep Adrien's trouble ran. His anxiety ratcheted up another notch.

The gun lowered. "You always liked playing the martyr."

Those six words shattered the tension.

Adrien's relief drizzled in. The prickle of his fear eased. "Easy to do when you've got a gun pointed at you and no way out."

The chilly smile warmed a bit. "You know me better than that. I might have given you a chance to turn around and reach the door."

Adrien eyed his uninvited guest suspiciously. "Before you shot me in the back?"

"Maybe." A shrug. "Maybe not."

"And hello to you, too. Such a nice way to greet an old friend." Though he wouldn't admit it, it felt good to see a recognizable face in this alien place. Having a home, belonging to a familiar group, sharing the camaraderie of those he'd fought with side by side. Nothing was left of his past but a big empty hole.

The assassin tucked his gun away and yawned. "I always liked you, Adrien. You were one of the more fearless of the Amhais. Fearless, but stupid."

Fearless. Right. He'd damn near shit a brick, and bravery wasn't the reason.

Strong fingers tousled thick hair that had never actually met a comb. "Where were you anyway? I was getting bored waiting in this dump all by myself."

Classic Morgan. Blunt and to the point. Insults were his way of being sociable.

Adrien didn't have to look twice to confirm what he already knew. The place was a dump. No reason to have it thrown in his face. "Like you haven't skulked in places a lot worse?"

"I only pass out in pigsties," came the sulky reply. "I do not live in one."

"If it so offends your finicky sensibilities, why are you even here?" Adrien demanded impatiently.

A snort. "I would have thought that obvious."

Adrien's hands suddenly itched to throttle. Welcome could be worn thin. "Coming from a psycho like you . . . uh, no."

Morgan grinned wickedly. "I came for your ale, which tastes like cheap horse piss, by the way." He simultaneously stroked Gisele's back, giving the Persian a quick scratch on the rump. "And your pussy."

That was the final straw.

Swearing in disgust, the cat's offended owner reached across the couch and angrily snatched her away. "It's bad enough you break into my house and drink all my beer," he steamed, stomping into the bedroom and depositing Gisele safely on the bed. "But I'll thank you to keep your hands off my goddamn cat." He stomped back into the living room. Settling his hands on his hips, he glared.

Blithely ignoring him, Morgan lit one of those noxious clove cigarettes he seemed to have a fondness for. "Whatever." An exhalation of white smoke followed as he rubbed his eyes with thumb and forefinger. "I could use another drink to chase off this hangover."

Adrien glared harder, mentally sending daggers. "There isn't any more."

Making a quick gesture with one hand, Morgan produced a small silver flask out of thin air. His move was so fast and so practiced Adrien almost didn't see it, even with his superhuman vision.

The lid came off the flask. "Never go anywhere without an emergency supply."

Adrien rolled his eyes and smiled reluctantly. "I should have known an alcoholic bog-trotting cockroach such as yourself would never be found far from booze."

Half emptied, the flask came down. "I resent that slur against the Irish half of my heritage."

"But you don't deny the alcoholic cockroach part?"

"No more than you could deny the sheep-fucking Englishman part of yours."

Irritation twisted Adrien's insides. "That's not true."

"That you're English?" Morgan countered in that irreverent tone.

Check and mate. He'd been bested.

And that ticked him off. Not that there was any truth that he had carnal knowledge of farm animals. "You haven't changed a bit. Still rude, very crude, and socially unacceptable."

Now that tension had faded, that old sense of familiarity had begun to return. Despite their seeming antagonism, they had more than a passing acquaintance. At one time they'd both been fighting on the same side. An enigma wrapped in a mystery, no one knew exactly why Morgan had chosen to hunt other occultic beings. No one was brave enough to ask. His reasons were his own.

Exhausted from the stress and pressure, Adrien felt like collapsing. Instead of doing that, he walked over and retrieved one of the rickety kitchen chairs.

Carrying it into the living room, he plunked it down a few feet away from the couch. He sat. Leaning forward, he folded his arms across its high back. He didn't lean too hard. Barely attached, the back threatened to collapse momentarily.

Adrien ordered his body to relax. Showing fear would be the worst thing to do. "No more bullshit," he said firmly. "Despite your warped sense of humor, I have a feeling this isn't a social call."

"You would be right."

"How'd you even find me?" He'd been careful to cover his tracks and keep moving.

Morgan gave a smile of clueless chaos. "Just lucky, I guess."

Uh huh. Adrien doubted luck had anything to do with it.

All appearances aside, everything Morgan did was usually calculated to the Nth degree. Adrien's instincts stood at attention. "How convenient. You used to lie a lot better than that. I've already pretty much figured out that chicken-shit Devon put you up to this."

Amusement tugged at Morgan's lips. "I did a search on your psychic aura through the astral realm. Once I got a current, I was able to pinpoint your physical location."

Oh. The explanation jolted Adrien. He closed his eyes and tried to block the dizzying sensations of ignorance flowing along every nerve ending. There was still so much he didn't know or understand about the abilities of occultic beings. The little bits and pieces he'd learned from watching Lilith didn't even begin to scratch the surface of what the Kynn were capable of. For the first time since his crossing, he wondered just what it would be like to be a fully skilled occultic being.

Adrien quickly shoved the thought away. The point of existing outside the Kynn collective was precisely that he didn't want to be one of *them.* He wasn't one of them. Had never wanted to be.

"So much for hiding," he mumbled. All the trouble he'd taken to lay decoy routes was for nothing.

Morgan finally deigned to explain. "All I needed was some object that you'd touched. The rest was amazingly easy."

Adrien sucked in a deep breath. Suspicion had just been confirmed. "The things I sent Devon," he spat bitterly.

"Yes."

A frown wrinkled Adrien's forehead. "I should have known he wouldn't be man enough to handle this himself." He thought for a moment. "Did you read them?"

Morgan snuffed out his cigarette and flicked away the butt. "Aye, I read them all."

Adrien bristled. "Thanks to Devon, I spent over thirty years trapped with a madwoman."

"Whom you have gotten even with." Morgan gave a quick thumbs up. "Sending Lilith's head to Devon was sheer genius. Got the message right through."

Hearing her name spoken aloud, sensations of despair washed over Adrien like the waves of an all-consuming ocean. The darkness, the emptiness, the long years spent alone. Lilith had cast him into this living hell. Devon had helped. Until he'd paid them both back in full, he'd never know rest, never find the peace eluding his damned soul.

Adrien dropped his head and stared at his arms. He closed his eyes and the memories all came flooding back. Fierce, unrelenting pain stabbed deep. They'd made him a demon.

Irritation threatened to morph into fury. Struggling for calm, he forced his mind blank. Right now was not the time to lose it. "Devon's next," he stated flatly. "And his wife."

Morgan tucked his flask away and leaned slightly toward him. "And this is the place where I step in and warn you to back off," he countered in a low voice.

Anger jolted through Adrien. He sucked in a breath. The threat he'd been anticipating had just materialized.

Not that he'd be willing to change his plans, he reminded himself. Following the only pursuit he felt he had left in life had kept him going.

Emotion tightening his throat, Adrien's lips trembled before he pressed them together. He considered his options for a few moments and then made a decision. He had a mission to accomplish. He wouldn't let anything get in his way of settling his final score. Not now. He was too damn close to stop.

He snapped out of the trance he'd fallen into. "I see you've switched sides. Protecting human lives must have begun to bore you."

Morgan sighed. "Not at all. Were you just threatening Devon I would step back and let you wreak your havoc. But threatening unborn children is another matter entirely. And why the worry? The Kynn have never even posed a threat to humankind. For the most part they are one of the more harmless entities in the occultic realm."

That wasn't quite how Adrien viewed things. "The Kynn also don't procreate. They recruit from human ranks. So what exactly will Devon's children be? Human? I doubt it. Despite the fact that I'm unwillingly Kynn, I was Amhais first."

"You're letting your antagonism toward Devon blind you to an entirely different situation," Morgan warned.

"I'm doing what I was born to do," Adrien gritted out, his voice rough with emotion. "Defending humankind from hell-spawned creatures. It seemed to me you once believed that, too. I've seen you kill to keep evil in its place. What changed?"

Morgan all of a sudden rose with an inhuman grace. Gone in an instant was the mask of the vapid jester. He'd slipped on another. Within seconds the detached and icy calm of the professional mercenary had taken over.

Obsidian eyes glittered with fresh menace. "I did not change. You did. You have become the thing you most despise: an entity preying on the weaker race."

Adrien gave a contemptuous sneer. "That's not true. I was the victim."

"Not anymore."

Adrien didn't want to listen. He didn't want to think about it. "I'm not backing off," he finally said. "Those children won't be born into this world as long as I am alive to stop it."

An intense gaze studied him. "Do not go there."

A volatile mixture of emotions coiled inside his heart, slicing from the inside out. "I'm not making a threat. Mark my words now; it's a promise." His mouth was drier than the Sahara but surprisingly his voice sounded strong and steady. "One I intend to keep."

In the attic of Adrien's skull, the small voice of conscience cried out in the darkness. Sanity lingered, a thing barely alive. It pleaded for Morgan to draw his gun and kill him. Better to die now than to discover he really was capable of killing a woman and her children. Maybe better to have salvation through death than damnation through living—and murdering—again.

No such luck. The gun stayed holstered.

Fueled by vengeance, insanity delivered a devastating jolt to his conscience. The voice in his mind went silent.

Guess that's that, Adrien thought with finality. *I'm going to do what I'm going to do—and so will he.*

Morgan retrieved his crossbow, slinging it across one shoulder with an easy strength. "So be it." He headed toward the door he'd mutilated. It would never close right again, much less lock. "I will give you a little time to think. I suggest you use it to look for your fucking brains, my friend."

Adrien jumped up and flung himself around like a petulant child. "What if I don't want to think about it?"

Awkward silence throbbed.

Morgan stopped. Turned. A smile tugged up one corner of his mouth. One hand held the strap of his crossbow, and a pair of designer sunglasses appeared in the other. "Consider this visit a warning." He slid the glasses on, obscuring his eyes. A psychological ploy of cutting off and separating. "The second one will not be. I will regret having to kill you for being a stubborn fool, Adrien."

Then he vanished from sight, walking out the door as if he hadn't a care in the world. The incredible energy electrifying the house was sucked away, leaving a cold sense of emptiness in its wake. Where he would go next—what would happen next—was anybody's guess.

Like a balloon with a slow leak Adrien exhaled a heavy breath. He felt limp and spent. His legs trembled beneath his weight, threatening to collapse.

Oh, God, he thought. *Why have you forsaken me?* He'd been born with an awareness of the occultic world, seeing the invisible menace of the supernatural in living color where others saw only indistinct shadow.

He tried to block Morgan's words from his mind but they kept echoing there.

"One way or another," he muttered, rubbing his face with both hands, "I think I'm fucked."

12

Strands of long red hair spilled across the white silk like a veil. His lover lay asleep in her bed, cheek pressed to her pillow, lips parted by the gentle breath that moved her breasts. She lay atop the covers, naked save for a sexy red lace bra and the skimpiest of panties.

Julienne had obviously planned to surprise him.

And what a present to come home to. Just what he needed. Sex.

Gaze sweeping her from head to toe, Morgan felt the blood rush from his head. Straight to the erection swelling uncomfortably in the confines of tight jeans.

She looked good enough to eat. A grin parted his lips. That's exactly what he planned to do. He'd devour every inch of her, beginning with those lush red lips. Slack in sleep, her mouth was open just wide enough for him to imagine slipping his cock into her warm mouth. Having just the slightest overbite, she had unparalleled oral skills.

Shrugging out of his duster, Morgan tossed it on a nearby chair. Devon Carnavorn would probably be surprised to learn that he'd settled in the mortal realm, in 1738, in the geographic region known as the Commonwealth of Virginia. That was when he had established his homestead and founded his coven. He had granted them the knowledge and power of the occult, his very blood, so that they would not only survive but flourish.

Visually exploring Julienne's ample curves, he couldn't help but think just how well the last of his sentinels had flourished. She was the first he'd ever taken as a lover. The first he'd ever offered to share immortality with.

Stripping off his shirt, he slipped onto the bed, scooting his body against hers. The softness of the backs of her thighs fit perfectly against his hard planes. The tantalizing scent of strawberries teased his nostrils. Her creamy skin beckoned for kisses and caresses.

Sliding his arm under hers, he cupped one breast. Fingers slipping under the lace of her bra, he slowly circled her nipple. He bent his head, nibbling at the soft flesh beneath her left ear.

Roused from sleep, Julienne moaned softly. Her body pressed against his, treating his cock to an enticing rub. "About time you made it back," she murmured, still half asleep.

Drawing in her sleep-warm scent, Morgan nuzzled deeper. "Just a little trouble that needed tamping down, darling."

"Mmm. I waited as late as I could. I didn't know you'd be gone all night." Her words were true. Behind shuttered windows the first wisps of day were peeking over the horizon.

Pushing down the lace covering her breast, he circled the little nub, causing it to pucker then tighten. "If I had known you were waiting half naked for me, I would have hurried back."

Julienne stiffened in pleasure. "You're here now," she breathed. "That's all that counts." She gasped, reaching behind her to grasp at his hip and pull him closer.

Morgan chuckled as he trailed his palm down her abdomen. "I will make it up to you," he breathed, aching for her more fiercely than ever. Though he'd have liked to take her right then and there, he owed her a little foreplay. Maybe it would help make up for running off without telling her where he was going.

She quivered as his hand massaged her flat belly. Her knees separated. "I don't know why you even had to go."

He pushed his hand between her legs to give himself a little space to work. The line of her skimpy panties rested just above her Venus mound. "Same old thing, different day. Just out slaying a few dragons."

Not that he was thinking about Devon or Adrien right this minute. He had more important things to think about. Like making this lovely creature cuddled against him one happy woman.

Cupping her intimately through the silky material, he slid his middle finger against her clit. The crotch of her panties was delightfully moist.

Julienne thrust her head back against his shoulder. "You always were all work and no play," she purred, her voice low and hoarse from the remnants of sleep and the beginnings of arousal.

He laughed softly and worked his fingers inside her panties. She grew wetter. Her hips began a slow sensual dance. "You are about to find out how much play I have in me," he teased.

"Keep that up, and I might be persuaded not to be mad at you," she gasped through delicious desperation.

Morgan nipped at the soft skin between her neck and shoulder. His own body trembled with his efforts at restraint. A burning tremor started to build deep inside his loins. "Persuading as much as I can, darling." A suction like moist velvet rippled around his fingers when he slid them through her honeyed folds. Heat thrummed through her sex.

She drew in a little breath as his fingers slid out, then plunged back in. "Persuade a little more."

"Gladly." He rewarded her by slipping his other arm under her body. Slipping down the cup of her bra so that her other breast was bared, he drew soft circles around the hard point of her nipple.

Julienne released a long, lusty groan. Her back stiffened. Fingers digging into his hip, her body convulsed with orgasm. Spiraling into her own pleasure, she writhed against him with a smooth rhythmic ferocity, a she-cat in feral heat.

Morgan damn near came right then and there. Control nearly shattered. He gritted his teeth and mentally imagined putting a cork in a hole. Not the best thing to picture, but it worked. He was supposed to be the older, more experienced lover.

Her climax subsiding into a steady quiver, Julienne gasped for breath. "Wow. I liked that."

Burying his face in the softness of her hair, he tightened his hold around her waist. "I did, too." It felt good not to be alone, to know someone waited for him to come home. Once, he'd been too cynical to believe in love. Lust, yes. He recognized its need and had fallen prey to it often. He enjoyed the thrill of pursuing the opposite sex. Chasing a woman down, breaking her resistance, wooing her into his bed . . . and then leaving her without a word.

He'd admit it. He'd been a bastard through and through.

Falling in love had changed all that.

The ball and chain had gotten him. Julienne had done more than keep him from destroying himself through his own suicidal excesses. She'd kept him sane. That gift alone was priceless.

She broke out of his hold and rolled over onto her back. "God, how you spoil me." She wrapped her arms around his neck and drew him down for a kiss.

Morgan gladly obliged. His tongue brushed along the seam of her mouth, teasing then invading. Her soft curves began to meld into his. Her hands rose, fingers weaving through his unruly hair.

A hard yank at the back of his head caused him to rear up.

"What the hell?"

Lying beneath him, Julienne tightened her grip. "Slaying dragons, eh?" She eyed him suspiciously. "You come home smelling like a bar and tasting like a brewery and expect me to believe you were working."

Busted.

Just when he was beginning to get all good and worked up, she had to go and ruin it.

To explain, Morgan tried to rise out of her grip. Fire snapping in her green eyes, she held firm.

"Ouch! Damn it. Have a care, woman. You will snatch me bald." The idea that he needed to start wearing his hair in a shorter style flashed through his mind. He'd never worried about his collar-brushing mane before. No man worth his salt would ever resort to hair pulling to win a fight.

But a woman would.

"I might. How considerate of you to leave me alone at home while you go out partying." She twisted her fingers deeper. "Then you have the nerve to come home and paw all over me. You damn horny drunk."

He frowned. "It seemed to me that you were enjoying yourself. Correct me if I am wrong, but you did come. And quite nicely, if I might say so myself."

She glared. "Don't think giving me a little finger-fucking is going to get you off the hook, mister. A demon courier shows up and *POOF!* You're on your way without a word."

"I told you—" he started to explain.

She cut him off. "That you were working. Ha! Liar. You weren't out killing evil wizards." She twinkled the fingers of her free hand in front of his face. Angry red sparkles appeared. "I've been practicing my spells. You'd make a nice snake in the grass."

Damn Julienne's grandmother for leaving those spell books

behind. Ever since Julienne had learned to read their enchanted text, she'd gone on a tear. Thank heavens she hadn't yet managed to cast a successful spell.

Still, there was a first time for everything.

He tried to pull away. "Damn it, let go." Desire had definitely been replaced with annoyance. He doubted he could get his dick up with the help of a hoist.

She held on tighter, pulling his hair harder. The sparks flashed hotter. "When you're working you smell like blood and sweat, like you've really put some effort behind swinging a sword." She wrinkled her delicate nose. "What I'm smelling on you right now smells suspiciously like *eau de twat*."

Aw, damn. Julienne's inhumanly acute sense of smell had picked up a female's scent on his skin. Only one female had caressed him that evening, and rather vigorously.

Adrien's cat.

Groomed within an inch of her life, her luxurious fur had also been sprayed with a conditioner that could be mistaken for a light perfume of some sort. Happy to see a visitor, the Persian had loved all over him. He almost hadn't been able to get her off of him. When he had, she'd simply moved to the back of the couch and continued rubbing her head against his.

A very friendly pussy indeed.

Morgan concealed a smile. Some perverse part of his personality couldn't resist teasing her temper. Just a little. "I love the way your jealousy manifests itself through delivering pain."

The sparkles vanished. Releasing her death grip on his hair, she wriggled out from under him and sat up in consternation. "God, what did I ever see in a lying bastard like you?"

Morgan rolled over onto his back. He stroked his palm across her bare arm. "My terrific looks, dazzling personality, and the fact that I can fuck all night probably helped sway you."

She jerked away, pointedly crossing her arms to cover her breasts and drawing her legs up. "No, that wasn't it." She sighed.

"It certainly couldn't be your charm. You turn into a jerk the moment alcohol hits your lips."

He pretended to mull her words. "I think it is genetic. Has something to do with the Irish in me."

She let out a snort. "Don't you mean it has something to do with the *asshole* in you?"

Unbuttoning the top of his jeans, he reached for his zipper. "If you are going to use that mouth of yours to wound, I might as well enjoy it."

Surprised brows shot halfway up her forehead. "The only fucking you're going to get tonight will be from your hand." She sniffed, beginning to slide off her side of the bed. "Go back to that other piece of tail you've got on the side."

Morgan caught her wrist. She resisted. He tugged harder, pulling her back down on the bed. "The other piece of tail actually has a tail. I wasn't with another woman tonight." The corner of his mouth lifted at the irony. "I was with a cat."

She clamped her jaw and shot him a disgusted look. "Oh my God! You're into bestiality, too? I thought the S&M was kinky. . . ."

He rubbed a hand over his face. "No. The cat belonged to someone I visited tonight."

"Ah, okay. Someone with dragons to slay, I suppose?" she asked cynically, still not entirely wanting to believe. "You said you were working, not visiting."

"The visit turned into work," he started to explain. "Sort of."

Julienne's delicate jaw set into a stubborn clench. "Sort of? Either you were working, visiting, or fucking with someone's pussy. Which is it, Morgan? This story had better start getting straight or you'll be sleeping alone for a very long time." She stared him down, waiting.

"All three, actually. An old friend contacted me. Devon Carnavorn. You could say we have a history. A *long* history."

She picked up on his inflection. "So he's not human?"

"Kynn, actually."

Her lips pursed. "I think I remember you mentioning them when I was going through my own nasty little changes."

"The bracelet I gave you is a Kynn design," he said.

"Ah, okay." Opening a drawer on her side of the bed, Julienne retrieved a beautiful, if very unusual, piece of jewelry. A silver slave bracelet was connected to twin rings by a delicate chain.

"I always did think it was beautiful." She slipped the rings onto her two middle fingers, guiding the length of chain down the back of her hand and clasping the thick bracelet around her wrist.

A unique adornment, the rings masked a danger. On the inside, where they would do the wearer no harm, two sharpened half-inch spikes protruded. When forced into skin, the spikes opened up a bitelike wound. Drawn across flesh, they would rip it open. The bracelet was a creation of simplicity, yet diabolically lethal.

She waggled her fingers. "We've had some fun with this."

Morgan flashed a grin. "Indeed we have." They'd found a lot of ways to employ the bracelet in their lovemaking. He liked pain during sex. The more Julienne inflicted, the more he enjoyed the experience. Kinky, maybe, but it worked for them.

"So," she said, probing for more information. "Did you and your friend catch up on old times?"

He grimaced. "Not quite in the way I had expected."

"Oh?"

"Devon came to me with a problem. His wife is pregnant—"

A grin tugged at her lips. "You're not the father, are you?"

He gave her a droll look. *Women.* Couldn't live with them, couldn't bury them in the back gardens.

"In this case, no. Devon is. And his wife is due to give birth in a few months."

Her eyebrows lifted. Nothing caught a woman's attention

faster than the mention of babies. Must be that nesting instinct they all seemed to have. "How exciting."

Morgan leaned forward, his voice deadly serious. "The reason I went tonight is because Devon's wife has received threats on her life. Another Kynn, someone Devon conspired to turn unwillingly, is determined to make sure his children are never born."

Julienne's gaze snapped to his. She stared at him gravely for a moment, then said, "Turning someone against their will is a crime by occultic law, isn't it?"

Her words were a definite understatement.

Morgan sighed and shook his head. "The entire situation is one tangled web of deceit and lies." He almost wished that Devon hadn't chosen to involve him. His link to the events was tenuous at best. True, Lilith has once been his lover. But that was a long time ago.

Thinking it through, both Adrien Roth and Devon Carnavorn had put themselves on a collision course that wasn't going to be easily resolved. Both men were angry, nursing old wounds. He'd given Adrien a warning to back off, but doubted it would do any good. Sooner or later the two enemies were going to meet—and there'd be hell to pay.

Someone was definitely going to die.

Morgan had a feeling he'd be the one doing the killing. Reluctance slashed through his thoughts like a blade, cutting his conscience wide open. At one time or another he could have called either man a friend. And friends, as he was too well aware, were few and far between in his line of business.

"Tough job," Julienne commented as if reading his mind.

She'd hit the nail right on the head. In this case he didn't want the job at all. He needed to think about it.

Trouble was he didn't want to think about either of those assholes right now. Not when he had a sexy redhead in bed beside him.

And a very unsatisfied libido.

Time to do something about that.

Morgan reached over, jerking a very surprised Julienne across his lap. Her backside stuck straight in the air, the perfect target for the flat of his palm. The thin string of her thong disappeared into her crack, leaving her wonderfully exposed.

"I think you owe me an apology," he said, bringing his hand down across her delectable ass.

She made a strangled sound of mock rage. "What for?"

Another sharp smack, just enough to add a little sting to her firm cheeks. "You accused me of menacing a cat and knocking up another man's wife."

Julienne squirmed and squealed, but there was no escaping. Hand coming up, she flashed her "fangs." "Careful, mister." She tipped her head coyly. "I'm dangerous tonight."

His hand stopped in midair. He angled a brow in challenge. "Do your damnedest."

She slashed. Above his right nipple a thin red welt appeared in his pale skin. Just deep enough to draw blood. "Mmm, my favorite." Her tongue traced her lips in anticipation. A moment later her tongue strafed his skin.

Desire rose in a very palpable form. Heat sizzled between them.

Pulling her to him, Morgan unhesitatingly drew his fingertips over her lips. A hint of crimson blemished the tips. Slowly, he smiled. This was the kind of sweet torture he definitely enjoyed. Oh, but she'd learned exactly what he wanted and how.

Catching his hand, she guided his fingers to her mouth. Her gaze captured his as she sucked. A million tiny fires twinkled in the depths of her eyes. The beast inside had been unleashed. All for his benefit.

"You taste good."

"So do you." Morgan couldn't resist. He claimed her stained mouth, sampling his blood on her lips. The overwhelming need to strip her naked and plunge into her sex had him sparking with frustration. His body a hot bundle of nerves, he forced himself to slow down.

Julienne took control. Her hands caressed him as if she couldn't get enough of him through touch alone. "The pants, the boots. Lose them now."

Sighing in mock agitation, he got up.

Julienne rolled onto her stomach. She placed her chin atop her hands and looked at him, eyes following the line from his square shoulders to his lean, muscular waist as he took off his boots. In a very few moments his tight black jeans followed

He got back into bed. "No stopping me," he growled, "from having you now."

She smiled and rolled onto her side, opening her arms. "Come and get it."

He snuggled into her warm embrace. Heaven. Sheer heaven.

Julienne lay half over him, her breasts pressing against his chest, legs tangled with his. Her fingers trailed along his chest, teasing one dusky nipple. His chest, abdomen, and arms were scarred from fights long past, proof he did not always win his battles. "What are you going to do about this mess you've gotten into?"

He shook his head. "I do not know yet." There had to be a way to make things right for Adrien while still preserving the safety of Devon's wife.

Julienne's exploring hand moved lower, easily finding his penis. She grasped his length, stroking gently. Her touch sent a hot rush to all his nerve endings. Her fingertips felt like feathers, stroking him with the familiarity of a lover who knew where his every sensitive spot lay.

Her hot mouth joined her hand. The feeling of her lips sinking over his cock set his head to spinning. She took him deep. He could do nothing but hold on as a tidal wave of pleasure inundated him.

Gritting his teeth, Morgan let out a slow, pent-up breath. Every stroke of her mouth sent another blazing pulse through his cock. Feeling like wet velvet, her tongue explored from crown to root. A squeeze to his balls nearly sent him rocketing into the stratosphere. She was putting those faux fangs of hers to delicious work. The metal scraped his most sensitive flesh, delivering just enough of a bite to be extremely pleasurable.

Fighting off climax, he closed his eyes and centered his senses around her breathing, her femininity, and her lush curves. The heat of her mouth seemed welded to his erection. The power she wielded over him through the simple act of oral sex made him that much more aware of her intense female domination.

Like lightning blazing through a rain-soaked night, a totally random and unexpected thought cracked through his skull. More than death could come from this tangled situation between the two men.

Hard to think when brutal tremors were beginning to stampede his self control. Lust coiled in his loins, too hard and hot to be longer denied. His body prepared for magnificent release.

He strained to hold his desire in check. *Just a minute longer.*

Definitely not the time to get inspired. The very pressure of her hands and lips was driving him mad. Damned inconvenient, too. Each fondle and caress sent liquid fire straight through his veins.

Still, in the back of his mind he knew Adrien Roth needed what he had now. What Devon had.

A woman in his bed—preferably one administering devastating sex with the skill of a whore and the enthusiasm of a cheerleader.

Never in his wildest imaginings would Morgan have guessed the answer would arrive with such serendipitous simplicity, during the act of getting a blow job. Fate always had a little twist waiting for the most unsuspecting, though. No one knew for sure how the future would unfold.

But one could give it a nudge in the correct direction.

Adrien Roth needed a little push toward accepting his existence as one of the Kynn. He'd never had a reason to want to embrace the gift he'd been granted. Perhaps the woman he'd met tonight could provide that impetus.

A plan was forming. One he'd do a little maneuvering to set in motion.

Later.

13

Hammer in hand, Adrien worked on repairing the damages Morgan's visit had inflicted.

The door had taken one hell of a hit. The weight levered against the barrier had obviously arrived with impatient force. The frame had shattered, split from top to bottom. The dead bolt . . . well, it'd never turn again.

The damages had gotten him evicted. Technically, it hadn't been his fault someone had broken in. But try convincing the old lady who owned the place. Calling him "trash and trouble," she'd evicted him. He had 72 hours to vacate the premises or she'd call the law. Didn't need that trouble at all, so getting gone was a good idea. ASAP.

"I should tell that fucker he owes me three hundred and fifty dollars next time I see him," Adrien groused around the nails in his mouth.

Then he thought about it. Uh, no. The next time he saw Morgan, they'd probably be busy trying to kill each other.

He'd already packed up the few things he owned. Not exactly how he'd planned for things to go, but when your back was against the wall, you improvised.

The balance of power had shifted. And not in Adrien's favor. It didn't mean he'd lost the war. Just that he had another obstacle to go through.

Adrien lifted his newly built frame into the space the old one had occupied. "Look's like it'll do," he grunted. At least not everything he touched turned to shit.

Carnavorn was afraid. Good. It didn't take a lot of brainpower to figure that out. Adrien had meant for Devon to be looking over his shoulder, wondering when he'd arrive. He hadn't expected him to sit back and do nothing, either. The man wasn't stupid and wasn't without his resources.

One thing Adrien had already figured out was that Devon didn't have the sanction of the collective, else he'd be fighting more than one enemy and he probably wouldn't have gotten as far as he had with his threats. What Devon Carnavorn had helped to do to Adrien was a crime by occult law. Adrien knew it. Devon knew it, too.

Therefore Devon had sent someone outside the Kynn dominion.

Check.

But not mate.

Morgan Saint-Evanston wasn't an entity anyone sane wanted to tangle with. In his days as an active Amhais, Adrien had witnessed him in action—pretty damn impressive. Because of that he knew what others didn't: entities weren't wholly invulnerable. They were still flesh, blood, and bone. And they usually had a vulnerability or two, an Achilles' heel that could be exploited. It just took knowledge of the enemy and determination.

It had also taught him that no matter how big and bad you were, there was always someone bigger and badder around the corner. Morgan hadn't always won his battles; the scars the assassin had etched in his flesh were a testament to that.

Adrien had been trained to kill by the best. And now he possessed the supernatural speed and strength to back up his knowledge. Let Morgan cross his path again, and he'd be glad to mow down the assassin on his way to Devon Carnavorn.

Nothing was going to stop him. Old allies had become new enemies. So be it.

Smashing his thumb with the hammer's head immediately whisked his mind out of vengeful thoughts. "Bloody hell!" He examined his smarting thumb, which was thankfully unbroken.

Gisele, who'd spent her time supervising the renovation, looked at him as if he were a freaking idiot. Her wide green eyes seemed to sparkle with a secret amusement.

Adrien reached out and gave her furry head a scratch. "Don't worry, Gizzy. I'll see that you're taken care of." He'd already decided to head straight for Arizona. Once there, he planned to stop and grab a hotel room for a few days. He wouldn't be staying any length of time. Just long enough to find a home for Gisele. As much as he didn't want to leave her, their time to part had arrived. He hoped to find her a place with a Persian rescue group.

His next destination would be Warren, California.

And he'd be paying a little visit to Hammerston Manor.

Gisele meowed her two cents on the subject, then released her trilling purr. Since he'd lost her meds, he'd had to make another trip to the farm supply store, run by a crusty old veterinarian who saw cats and dogs on the side to supplement his income. Adrien had also lost the beautiful custom tag he'd picked out to match her faux-jeweled red leather collar. He vaguely recalled sticking them in the pocket of his jacket.

That, alas, was gone.

He'd forgotten to get it back from Cassie Wilson after dropping her off at her home. He knew where she lived. And though it would've given him a logical reason to see her again, he'd decided it was better not to retrieve it. His sexual attraction to her had been incredibly strong. Something about her stirred emotions he'd sworn never again to fall victim to. He'd only had a glimpse of those pert little breasts and her slender hips, but that was enough to get his fantasies fired up.

Hinges installed, he propped the door into place and screwed the necessary parts together.

"You should be ashamed of yourself," he muttered under his breath. "Jesus, she needed help, and all I could think about was my dick." *She needs a man like me like she needs the fucking plague*, his pessimistic mind finished.

A few minutes later the door was finished. It opened and closed just like it was supposed to. His landlady should be pleased. The door he'd purchased was a lot nicer than the old one, which had seemed to be little more than cardboard anyway.

Hot, sweaty, and tired, he ran his hands over his face, then down to his aching shoulders. His T-shirt clung to his body like a second skin, and he was ready to shed it.

"First, a beer." Shaking his head to move his long hair off his neck, he pulled off his damp T-shirt and tossed it onto the floor. "Then I'll make us something to eat."

He grinned when the Persian began to weave in and out between his legs, nearly tripping him with her eager display of affection. His heart nearly constricted in his chest. God, he hoped the people who took her would treat her decently. She'd been a good companion. He hated losing her.

That's the way it has to be, my girl, he thought sadly. Someone in his life needed to be safe. "I've got a can of tuna with your name all over it."

He glanced once more at his handiwork. What he'd done wasn't the work of a master carpenter, but it would suffice. A jack of all trades, he was a master of none. All his life he'd thrown his back and hands into laboring.

Lilith had introduced him to an existence of decadent ease; he'd spent over thirty years as her prisoner-consort. Only the need to vacate during Hitler's *Luftwaffe* blitzing of England had given him the chance to escape her hold. Lilith had been desperate to flee from the intense bombing. She'd not taken the turn of the century well and was loathe to step into a more modern era as times progressed, technologically and socially. She was too mentally unstable to accept change, wanting to remain forever in the genteel age that had spawned her. Her fatal mistake was to trust him.

After all, I learned to deceive from the tongue of my own mistress, he thought wryly.

Lilith's jewels had financed his passage to America, her head his sole companion. Like a hound on the scent of its prey, he was determined to sate the vengeance burning in his heart.

Heading to the fridge, he retrieved a bottle of beer. He gulped down half before pressing the cold bottle to his forehead. Outside, an unseasonably warm day was giving way to the coming chill night never failed to bring to the desert.

A knock at his front door instantly caused his heart to skip a beat. He wasn't expecting company. The only person who'd set foot in the house since he'd moved in was his landlady, and he'd already hustled her and her alley cat out the door once today. He didn't like the way her scraggly-eared, snaggle-toothed, uncouth tiger-striped tom had sniffed around Gisele.

Beer in hand, he opened the door. His jaw nearly dropped to his knees. On his doorstep stood the very woman he'd just been thinking about.

Cassie Wilson smiled and held out his jacket. "A. J.?" She spoke his name timidly, as if she wasn't sure it belonged to him. "I think you forgot something."

"Uh, yeah." Befuddled and tongue tied, Adrien reached out and snatched it from her. "Thanks. Been needing that."

Her smile grew wider. "You could have come by and picked it up any time."

He felt the perfect fool. "Just a jacket," he mumbled. "Nothing special."

Cassie stood on her tiptoes, trying to glance in. "Long drive out here. You're not an easy guy to find."

"I'm not supposed to be," he blurted rudely.

A flicker of hurt crossed her face. She recovered in an instant. "I see you've got a beer there," she said conversationally. "Got another?"

A blatant hint.

Adrien stepped aside. Cassie passed him with a smooth slink. She walked around his small living room. "Nice. Cozy bohemian chic. I like it."

Adrien closed the door, tossing his jacket on a nearby chair. What the hell had possessed him to invite her in? He should have thanked her and sent her on her way. She was just a stranger he'd helped. End of story. "It's just a place I rent."

"Been here long?"

"No."

An arched eyebrow of interest rose at his reply. She noted the absence of personal items. "You just move in?"

He shook his head. "Nope. Moving out, actually." He hoped she'd take the hint and leave.

She didn't.

Cassie ignored his rude behavior. "How about that beer?"

Finishing his first, he retrieved two more bottles. Twisting the cap off one, he handed it over. She waited until he'd uncapped his own, then clinked her bottle against his. "Cheers." She drank down a healthy swig.

"Cheers."

Almost unsure about the surreal turn his evening was taking, Adrien didn't bother with his beer. His gaze was riveted on the stunning woman standing so casually in front of him. Her skin reminded him of fresh cream. Her eyes were wide and intelligent. She had enough makeup on to cover the fading bruises, but not so much that she looked artificial. She'd let down her hair. Styled in a sharp and sassy manner, a mass of curls framed her face. He wondered what it would be like to brush her hair aside and nibble the nape of her neck. Just the idea of touching her intimately sent a warm stirring of desire straight to his loins.

Oh, God, he inwardly groaned. *Let's not go there.*

His rapidly deteriorating thoughts weren't helped by the fact she was dressed in a charcoal gray jacket-style dress that brushed her legs mid-thigh. She'd paired it with a pair of silky garters and hose, along with a pair of open-toed high spike-heeled sandals. The dress buttoned just below the valley between her breasts. She wasn't wearing a bra. A single strand of pearls graced her slender neck. It was the classiest damned ensemble he'd ever seen a woman clad in, and his only desire was to rip it off her. Definitely hard to keep his eyes locked on her face and away from her beautiful body.

Cassie lowered her bottle. She also looked him up and down; her gaze ate up the well-worn jeans he'd donned that morning and the scuffed work boots, then made its way back up his body, pausing on his bare torso. He inwardly groaned when her eyes recognized the signs of abuse.

Embarrassed, Adrien backed off and reached for his discarded T-shirt.

"Don't." Her word was a command that stopped him in his tracks. She took his beer out of his hand, setting it down on the table alongside her own. Then she slowly unbuttoned her dress.

"I know there's no need to thank you. But I want to." She let the dress slide off her shoulders. Except for her garter and stockings, she was completely naked. She struck a seductive pose, briefly cupping her breasts before running her palms over her flat belly and gently rounded hips.

Adrien's brain turned to mush. He held his ground even as he felt his blood pressure and temperature rising. Few sights in this world struck a man speechless, but a naked woman was a guaranteed tongue twister. He couldn't resist admiring the view, visually drinking in every inch.

Starting at the tip of her sandals, his gaze traced the lines of her slender legs, slowly going higher, lingering at the vee between her legs. Her pubic mound was hairless, slick and smooth. Breath hitching in the back of his throat, he mapped out the path to her breasts: small but pert nipples like ripe cherries atop vanilla ice cream. She looked good enough to eat, in more ways than one.

Before Adrien could think to stop her, she stepped up in front of him. Another whiff of her perfume sent his head to swimming and a tremble straight to his knees. Running her hands over his bare chest, she traced a prominent scar under his left nipple with the soft pad of one finger.

"Mmm, I know there's a story behind these." Her tongue snaked out to trace it. The velvety moist warmth was tantalizing and utterly seductive. She glanced down at the readily apparent sight of his growing hard-on.

Straining for breath and his deteriorating control, Adrien gasped out, "There is." He wasn't really listening. He was staring at her mouth, half wondering what those delicious lips would feel like wrapped around his shaft.

He tried to step away from her, but Cassie moved a little bit faster than he did. She dropped to her knees and caught his hips, pressing her lips to the front of his jeans. The hot air she exhaled through the material made instant contact. Penis surging against the too-taut material, a soft moan escaped his throat. That was it. He was a total goner. Once, twice, he was a man sinking under the waves. He'd willingly drown just to make love to her one time.

Cassie's hands found his beltline. She wriggled her fingers inside his jeans and slid them together, expertly working open the top button.

Gritting his teeth, Adrien grasped her wrists. He pulled her hands away from his zipper. "If you don't stop now," came a voice that didn't sound like his own, "I don't think I can, either."

Still on her knees, she looked up at him. Her naughty smile vanished and her wide eyes held a measure of surprise that he'd stopped her explorations.

"What's wrong?" she asked. "Don't you want me?"

Adrien lifted Cassie to her feet. "Want you?" he parroted, just barely under his breath. "What man wouldn't?"

He wasn't sure, but he thought she blushed.

Cassie giggled and crossed her arms demurely across her exposed breasts. "I have to admit you've been on my mind." One slender hand went down to cover her slick mound. "Um, in more ways then one." She cut him a quick glance and blushed a shade redder. "Maybe I shouldn't have been so aggressive. I just . . ."

Needing to quench the heat sizzling in his veins, he picked up his beer and finished it. "Don't apologize. I've been on my own a long time." He shook his head. "It's strange to have a woman walk through my door wanting to screw me. It wasn't anything I was looking for."

His words were like a dash of cold water. In a blink, her attitude changed. She held up a hand to halt the all-too-familiar words. Her smile faded. She stiffly picked up her dress and put it on, then straightened her back, held her chin high, and looked down her nose at him.

"If you're uncomfortable, A. J., I can go." She worked each

button closed. But behind her civil tone was a hint of arctic wind. And if he weren't mistaken, he also detected a touch of hostility. She thought he was rejecting her outright. She bit her lower lip to keep it from trembling. "Thanks for helping me. I returned your jacket. Good-bye."

Adrien caught her arm when she turned to depart. She barely gave him a glance. Before he could stop himself, his gaze dropped to the level of her breasts. In one gut-wrenching moment he imagined what it would be like to make love to her. God, how he'd love to push that jacket aside and run his tongue around one little pink nub. Just a taste . . .

"Wait a minute. I'm being a clod about this."

"Yes," she agreed. "You are."

"What I'm trying to say is that I wasn't expecting this. It isn't every day a beautiful woman walks through my door. Does that make sense?"

Cassie relaxed and her gaze softened. The frost was melting. She nodded. "Sure." She fidgeted. "Can we please start over?"

Adrien couldn't help smiling. "I'm willing."

Their gazes locked. "Maybe we could have dinner or something?" she suggested.

Mentally he grimaced. Going on a date hadn't been on his agenda. "I had other plans," he started to say.

Crushed, her face fell. Disappointment welled in the depths of her eyes. "I understand." She sighed. "Guess we didn't need that starting-over part after all. I should get going."

Dropping his head and staring at his hands, his stomach clenched at the idea. Damn, he felt like a total heel. Where were his manners? He winced. His mother would have smacked him royally for treating a lady so.

Something in the back of his mind prodded. A morass of emotions coiled like tiny writhing snakes inside his skull. For a moment he wanted to grab her and just kiss the hell out of her.

But with every fiber of his being he already knew one kiss wouldn't be enough. Just looking at her made his body ache with a yearning he hadn't known in a long, long time.

Lungs suddenly aching with the need to drag in a breath of air, Adrien's head snapped up. Before he could control his mouth, a bunch of words leapt out. "Dinner sounds great. In fact, it sounds like just what I needed. I haven't had a thing to eat all day." Adrien couldn't believe what he'd just said.

Her face lit up like sparklers on the Fourth of July. She smiled, and his heart dropped like lead. Right at her pretty little feet in the sexiest shoes he'd ever laid eyes on. Easy to imagine one high heel digging deep into his ass as he . . .

Oh, hell!

You can't have her, he warned himself.

"Really? Me, either. I wasn't able to eat anything. Too nervous trying to get up my nerve to drive out here." She seemed hungry for companionship. Any companionship. Even that of a strange man who'd helped her out of a bind.

His heart wouldn't slow to a normal rhythm. As hard as he tried to block his attraction to her, he just couldn't help his body's physical reaction. He had an attraction to her. A foolish attraction. A pointless attraction. He'd hurt her. His life was too screwed up for her to salvage. This was just another tragedy in his poor excuse for an existence on the face of planet earth.

So why was he standing here, grinning like a fool and feeling as though his feet had magically lifted off the ground? How was it this woman was managing to reach him on levels he'd believed incapable of penetration? Damn her. She'd somehow managed to knock a brick out of his emotional wall. He'd have to put it back and cement it in—fast.

Instead another brick fell away.

Women like Cassie Wilson didn't come along every day.

"I'm glad you did," he heard himself saying.

She giggled as her gaze swept the length of him. Bare torso, the rest of him clad in skin-hugging jeans and boots. "Me, too. The eyeful of beefcake was worth a tank of gas."

Adrien glanced down, realizing he was still half undressed. He'd been working hard and sweating like a pig all day. He must stink to high heaven. "Let me take a quick shower, and we'll go somewhere."

Heading toward the bathroom, a smile easily pushed aside his frown.

He couldn't believe he had a date.

14

Cassie dipped her tortilla chip into the clay bowl, ladling up salsa, and guided it toward her mouth. Her eyes rolled heavenward as she chewed, then swallowed. To cool her burning tongue, she quickly took a sip of her margarita. Her eyes were watering from the hot sauce.

"Damn! I love this stuff, but it'll set your mouth afire." She dunked another chip.

Adrien sipped his drink, Mexican beer with a twist of lime. "I don't think I'll dare it."

Cassie laughed and opened her menu. "This place has the best food in town." She scanned the selections. "I don't know why I look, I already know what I want—everything! Combination plate, here I come."

She'd suggested the ramshackle hacienda on the edge of town. On the outside it wasn't much to look at, but inside it brimmed with the warm ambience of old Mexico, from the lanterns on the quaint tables to the Saltillo tile on the floor. Mariachi music played in the background, courtesy of a live band.

The place was packed, but a table was found for Miss Wilson posthaste, one away from prying eyes. It was evident that Cassie expected—and got—VIP treatment.

Adrien had bypassed dressing up. He'd put on a decent pair of jeans and a Western-style shirt. His long hair was tied back with a strip of leather thong. He fit in. Few gave him a second glance.

He set aside his own menu. "Since you recommend the food so highly, I'll take your lead and have the same." He took another sip of his beer, then put his hand up to summon the nearby waiter. He wasn't really hungry. All he wanted to do was look at Cassie. She filled that empty space inside him, that space going beyond physical needs. She filled his spirit, and he liked the feeling. She was the perfect combination of brass and charm.

Ordering for both, she handed her menu back to the waiter. "You're so easy, A. J. Are you going to let me make all the decisions?"

The sound of a stranger's name jarred. "Adrien. You can call me Adrien." Then he shrugged. "I'm a pretty easygoing guy."

Cassie accepted the name change without comment, most likely assuming that the A and J were simply initials of his first and middle names. Most people did. She planted her elbow on the table. "So, what does a 'pretty easygoing' guy do in a place like Broadview?"

A tricky question. Not one he could answer truthfully, so he told the lie he'd practiced the most. "Well, I'm not working right now, but when I do, I'm a repo agent."

It wasn't entirely an untruth. He'd worked in the field for several years. It was one of the few occupations where he could work alone at night and not be questioned about keeping odd hours.

"At least you work. Most guys I date are deadbeats. They think just because I have money that I should write a check at the drop of a hat." Cassie's hand lifted to her face. "That's what Kevin and I were arguing about that night he beat me up. Money. Such a stupid thing, too. Sometimes I wish I didn't have it at all."

"Most people wish they had more."

She blinked. "Do you?"

He shook his head. "No, I don't. I have the things I need. My bike, my clothes—"

"Your cat." She laughed. "I found her tag and medicine in your jacket. I saw her throwing evil looks at me. Is she always so unfriendly? She's very pretty. A Persian, right?"

He laughed. "That would be Gisele. And she is a Persian. She's not good with strange people. She and I, it's been only me and her for quite a few years."

"Then there's no wife or girlfriend on your horizon?" Cassie was probing, seeking the answers he normally would have danced around and avoided. He wasn't supposed to be getting involved with any woman. That was the rule. A hitch rose in his throat. To quell it, he quickly dunked a chip in the salsa and bit into it.

"I was married," he admitted. "A long time ago."

"Oh? What happened?"

"She died." An honest, brutal reply.

Cassie put her hand on his. "I'm sorry."

The waiter arrived with their food, two huge platters covered with a variety of Mexican delicacies: enchiladas, tacos, tamales, beans and rice, along with tons of hot salsa and guacamole. A feast fit for a king.

They both dug into the hearty meal with gusto. Cassie obviously wasn't watching her weight. Come to think of it, she bordered on bony, and her skin was just a bit too pale—you could see the thin green lines of her veins underneath her flesh.

"What about you? What's your history?"

She forked up some rice and guacamole, chewed, swallowed.

"Five husbands, five strike-outs." She blotted her lips with a cloth napkin. "The last was Paulo, my Italian boy toy, when I still lived in California. I should have known I was playing with fire. He was all of twenty to my thirty-one. We were married nine months."

Her mention of California made his ears prick up. Devon Carnavorn lived in that state. But he didn't want to think about that. He wanted to focus on the lovely lady across the narrow table. If he wanted, he could lean over and easily kiss her. Instead, he toyed with his food.

Cassie cocked her head. "Correct me if I'm wrong, but I keep thinking I hear an accent in your speech. It's faded, but it's there."

Adrien cleared his throat. He'd worked for decades to affect the flat tones the American people spoke in. "I was born in England," he said, then lied. "My parents moved to the States when I was a kid. I guess it still lingers."

She clapped her hands. "Oh, I knew it. I can just hear the hint. I love an accent. I wish I had one. My grandfather kind of had one, too. His family came from Scotland. I love the rolling burr. It's fabulous."

"It's been a long time since I was there."

"Ever think of going back?"

Adrien shook his head. "No. I've cut my ties with that past."

"Too bad. I have always wanted to live in Europe."

"Why don't you?"

Cassie's gaze went vague. "I might. If I find a reason to get over there."

They continued their meal, keeping the talk light and chatty, discussing the area, local economy, and job opportunities. As dinner wound down, they turned to the local sights.

"Have you seen the sunken gardens?"

"I've heard of them. But I believe it's closed at night—that's the only time I ever get around."

She smiled. "You've got to see them. The place is like Eden must have looked when the earth was new and only man and woman walked there."

"Maybe sometime I will." How the hell could he tell her that walking around in the daylight would turn him into a crispy critter?

"Why not tonight?" she said impulsively. Her enthusiasm was catching. She certainly seemed ready to do anything on the spur of the moment.

"How?"

Her grin was that of a mischievous child. "How the heck do you think the city could afford that thing? My money financed every bit of it, as well as a new wing on the hospital and donation of Grandfather's books to the library. I know the guards, and they'll let me in any time. I love going there late at night. It's peaceful." She pointedly raised her eyebrows. "And private."

Caution went with his sense. "Let's go."

Perfectly landscaped gardens were impressively arranged, lush with exotic plants from around the world. A cascading waterfall was surrounded by lush tropical plants and flowers. Cassie and Adrien followed the cobblestone path, hardly saying a word, both appreciating the beauty and tranquility. It was a night for whispers, for kisses, for love to blossom.

Adrien could hardly protest when Cassie drew him into the shadow of the gazebo; it was serene, peaceful, and deliciously cool. He pulled in a deep breath. Being alone with her and having her so close gave rise to a number of fantasies, all of them centering around naked bodies and heavy breathing.

Cassie sat down on an elaborate wrought-iron bench. "I come here when I feel lonely or sad." A wistful tone colored her words. "It's forever spring here, forever unchanging. I wish . . ."

Adrien leaned back against the railing, studying her. "What?"

An awkward silence fell between them. The moment stretched out, a microcosm of their two clashing worlds.

Cassie shook her head, reluctant to answer. "I guess I feel so empty sometimes." She sighed and closed her eyes as though a searing pain was cutting through her. "Seems like there's not much left for me anymore."

He stared at her in disbelief. "You're young, beautiful, and set up pretty well in life from what I can see."

Her gaze skittered away from his. "All that's meaningless when you're alone, Adrien. What is life without true love anyway? It's nothing. It's like the vows say: for richer or poorer, in sickness and—" Her voice cracked, becoming almost unintelligible. "In health. I have no one. I'm all alone. No one would miss me if I vanished tonight."

Adrien knew exactly how she felt. They were two very empty people searching for a connection. He'd long ago shunned the idea of taking a bloodmate. But the idea was insidiously taking root in the back of his consciousness.

"I'd miss you."

Cassie gnawed her lower lip a moment. "You just met me. Tomorrow you'll be gone and probably won't ever think of me again."

He couldn't help himself. Cassie seemed such a frail woman, a tiny little thing. If he tried, why, he'd bet that he could span the width of her trim little waist with both his hands. When he'd picked her up off the ground she'd seemed to weigh next to nothing. "I wouldn't be too sure about that. You're not an easy lady to forget."

Cassie responded with a faint smile. "You flatter me."

Adrien was out of practice and lousy at seduction. Not that he had it in his mind to seduce Cassie Wilson. No way, no sir. They were going to finish out the evening, he'd take her home, and that would be that. He wouldn't be climbing into this woman's bed tonight.

Or any other night.

He couldn't. Not since he knew that when he made love to her, he'd also psychically be draining away the sexual energies generated by her passion. Like a leech, he'd drain her dry.

And then he'd want more.

Still, a thought in the back of his mind niggled. There were other ways to satisfy a woman without making body to body contact. Cassie, he instinctively knew, would enjoy the orgasms he'd give her. They were both adults. If it was what she wanted and what he wanted, then why not? It wasn't like they'd be starting a grand love affair.

"You deserve the flattering. And a whole lot more." Thinking of Cassie writhing in pleasure somehow emboldened his taking the idea from planning to doing.

Without knowing quite what moved him, he reached out and cupped her chin. Tilting back her head, he threw caution to the wind and kissed her, the beginning of a slow exploration of her luscious mouth. She tasted of strawberry lip gloss and margarita salt.

Pulling her to her feet, he snaked an arm around her waist. When his mouth covered hers, all doubts melted away. He felt her press closer, her hand sliding across his chest. Her lips were warm and sweet under his. It was a kiss their drained, battered spirits needed for nourishment.

The intensity of their clinch grew steamier.

Cassie wrapped her arms around his neck and pressed closer, sighing gently. Their hands roamed with a familiarity born of instinct, coming dangerously close to carnal knowledge.

Just as things were in danger of getting out of hand, Adrien grasped Cassie's shoulders and gently drew their bodies apart—the last thing he wanted to do, but he also didn't want to end up going too far and doing something he'd regret. If he was going to do this with her, he had to take it slow. And keep himself under absolute control.

"Whoa," he said, the single word clearing his throat if not his thoughts. "I think we'd better slow down a little."

Cassie tipped back her head to look up at him. Her lips were moist and enticing, inviting more kisses. "I don't want to stop." She tried to guide his hands to her hips, but he stepped back, drawing a deep breath.

"I don't either," he hedged neatly.

A hint of fire burned within her gaze. "It feels too right, Adrien. I know you feel it, too."

"I do," he whispered. "And it scares me." He blew out a quick breath of nervousness. Inside his chest his heart did back flips. "More than you can know, Cassie. I—I'm not what you think I am."

She looked up at him through jaded eyes. "Is anyone what he seems?"

Caught in the moment, Adrien drew her small body close. He couldn't help but relish the feel of her curves against his. He could almost feel those legs around his waist, see that mass of gold curls spilling over his pillow. Encircling her in his arms, he kissed the top of her head.

He wasn't planning to seduce her. It just happened. Desire ignited like pure oxygen meeting flame.

When his palm cupped the back of her head, Cassie didn't resist the pull. She melted willingly. Without another word, Adrien bent and claimed her lips. His mouth sought to conquer, his tongue darting into the softness, circling hers in an erotic duel of teeth and tongues. Her mouth was warm, liquid, and all heat. He fought the primal urge to tear off her clothes and feast his eyes on her naked porcelain skin.

Adrien cupped her left breast, tracing the taut tip with his thumb. Cassie pressed herself closer. She shivered beneath his slow caress.

He frowned. This was what he needed to survive. Oh, God, the ache to take her, consume her, was fierce. Desire smoldered, threatening to burst out of control, a wildfire that would consume everything in its voracious path.

She caught the look. "Something wrong?"

He had to be honest. "I want you so badly it hurts."

Her palm moved restlessly along the front of his tight jeans. "I'm willing," she whispered. "Any way you want, go ahead." Her uplifted gaze held absolute trust.

He trailed his fingers down her cheeks. She was so gorgeous that it hurt just to look at her. "I want you," he admitted. "But I can't go all the way. I can't penetrate you."

"Why?" she asked.

The explanation he couldn't give stumbled when reaching his tongue. "I didn't bring a condom," he lied instead.

She nodded. "Makes sense." A pause. "I'm on the pill, if that helps."

He semi-shook his head. "Let's be safe."

She quirked a wry smile back at him. She'd obviously not thought any further about protection past the birth control she already used. "You're probably right. In today's world it's better safe than sorry, right?"

"It doesn't have to ruin the fun," he assured her. "It just means I'll be a little more inventive." Holding back would be sheer hell. He silently swore that oral sex was as far as he'd go with her.

That perked her interest. "Mmm. I can handle inventive."

They kissed again. As she stroked lightly against his sharp jaw with her fingertips he maneuvered his hands to unbutton her jacket, easing it down over her slender shoulders.

"I want to see you," he murmured against her hair. A flame of desire shot down to his balls, making them tingle, tighten. His hands found and teased her bare nipples, making them newly erect. She made a soft sound, a half gasp, a half laugh. But she did not pull away. When she looked up at him, her eyes were full of desire. A shudder of longing crossed her face.

He smiled. She welcomed sex the way a cat anticipated a bowl of cream. His cock was pulsing furiously; he knew she could feel the unmistakable urgency radiating from his body.

"If you change your mind," she hinted.

"Wish I could," he murmured, stroking those tender tips, circling the pink aureoles with his fingers. "I won't do anything if you tell me to stop."

"Don't stop," she gasped. "Please."

Smiling, he caught her around the waist. His head dipped and his mouth found a hard tip. He kissed her nipples, gently biting, then rasping away the ache with his lips.

Cassie squeezed her eyes tighter, her breathing ragged from the sensual motion of his mouth.

"You like that?" He tugged on one nipple until she released a soft gasp.

"Yes, ah, hell I do. . . ." She opened her legs and let his hand find the spot he was aching to touch.

Pressing her against the wall of the gazebo to support her, he dropped to his knees. The tips of his fingers traced her belly, his mouth following the gentle journey. He ran his hands over her hips, then grasped the firm cheeks of her ass, giving each a playful squeeze. He wanted to lick, suck, and taste every inch of her as she hovered in a state of peak sexual arousal.

Adrien eased her legs apart, slipping an exploring hand between her thighs. He ran his palm up her inner leg, stopping when he found the tender slit. He slid his fingers along her soft labia, stroking.

Cassie writhed in sweet agony as the pressures mounted within. Her need only heightened his desire to explore. He dipped one finger inside her, swirling it. She was taut and warm, already dripping with the juices of her arousal.

She moaned when he found her clit. He moved his index finger in a stroking motion, beginning a sensual tease, taking his time to discover all the hidden places that made her whimper.

Her moans increased in demand. "God," she gasped, starting to quiver and quake. "I think I almost came."

Adrien slid two fingers inside her honeyed depths. "Let's make sure you do." Her inner muscles clenched, drawing his fingers even deeper. Grasping one of her legs, he draped it over his shoulder to gain full access. He tongued through her soft folds with a long slow motion.

Hands tangled in his hair, Cassie moved her hips in a rhythmic motion. She met the thrusts of his fingers with increasing fervor, her need increasing the rippling motions deep inside her.

Trembling with pent-up pressure, she cried out. "I'm going to come!" Wanton fierceness made her voice quaver.

She lifted one hand to her left breast, twisting the bead-hard tip of her nipple and adding to her own pleasure. She vibrated with tension, clearly on the edge of a mind-blowing orgasm.

To help her out, Adrien's fingers delved deeper as he nibbled her tender clit.

Cassie's words became little more than lustful moans. Her hands scrabbled at the trellis composing the gazebo's walls, finding, then clenching the slats with eager hands. She quivered, peaking. Her body arched as orgasm ripped through her, sending a shiver from her shoulders to her toes. Her expression clouded with passion, alight with the delights his touch had unleashed.

Adrien wrapped his arms around her, holding her as she regained her composure—and he regained his. Her passionate reactions were close to causing his own desires to spiral out of control.

Hands covering her eyes, Cassie giggled and sagged weakly against him. "Wow," she said, peeking through her fingers. "That was *yes yes yes* fabulous." She grinned down at him. "Can I return the favor?"

Adrien climbed to his feet, offering her a kiss flavored with her own musky spices. "That was for you."

"I'm an excellent cocksucker," she informed him.

He leaned close to her ear and whispered. "I can't."

She smiled, but he detected a hint of puzzlement in her eyes. "It feels like you can."

Regret stabbed deep. "Let's just leave it where it's at." His throat caught. A nice memory for him to take with him, but that was all.

"It's a really crummy way for me to say 'thank you.' "

He traced a fingertip over her lips. "You've given me much more than you know."

For a brief moment she'd made him feel human again, as though he still belonged in this world.

But he didn't. Not anymore.

A little rip opened in the fabric of his heart. *I wish I did.*

15

Cassie dropped her purse on the small buffet table in the foyer. "Make yourself comfortable," she tossed over her shoulder.

She ran her fingers through her tangled hair, mussing it further. She loved traveling by motorcycle. Adrien handled the great machine the way a lion tamer handled the great feline beast, with confidence and an absolute lack of fear.

Adrien shook his head as he walked farther into her luxurious living room. He fiddled with his jacket, touched a chair, looked at everything except her. The expression on his face spoke volumes. He was out of his league and knew it.

"Nice place." He took off his jacket and tossed it across the back of a chair as if the worn leather material belonged against the fine Italian fabric. He shoved his hands into his pockets and shrugged, as if to say "screw this stuff, it ain't for me."

Nerves on edge, Cassie cleared her throat. "Would you like something to drink?"

Adrien stopped her as she was reaching for the bottle. His arm curled around her waist, and he pulled her close. "There's something I want a lot more than a drink."

Cassie licked dry lips, turning her head away from him. "What?" Her voice came out a little shakier than she would have liked.

Lifting his hand, Adrien trailed his fingers across her neck, tips of his fingers lightly touching her jugular. "A taste." Head lowering, his tongue snaked a moist trail down her jugular. Then he nipped, not hard enough to break skin, but enough to send a shiver of delight straight down her spine.

Entranced, Cassie's head dropped back. "Oh, God. That feels so wonderful."

Just as she believed he was going to kiss her, Adrien drew back and took a deep, steadying breath. She could literally see the tremor go through his body, hear the strain in his voice when he stepped away. "Sorry. Almost got carried away."

She smiled. "I wouldn't mind if you did." He inhaled quickly when she took a step toward him. "Don't scare you, do I?"

"You're a hard woman for a man to keep his hands off."

"Who says you have to?" Cassie boldly placed her hands on his hips and pulled him closer. Adrien stiffened, then relaxed, letting her reel him in. "Having second thoughts about coming in?"

"No. I wanted to." He paused, frustration apparent in his features. "It's not you. It's me."

She tipped back her head, still amazed by how tall he was. Beside her five-foot-three frame, he was a towering oak. "Now that you're here, you're uncomfortable?"

He shook his head. "Not uncomfortable. I'm just trying to be a gentleman."

Cassie couldn't help laughing. "And I'm definitely not trying to be a lady. The way you touched me a minute ago has me thinking all kinds of naughty thoughts." She worked herself back into his embrace, letting the moment ease his tension. "Feel better?"

He stroked her hair. "I could hold you all night."

Standing on tiptoes, Cassie reached up and pulled his head down, offering her lips. "Then do."

Without hesitation, Adrien claimed her mouth. Tangling tongues explored the velvety softness of each other's mouths. Tightly wound nerves began to relax.

Cassie moaned.

Adrien groaned in response. Picking her up, he carried her to the couch, tumbling both their bodies onto the soft cushions.

He grinned. "You make me want to do more than taste you."

She smiled. "Is that good?"

He leaned close. "In my case it's pure poison, honey," he whispered, passing his lips across her ear.

She shuddered; the sensation was one of exquisite pleasure. But his words seemed at odds with his actions. What a strange thing to say.

"You like that?" Her hair, a golden cascade in his hands, became a weapon he used to tease her, to taunt her. With one thick strand, he traced the contours of her ear, the smooth lines of her neck, the soft spot under her chin. His lips followed suit, leaving a trail of warm heat all along the way.

Cassie pulled him closer. "I want you, Adrien. Not just tonight, but every night after that. I feel so . . ." For lack of words, she simply decided to show him how she felt by guiding his hands to her breasts, and then lower. Her hands tugged at his shirt. Somehow she worked open the buttons despite her trembling fingers.

His attitude all of a sudden changed. After her climax he'd acted energized, almost invigorated. Now he was coming down off his high, starting to close down and put that invisible shield back into place. "We shouldn't."

Cassie pressed a finger across his lips. "I think it's time for a little payback." She explored the length and breadth of his chest, traversing every inch of his pale skin. She paused at numerous scars, kissing each one as though her touch could obliterate the old wounds.

"What happened here?" She boldly traced a scar above his beltline.

He seemed to have lost the ability to speak coherently. "Uh, I was with . . . oh . . . damn . . ."

Cassie lowered her eyes, finding the hard bulge in his jeans. If she had doubt of his desire for her, this quelled it. She placed her hand lightly on his inner thigh, then added a little pressure.

Instead of giving in to her stroking, Adrien unexpectedly pushed himself off the couch. He quickly straightened his shirt, redoing every button she'd undone.

Cassie studied him. He was again cloaked in his ill-at-ease attitude. Every time she attempted to get intimate with him and turn the sex play around, he became positively rigid and stopped her. It was clear he wanted her: his hard-on alone was enough evidence. He seemed to crave sex, but without the ability to enjoy it.

She sighed. The only way to find out what was bothering him was to ask. "Am I doing something wrong?"

"No." He shook his head. "Nothing at all."

"It's all right for consenting adults to sleep with each other on the first date." She studied him for a moment. "Or do you think I'm being too easy?"

Adrien swallowed hard. "It's not that I don't want to. . . ."

Cassie raised an arched eyebrow at him and frowned. "Then why aren't we?"

He faced her, hands on his hips. "You want to know the truth?"

Cassie nodded.

"Well, the truth is, I'm not looking for a new piece of tail," he said bluntly. "Before I met you, I made plans. Just because you've stumbled into my life tonight doesn't mean I can drop them."

She blinked. "I'm not asking you to, Adrien. I'd like to make love to you, even if it's just a one-night stand. And I don't think I've ever suggested that I'd tie you down and hold you captive here."

Her words caused him to wince a bit. "I—I have—relationship issues."

"I'm not asking for a relationship. Just a friendly fuck." Cassie tried to make her voice conversational, nonaccusatory. The last thing she wanted to do was jump all over his hesitations like a nasty shrew. Adrien was the kindest, sweetest man she'd ever met. He treated her with something few men ever had: respect.

He hesitated a beat, then admitted, "What scares me is that once I've had you, Cassie, I won't walk away. And that's a problem. I have to go. I have no choice. If you don't mind, I'd rather not know how it could have been with you. I don't need any more regrets in my life right now."

Cassie realized it was fear backing him into a corner. His thoughts were not on just sex. His thoughts were on the *what's going to happen next?*

A little thrill of warmth filled her. She was more than a casual fuck, to be found then forgotten. Adrien was thinking about her, wondering why she'd burrowed so deeply into his mind. She knew he was.

The same thing was happening to her, too.

The night Adrien had dropped her off, all she could think about was being with him. Now that she was with him, she was thinking about the next time they might be together. It was like stepping aboard a merry-go-round, only instead of stopping and getting off, the damn thing whirled faster and faster until you were dizzy. She felt as giddy as a sixteen-year-old girl experiencing the first blush of true love.

Except that he had no plans to stick around. Hell, he'd already packed and was ready to leave town.

Was it fate or just bad luck?

What exactly had brought Adrien into her life? Why now, at a time when she couldn't really offer a long-term commitment either? Like him, she had plans that couldn't be changed. Mainly, her cancer. If he stayed around, he'd eventually find out the truth.

Cassie slid off the couch and took both his hands in hers. "I guess it wasn't mean to be," she whispered, fighting to swallow the lump that had risen in her throat. Her eyes blurred, but she blinked back her tears. She didn't want to cry. That would be a tad too emotional and would probably send the man running back to the desert hills.

The corners of his mouth twitched. Cassie felt her body heat at the remembrance of those lips in action.

Adrien drew away, putting distance between them. Cutting her off, physically and emotionally. "I'm sorry. I really wish we could have had something." His words seemed sincere.

She drew a breath, hoping the answer she gave was the right one. "It's okay. Shit, I always have bad luck with men. What makes me think that would change now? I'm always right back to square one."

A pained expression flashed across his face. "Me, too, damn it. Me, too."

She gave a small mirthless laugh. "What a pair we are. We want each other, but can't manage it for one reason or another."

His shoulders slumped. "No." His lips pressed into a thin line. "Sometimes even when things can be right, they're wrong anyway."

"So what's next? You and the cat hit the road?"

"We will be." He paused. "At least until I find Gisele a home."

"Oh, why?"

"I have to give her up. Got business to take care of, and I won't have time for her anymore. You know anyone who could take her?"

Cassie went into instant calculation mode. "I will," she said, surprised at how easily the offer came out.

He stopped short, surprised by her offer. He clearly hadn't been expecting it. "You will?"

By the look on his face, Cassie could tell he really loved his cat. Damn, a man with a soft spot for animals. Could he get any better? She hadn't rhyme nor reason to want a pet at all. But if she had Adrien's cat, maybe he'd keep in touch, make a trip or two through town to see Gisele.

And that would mean he'd have to see Gisele's keeper, too.

She shrugged, pretending nonchalance. "Why not?" She gestured around the room and winked. "It isn't like she won't have a nice home." *What the hell?* she thought philosophically. Worth a shot.

Sheer relief colored his features.

"I'd really like that," he said. "Knowing Gisele is safe would really be great. And that she's with you . . ." He caught his breath and swallowed. "Well, I feel even better."

Heart in her throat, Cassie reached out and placed a hand on his forearm, fixing him with a level gaze. "So let's go get the damn cat."

16

Rachel Carnavorn sat in the library. Tired of staring at the same four walls in her bedroom, she'd settled downstairs for the evening. A scene of warmth and serenity surrounded her: fire crackling in the hearth, a single lamp lighting the room. In her lap was her latest creation, a fine piece of needlework she'd spent the last few months painstakingly creating for the children's nursery.

Outside, the rain beat a steady tattoo against the windowpanes. A night fit for neither man nor beast, ribbons of lightning danced across a sky dressed in luminous purples and dazzling pinks. By day the room was normally swathed in shadows, as was most of the manor; windows were covered with heavy draperies. In the evening, after the sun had given way to night's dusky cloak, the drapes were drawn aside.

The peace of the evening shattered when thunder boomed. The house shuddered, shaken to the foundation by nature's fury. The wind kicked up, howling, a thousand angry demons clawing at every crack and crevice.

Startled by the ominous turn of the storm, Rachel jabbed her needle straight into the soft pad of her finger.

"Ouch!" She quickly drew her hand away from her embroidery, taking care not to stain the snow-white linen. A drop of crimson welled from the prick. Without thinking, she popped her finger into her mouth, tongue soothing away the ache. The salty taste brought a rumble to her stomach, followed by a great roll of nausea. A cup of steaming green tea and a plate of cookies sat within arm's reach. She reached for the tea, sipping it slowly to calm her stomach. She'd tried nibbling a cookie, but it had done little to sate her hunger. Her diet was strictly liquid, and she simply could not stomach normal food. She hoped her strange craving for living sustenance would lessen after the birth of the twins.

A punt to the ribs reminded Rachel that she wasn't alone or the only one disturbed by the furies. Cramped and weary from sitting in one place, she pressed a hand to her bulging belly. Under the soft folds of her gown, the twins tussled for a more comfortable position.

"Settle down, children," she crooned, more to herself than the babies. "No reason to get excited."

Devon was at work and she was alone, again trying to lose herself in the long, aimless hours enveloping life since she'd conceived her twins.

My life's changed so much since the store closed. A little over seven months ago, she was a failed businesswoman drowning in a mountain of debt. Desperate for work, she'd brazenly talked her way into a waitressing job at a popular nightclub, never dreaming that walking though those doors would alter her destiny in ways she would never have dreamt.

Mystique.

The word more than perfectly described the aura surrounding the enigmatic man who was to become her husband. Not only had Devon changed her life, he'd opened her eyes to an invisible realm, a realm many humans would even fear to imagine.

Yet when Devon had invited her to step into his world—that of the Kynn—she'd put aside fear and doubt, taking the step that would make her immortal. Her decision hadn't been made lightly or in haste. She'd at first rejected his "lifestyle" of sexual vampirism. The senseless murder of her friend had changed her mind. The human side of existence was no less destructive to fragile lives and even more fragile souls.

Putting aside her cup, Rachel picked up her needlepoint. Rapunzel's hair was a cascade of golden locks, each curl painstakingly produced stitch by stitch. She was guiding the needle through the white linen when the firm *thunk* of a heavy object struck the window nearest her lounge.

Heart leaping to her throat, Rachel struggled to rise, feeling every bit like a beached whale. She hurried to the window, peering out into the murk. A strange veil of fog had settled across the land. Half shadow, half light, its depth radiated an otherworldly illumination. The wind had fallen strangely silent. The rain, too, had ceased. It was as if the entire house was wrapped in a womb of mist.

A quick movement caught her attention. A large black raven scuttled back and forth across the wet cobblestone patio.

Rachel smiled, heaving a gentle sigh of relief. The bird had probably gotten caught in the storm and sent astray by the high winds. As though challenging the edifice knocking it senseless, the bird hopped up on the window's ledge and began to peck away most insistently at the glass.

" 'Tis some visitor,' " she laughed as she quoted, " 'tapping at my window.' " Not quite her chamber door, but close enough, she supposed.

She rapped back on the glass. "What do you want?"

The raven ceased its pecking. It looked straight at her, a sense of seeming intelligence gleaming in the depths of its eyes.

The air around her grew dense, making it hard to breathe. Her breath caught, face paling as comprehension flooded her brain. This *thing* perched on the ledge was no mere bird. The Kynn could manipulate their physical forms, blend with shadows, become invisible, travel the four winds as a surfer would ride the waves. Shape-shifting was another facet of their natures, yet another gift they had been granted by the touch of an unknown god. She herself had no chance to learn the wherefores, nor could she use the talents her husband employed so effortlessly. Pregnancy had dulled her abilities, even as it heightened her perceptions.

The raven was an omen.

But what purpose did it serve?

She rapped the glass again. "You want in, don't you?"

The stately bird of yore nodded. Each strike of its beak on the glass was ostensibly a signal that it was trying to communicate.

"Why have you come?"

The raven paused its pecking. Then its beak went down, pointing.

Rachel glanced down, her gaze falling on the strange symbols burned into the window's sill. Those symbols marked every entrance. Be the visitor human, the symbols affected them naught. If the visitor wasn't human no entry could be gained unless invited. As one very new to the occult and its ways, she didn't understand how such symbols could offer any sort of protection. Apparently it was not so much power, but respect of the boundaries of sanctuary. Respect for home, hearth, and inviolable space. Step outside, however, and all bets would be off.

She didn't like the idea of being a prisoner in her own home or living under the specter of dread of what might happen. Still, Devon Carnavorn had a lot of enemies. She knew that. She also knew word of her pregnancy had sent unwelcome ripples through the Kynn community. Change, of any sort, was not welcome.

Rachel set her palms against the glass, bending closer to the bird. "Before these runes, you can't lie to me," she said, invoking ancient rite and ritual. "Have you come to do harm?"

The raven hesitated, then gave its answer. No.

Should she let the creature in? Or should she turn away, drawing the curtains and shutting it out?

It seemed to Rachel that the raven spoke then. Although she knew it was impossible, she believed she heard the echo of words resonate through her mind.

Watcher. Protector. Guardian.

The wind, the storm was under its command. Without doubt, there was a reason it had isolated her, cutting off the manor from prying eyes.

Rachel unlatched the window. "Enter freely and of your own will."

The raven took wing, passing her by.

She turned to find her visitor had assumed human form.

Head held high, the man exuded an aura of calm and confidence. Glancing at her in brief acknowledgement, he paced through the library as though marking his territory, noting every angle, every exit. Absolute in his control, he moved as if he belonged within those very walls he'd invaded.

As if it were his right to be there.

Satisfied they would in no way be disturbed, he came to rest in front of the fireplace, allowing her a clearer view of what before had been a dark faceless shape in motion.

Involuntarily, Rachel stepped back.

Now that he had stopped, she could see he was clothed entirely in black. Basking in the fire's comforting warmth, he preened. Droplets of water flew when he fanned out the folds of his coat, settling it more comfortably on his shoulders. That done, he swept a mass of black curls away from his chiseled face.

Head thrown back, his dark stare was probing and direct, flinching from nothing as he, in turn, studied her. He must have liked what he saw, for a brief smile played at the corner of his fine mouth. By the aura radiating from him, he was all male; very much the alpha.

Looking him over, Rachel felt her skin heat in an unavoidable feminine reaction. His sculpted physique, guarded stance, and constant attentiveness marked him as a professional.

The stranger let her look a moment, then turned his head, dismissing her. "About time, damn it. I thought you were going to keep me pecking away all night." His words were tinged with a brogue, thick but clearly understood. By his manner of *noblesse oblige*, she knew he was not one of her own kind, but something else, something older. . . .

Whatever he was, he was an incredible specimen of masculinity.

"Hello to you, too." Rachel indicated the door leading into the library. "Perhaps walking up and ringing the front doorbell would have been easier. I'm sure Simpson could have shown you in with less trouble."

Her visitor rubbed at his temple. "Might have been wiser. I certainly misjudged the distance to that window."

"Quite a landing," she commented.

He flagged a distracted hand. "The view is all different. My perception of space and distance was off a bit." His pronouncement was totally disarming. He stated the fact as though anyone and everyone should possess and understand the abilities—and hazards—of shape-shifting. To become a raven, one would see as a raven, though Rachel was under the impression such a bird had good eyesight. Perhaps she was mistaken. Or perhaps flying was a bit disorienting when traveling on the tail of a storm.

No matter the explanation, his words put her at perfect ease. He neither hid what he was nor cared who knew. She perceived that his hard-nosed edge was tempered by a fair amount of blarney and a rogue's charm.

She had to smile. "Obviously."

Another rub at his temple. "I suppose I will survive." As he spoke, his hand dipped into a pocket. A cigarette case emerged.

Rachel cleared her throat, pointedly patting her belly. "You mind?"

A dark brow rose. "Ah. How thoughtless of me." He extended the case. "Make yourself welcome."

Floored by the brash cheekiness, she shook her head. "Could you refrain, please?"

He appeared to think over her request. "No," he said and lit up.

Feeling the weight of carrying two babies, Rachel returned to her chair. With a gasp of mingled agony and relief, she said, "Now that you've made a pest of yourself, would you care to sit down and tell me why you have come?"

Her visitor exhaled. "I shall stand. My visit will be brief, as I imagine your husband will be arriving shortly."

She relaxed, her heart assuming a normal beat. "Then you are a friend of Devon's?"

He considered the smoke, which rose around his head like a halo. "You might say we have a bit of history," he conceded. "It is because of that history that I have come."

"And who are you, if I may ask?"

The hand holding the cigarette came up with a flourish that sent ashes scattering every which way. "My name changes as the times change. What it was yesterday or may be tomorrow is irrelevant. It will mean nothing to you either way."

Rachel cocked her head. Odd did not begin to describe this man. He was almost larger than life. "Then I would venture your name to be Lucifer, perhaps?"

A hint of amusement lit his gaze. His fine mouth turned up in the barest hint of a smile. She had the feeling he didn't indulge himself often. "Mistaken for often enough. But, no. I am not that entity."

"I see."

"Not yet, but you shall." Flicking the butt of his cigarette into the fireplace, he again reached into another pocket, withdrawing a bundle of letters. "Today I am only the messenger." He stepped forward, handing the packet over.

Seeing them, Rachel felt a chill wash over her body. Her pulse quickened to double time. "What are these?" The words barely emerged, sticking in her throat. Panic threatened to flood her senses. She gripped the letters tightly, unable to look at them, certainly too afraid to open them. Apparently someone had done that already. Had she somehow been lulled into trusting a being whose motives were to take her life?

A look of understanding crossed her visitor's face. Sensing her fear, he took a step back, a silent signal he was not her assailant. "I believe you have received an unusual package—along with a threat against your life."

"Yes," she stammered. "Devon told me that was taken care of."

He nodded, saying somberly, "That is why I have come. Devon has hired me to execute the man who wrote those letters."

Rachel felt her guts twist around shards of fear. "Has that been done?" She was almost frightened to hear his answer, even as she welcomed the relief it might bring.

He shook his head. "Before I will do that, the whole truth must be known to all concerned."

Rachel struggled for self-control. Bile rushed upward and burned the back of her throat. She swallowed it down. "I—I don't understand."

Stepping back, the stranger returned to his haunt before the hearth. "The beginning of the story goes back well over a century, to Devon's first mate, Ariel."

His words delivered a rapier thrust to her heart. A stirring of memory was awakened in her brain. "Ariel," she murmured. "The woman who brought Devon across."

"Yes. His sire."

An eerie feeling raced through Rachel's veins, sizzling and electric, a feeling that this man was about to hand her a key to the dark rooms of Devon's past. "My husband told me that Ariel was murdered by those who hate our kind—those who also would not welcome my babies."

Her visitor blinked, his careful expression betraying no emotion. "Ariel was slain by a man named Adrien Roth. Once a hunter of the Kynn, he is the man who sent the rather gruesome gift you received."

Rachel felt her forehead cool as the blood drained from her face. "My God. That isn't Ariel's head he sent?" She waited, afraid of the answer to come.

His gaze flicked to her face, apparently checking to see if he should continue his narrative. He went ahead. "No, the head belongs to Ariel's sister, Lilith." He swore quietly under his breath, saying something in a language she couldn't understand before continuing. "How the pieces all fit together are in the letters Adrien wrote, a bit of history in Devon's past that he wishes to conceal from you."

She stared up at the nameless stranger, in shock. Everything Devon had recently attempted to hide from her was beginning to fall into place with a sickening thud. "And to keep that truth from coming out, my husband hired you to take care of the problem?"

He answered bluntly and immediately, "I believe Devon has no right to order Adrien Roth's execution. That, my lady, is a decision I feel must fall to you." His reasonable tone was like fingernails scratching down a chalkboard. It sounded horrible.

Rachel recoiled as though he'd hit a nerve. The directness of his words threw her completely off balance. Her hand rose to her chest as if to still the organ hammering in her chest. "Me?" The single word passed her lips as the barest of whispers.

"Read the letters, all that Devon has concealed from you." He spoke precisely in a low-pitched voice meant to carry no farther than her ears. "If you decide Adrien Roth must die, I will kill him at your word." He spoke matter-of-factly.

Rachel shivered. This man was a mercenary, and her husband had hired him to do a job that would curdle the soul and senses of most reasonable men.

In response, the fetuses in her womb shivered too, sending a roll of painful sickness through her bowels. This was something she didn't want to think about.

She looked at him with a hardening resolve, saying, "Wouldn't I want him dead, this maniac who threatens my children's lives?"

He was silent for a moment, as if considering every word he had yet to say. "You may find it a thin line to walk, but I believe your sense of justice will prevail. Think long and hard about the path you choose. The choices you make today will come back tenfold tomorrow."

Deeply touched by his words, Rachel suddenly felt very cold and alone. The weight of the world was on her shoulders, and she was the only one holding it aloft. "Then can you read the future? Foretell what is to come?"

A flicker of faint amusement passed over his face. Soft laughter filled her ears, surprising her. "I tell no prophecy. Only truth."

Taking a breath, Rachel placed her hands on her mountainous belly. She could feel the stirring of life inside her, her ever-restless offspring. "What's going to happen to my children?"

The stranger paused and gave her a long look. The depth of

his black gaze bore no good tidings. "Your children will be born. But for their lives you must give your own."

Rachel looked at him in confusion; it took a moment for comprehension to fully dawn. When it did, anxiety filled her. His words cemented something she'd suspected a long time, something she hid in the depths of her brain, daring not to mention it to her husband: that she would not survive the birth.

Slowly, with as much calm as she could muster, Rachel packed away her fear and doubt, her dread and uncertainty. Falling apart would do her no good, serve no purpose. "Will they . . . ?" The rest of the question lodged in her throat. Her voice wavered; she was crying softly now and simply could not say the words. The hope she harbored withered, but did not entirely fade.

"They will be more than Kynn," he said. "Much more. There will also be choices they must make. As their father did, as you did, too. Their choices will be their destiny."

Rachel was conscious of a deathly weariness creeping through her body. Rationally she knew she should get up, but the lassitude of the last hours had depleted her strength. She could not move. Lids heavy, her eyes slipped shut. Letting exhaustion have its way, she lapsed into a brief, uneasy sleep.

When she opened her eyes, she found the library empty. She turned her head. The window was closed.

And locked.

A thought flashed through her skull. Was she going mad? Had she imagined the entire episode?

Her visitor had departed with nary a sound, nor a word good-bye. He'd found it unnecessary, giving her the privacy to mourn. She knew he was gone, for the silence outside was shattered by the storm, again unleashed to vent its fury. The scent of his strong tobacco still lingered, an indelible mark of his brief presence.

The news he'd delivered was chilling to a woman's heart, but the lives of her offspring were more precious than her own. She could no more consider not having them than she could contemplate cutting off her own arm.

Her gaze fell on the stack of letters in her lap, solid proof.

Bound together with a rubber band, they both repelled and beckoned. By the address scrawled on the front of one envelope she could see they had been delivered to the nightclub, a place where she would not see or have a chance of finding them.

These were not meant for my eyes, she thought with icy rationality. *Only for Devon's.*

Stiffly, with fingers that would not cooperate, she removed a letter from its envelope and began to read.

17

Cassie Wilson opened a door at the end of the hallway. An opulent room spread out, ready to be occupied. "This okay?"

Almost reluctant to step into the bedroom, Adrien nodded. "It's more than fine." A small laugh escaped him. "Much more than I expected for a cat."

She grinned and led him over the threshold. "I want her to be comfortable."

Inside the room, Adrien set the kitty carry down. He tried to keep the surprise off his face as he looked around. When Cassie had promised that Gisele would have the very best, she hadn't been kidding. The room was more than a room. It was a freaking suite, complete with a huge, flat-screen television, stereo system, and a small wet bar. The bed . . . Hell, it occupied more space than a bed should be allowed to. Practically the size of a small island. He wouldn't doubt the attached bathroom had a tub the size of an Olympic pool.

"It's definitely better than what she's used to." He unlatched the door. Gisele darted out and ran for the bed. Settling on a pillow she immediately set to grooming her long hair.

Cassie looked at the cat, happily licking every inch. "Lord, if I could lift my leg and lick my pussy I wouldn't need a man."

Adrien had to bite his lip to fight back a laugh. Cassie usually said anything that came to her mind, no matter how shocking it might sound. He liked that in her. She didn't beat around the bush, but presented herself up front. Take her or leave her, but you couldn't ignore her.

"You sure she won't be a bother?"

"Of course not. Except for myself and Marta, my maid, no one else lives here." She sighed. "It's just a big empty husk. Not like the days when Granddad was alive. Then the place fairly burst with life."

"Then you're on your own?"

She appeared to be thinking this over, and she wasn't smiling. "Pretty much. Daddy died when I was twelve. Mom—" Her face twisted into a frown. "Well, she hates the place. Hard to be a socialite when you're out in the middle of nowhere."

No puzzling over that. The whole area was mostly composed of farm and ranchland, most of which was next to wider stretches of pure nothing. Cow shit and wheat fields clearly didn't appeal to the sophistication of high society. A whole lot of nothing going nowhere.

"So, no brothers or sisters either?"

A resolute shake of her head. "I told you, it's just me. Having Gisele here won't be a problem. She'll be taken care of. I promise."

He raised his brows and took another glance around the room. "I have no doubt."

She smiled happily. "I'm glad you let me talk you into spending the night. It'll help her settle in if your smell is here." She sounded so reasonable that it made him seem unreasonable to want to leave so soon.

He shook his head. "You were pretty damn persuasive."

A suggestive smile curved her lips. "I begged and pleaded, is all. Besides, why travel on the weekend? The highways are full of maniacs. Take a few days, get Gisele settled in, and then you can go off on your own." A little pause followed by an endearing look. "That is, if you absolutely have to."

The air sizzled between them, snapping with the physical electricity of two people who clearly set off sparks when near each other.

Damn. Cassie could give a look that could melt a heart made of steel. And cause a man to turn to steel in other parts of his anatomy.

Disconcerted, Adrien took a couple of hasty steps back. He shoved his hands into the pockets of his jacket, firmly locking down the temptation for them to go roaming over her body.

He took a deep breath. "It's business, that's all."

She said nothing. Just looked at him with those big, beautiful long-lashed eyes of hers.

He hesitated, then forced himself to spit out the words he didn't want to say. Again. "Something I've needed to take care of for a long time."

Disappointment creased her smooth forehead. Even so, she bravely lifted her chin and pretended he wasn't brushing her off, however gently.

She bent her head. "I guess I can understand that." Strands of long blond hair slid down to caress the top of her breasts in the most alluring manner.

Adrien gritted his teeth as a shiver crawled down his spine. Damn. He knew the delights that lay under her clothing. Hard to keep from ripping that thin confection right off her so he could suck and fondle her delicious little pink nipples.

Oh, God. Could it get much worse?

He felt as if he was burning up. His body's heat felt like it was spiraling out of control, liquid heat pouring straight into his veins and spreading like molten lava. Sexual hunger purred beneath the surface of his senses; he could see, smell, sense, and had certainly tasted the intensity of her desire. His own lay coiled, clenching his balls into tight painful knots.

Lids shuttering down, he groaned silently. Even with his eyes closed he was still too acutely aware of her presence. Consumed by the insistent throb in his loins, it was all he could do to keep from throwing her on the bed right then and there.

Her voice broke through the darkness. "Adrien? You okay?"

His eyes snapped open. "Sure." His hands came out of his pockets to rub at his temples. Better that than taking a grab at his cock, which was exactly what he wanted to do. He'd have to take care of the pressure later, in private.

Masturbation wasn't an attractive option, but it was the safest. Without taking in her sexual energy to replace what his own body expended, climax would weaken him. He'd feel like shit in the morning.

But he'd survive.

Adrien tried to put his thoughts back into coherent order. "Thanks."

The sooner they got this awkward dance over with, the sooner she'd leave and quit playing mind games with his libido. Not her fault. She couldn't help the erotic vibrations her body sent out. That was the way nature worked between men and women.

Between Kynn and victim.

"What for?"

"For all you're doing. For Gisele." *For me.*

She sighed. "Wish I could do more." Her gaze slowly drifted toward the bed. "If you change your mind, I'm right down the hall." The more he resisted, the more she seemed to want him.

He shook his head. *No.* "Thanks, but—"

Cassie held up one hand. "No need for thanks. I'm just glad you're staying a few days."

"I am, too." *For Gisele's sake*, he thought. Not his. Yeah, right. *Tell yourself another lie.* He'd agreed to stay because he wasn't ready to face Devon. He knew he had to, knew it was coming. Had planned for it, imagined it, played and replayed in his mind what he would do.

Hands trembling, he caught his breath. It dismayed him to realize that when the hour of action had arrived, he was doing his level best to put it off. Because he wasn't ready. To go, to kill.

Or possibly to die.

Putting it off would only delay the inevitable.

Still, putting it off two more days wouldn't hurt. He'd waited nearly half a century for this time to come. Forty-eight hours one way or another wouldn't matter. Hell, in his world time no longer mattered.

"So I guess this is good night?"

"Looks like it."

"If you need anything just buzz Marta."

"Sure." He wouldn't.

Cassie knew that. "She'll bring it right up," she said anyway.

Adrien had to work hard to put the bricks back into the wall, protecting his emotions to keep this woman's hands off his heart. Be pretty easy to hand it over, and gladly.

Something he was in no position to do.

"Thanks."

Resignation. She carried no sledgehammer to knock it down again. The temptation of her body wasn't enough to bring it down.

"You're welcome." She reluctantly walked toward the door. Reaching the threshold, she stopped, turned a little. "Sleep well."

He nodded. "I'll try."

Alone, Adrien blew out a breath. God, sending her away was the hardest thing he'd ever done.

Exhausting, too.

He stripped off his jacket and tossed it onto a nearby chair. Might as well get settled in, though that mostly pertained to

Gisele rather than himself. Unpacking her supplies, he set up her small litter box in a corner of the bathroom. As he'd suspected, it was larger than most people's living rooms.

His own travel bag was packed with the bare necessities. Cassie didn't seem to believe in paring down. The bathroom was stocked to the hilt with every conceivable item imaginable, and a few that were not. He wouldn't have to use his stuff at all.

Undressing, he flipped his jeans over the top of the shower door before stepping inside. He turned on the taps, settling on a temperature close to scalding. Water sprayed his skin from all angles. Perfect. The steam would also freshen his clothing, a trick he'd learned when facilities were few and far between.

Once Gisele was settled in, he'd be hitting the road.

A pang filled him when he considered the idea of leaving her behind. Saying good-bye to his faithful companion was going to be hard. But he'd already made up his mind.

Gotta go.

The time to settle his score with Devon Carnavorn had finally arrived. Oh, yeah. And there was also the problem of Morgan. No telling when or where that psycho might strike. Once he left Cassie's place anything could happen. It wouldn't be pleasant, that was for sure.

Lathering up, Adrien rinsed off and quickly finished his shower. Towel tucked around his waist, he padded into the bedroom.

Discarding the towel, he stretched out on top of the bedcovers. The comforter beneath his back felt smooth and cool, delicious against his freshly scrubbed skin. Most likely it was real silk, or some fabric comparably close.

Gisele claimed the pillow beside his. Furry paws kneaded the pillow into just the right shape before she plunked down. Her purr came out like a buzz saw.

Adrien reached out and scratched her head, just behind her ears. "I think you're going to be very happy here, my girl."

Gisele purred louder. Of course she was happy. Luxury and Persians went together like strawberries and cream. A moment later she closed her eyes, content in her world.

Adrien wished he felt that way. Loneliness clenched the remnants of his tattered soul, the abyss inside deep and seemingly unending. Even if he could climb out of his darkness, where would he go, what would he do? He didn't belong in the human world, hovering at its fringes like an earthbound spirit.

If only he could let go. If only he could embrace the Kynn world. Then he would belong.

An angry frown twisted his mouth. No, no, no! The gift of immortality had been a disease, an infection inflicted upon him against his own free will. To embrace it would be to accept what was done to him.

To accept would be to forgive.

Something he would never do.

Forgiveness wasn't in his heart. Not now. Not ever.

It wasn't just a matter of finding Devon and killing him. He could have done that at any time. No, he wanted Carnavorn to lose more than his life.

His throat tightened with emotion. "Just like he took everything from me," he gasped through the pain razoring his heart.

He no longer had even a picture of his wife, Anna. The cameo bearing her likeness had been taken from his possession by Lilith, along with the plain gold band marking him as a wedded man.

He and Anna Nichols weren't married long, only a few weeks, when he'd been nabbed by Carnavorn's lackeys. His shy young bride knew nothing of his secret calling as an Amhais. He hadn't had time to ease her into his life and the secrets he guarded as a shadow-stalker. His vanishing had been her heartbreak. He later learned she'd died of grief, killing herself and their unborn child by starving herself to death.

After slaying Lilith, his singular desire became not merely to slay Devon, but to do it at a time when Carnavorn had attained joy in his life. Adrien had sworn he'd be there, waiting in the wings to snatch happiness right out from under Devon's nose.

Adrien rubbed his eyes, suddenly moist with the memories that had crept up on him. Thinking of the past would do him no good. It would only bring back the bad memories, the ones that made him want to pick up a weapon—any weapon—and end his life himself.

His suicide would be Devon's triumph. He wouldn't give him that. Not ever. Though he might yet hand over his life, it would be as a warrior.

"I'll take this all the way to hell if I have to," he muttered viciously.

As his mind drifted, sleep once again initiated the devious spell that would again plunge him into nightmares.

18

Barely daring to breathe, Adrien crept down shadowy paths in his skull. A multitude of ugly beasts crouched in the darkest recesses of his mind. Now and again one of the creatures would raise its head, opening up steely eyes. Like mirrors casting back distorted reflections, he couldn't look long or hard into the depths of their twisted realm. These things were his sins, his failures.

He couldn't look, because if he did he'd find the eyes of the beasts living inside him didn't suppress the lies.

They revealed the truth. . . .

Warwickshire, England—1906

Heels of his feet digging into the cheeks of his bare ass, Adrien knelt on the floor. Hands across his lap, he stared at the floor. The silver collar ringing his neck dug into his skin, uncomfortably tight.

A woman's voice sulked. "You ungrateful cur! I bring you a gift, and you toss it back in my face."

Adrien refused to raise his head. He continued staring at the floor. "I won't do it," he grated between clenched teeth. Slow horror crept up his spine. What she'd proposed just wasn't possible.

Lilith laughed. "What you say and what you will do are two different things." A pressure settled on the top of his head. Long fingers tangled in his hair, wrenching up his head. "Look at him, pet. Isn't Sean so pretty? I've gotten him just for you."

Adrien tried to keep his eyes closed. He didn't want to look again, see the man Lilith had brought for his first claiming. But the hunger burning inside his soul wouldn't be denied.

His lids fluttered up. Candles flickered throughout the chamber, giving it a strange, sensual glow. The heat they generated clung to his skin. A thin sheen of perspiration coated his naked flesh.

Vision adjusting, his gaze immediately settled on the beautiful young lion spread across the loveseat, sipping a glass of red wine. He sat as if posed, treating anyone who cared to look to a full unhindered view of his lean body.

Adrien found himself unable to pull his gaze away. His mouth opened on a deep breath even as his hands curled into tight fists. Not from disgust. Envy. His reaction surprised him, caught him off guard.

The chamber seemed to shrink around him. He could hardly breathe as his hungry gaze skimmed broad shoulders, a flat abdomen, narrow hips, and long muscular legs. *Oh, God.* Despite his repugnance with the idea of taking another man sexually, he couldn't help his silent admiration. The man was gorgeous, a blond vision of sheer perfection.

A sudden spurt of unadulterated desire pierced his daze. The demon inhabiting his body raised its head in keen anticipation.

Scenting its victim, it centered on his desire. It whispered in his ear, whetting his basic primal instincts.

What he needed.

Adrien felt his brain twist from the ferocity of carnal hunger the beast forced upon him. His cock twitched. He kept his hands pinned firmly against his penis, forcing it down. No way he'd admit the sight aroused him. That he hungered for the flesh of the forbidden.

He scowled fiercely, feeling shame claw its way through his conscience. He'd never desired a man before—not at all. He wanted to perish the thought, but it refused to budge. Anger at himself conflicted with his growing sexual tension.

Rage simmered inside him, warring with unnatural lust. *It's not my desire.* His breathing came faster. His stomach clenched.

It was the thing. Inside him.

"I'm not fucking another man," he growled.

Sean smiled lazily. "Why not?" He laughed softly and fingered a long scar above a dusky nipple. "I've been the first for many of your kind."

Lilith laughed, too. "What you say and what you'll do are two different things." She tightened her grip. "The hunger's alive inside you. What it wants, it gets. Your will is no longer your own, Adrien. Accept that."

He shook his head. "I won't do it."

Another laugh, mocking and amused. "We'll see, pet."

Leaving him to stew in misery, Lilith sauntered across the room. Reaching the loveseat, she slipped off her robe, the only thing she wore.

She sat beside Sean. They kissed, tongues tangling in an erotic meeting. The air around them reeked of sweat and raw lust. Adrien had already been forced to watch as they made love.

Well, not forced.

He'd watched not because he wanted to, but because he simply couldn't resist the siren's call of his own starved libido.

Stroking her fingers through Sean's long hair, she gave his shoulder a soft kiss. Her hand stroked his bare chest, then down his abdomen, going lower to caress the cock nestled in a thatch of tight blond curls.

"Oh, he's so pretty." She worked her hand slowly up and down the length of his burgeoning erection. "And so damn hard."

Adrien shut his eyes and gritted his teeth. He swiped his tongue over suddenly parched lips. He refused to let his mind think about going down that path, the one that would have him taking a man as his first. Just as he refused to think about how his own traitorous body was reacting to the sight of another man, naked and aroused.

Sean continued to stare at him.

He shut his eyes. Damn his weakness. How could shivers of disgust be turning into quivers of anticipation? Of excitement.

Because he now shared his mind, his body, with the will of the Kynn collective. Voices whispered at the back of his brain, telling him of pleasures unbound.

Adrien wanted those pleasures, too. And because of his weakness he burned with shame, with embarrassment.

"Come and get him," Lilith urged. "Come and claim what is yours."

He drew a breath, wanting to deny it all.

Moving into a crouch, Adrien slowly rose to his feet. A black veil momentarily settled in front of his eyes. His head swam. For a moment he feared he would pass out.

No such luck.

His vision cleared. A thought formed. The window across the room beckoned.

Freedom.

Not because he could shift into mist and pass through it.

No, that ability was not his. Would never be his as long as he wore the slave's sigil of pure silver around his neck. Etched with ancient runes, the spell cast into it muted his abilities as long as he wore it.

The glass, he thought. Reach the window. Shatter the glass. Then he could tear his throat and wrists with the shards, end his life. End this living hell.

He started to move. To his horror his body wouldn't obey his commands to rush toward the window. Instead he was moving toward the lovers locked in intimate embrace. Propelled by a will other than his own, he found himself settling on the floor in front of them like a faithful hound come to beg for petting.

Lilith glanced down at him. "I knew you couldn't resist him." Her hand jacked Sean's rigid cock. He closed his eyes and moaned softly with pleasure.

Despite his revulsion, Adrien wanted to touch him.

Ached to touch him.

Rising to his knees, Adrien parted Sean's legs, his palms settling just above his knees. Flesh to flesh, he sensed the hum of energy under Sean's skin; vibrating up through his arms, his chest, straight into his cock. The sensation was akin to grasping a bolt of lightning. Pure human energy distilled to its basest, most powerful form.

Hardly daring to breathe, Adrien slid his hands higher, to the crux of Sean's thighs. Sean's cock was hard as a rock and ready for action. He tried to lift his hands away from Sean's skin. He couldn't. His palms seemed glued down.

Long seconds passed. "I can't do this," he gasped. "It's an abomination toward God."

Lilith's hand covered one of his, then guided it toward Sean's erection. "We were created by God, too," she said. "For is he not creator of all that is in heaven and on earth?"

And hell, Adrien reminded himself. Reaching deep down inside himself, he tried to find the strength to back away from this forbidden fruit.

He couldn't. He was so aroused that he ached. The temptation was too great, his hunger too long denied. Willpower faded, resolution faded. Damnation swept in and consumed his soul.

His fingers closed around Sean's cock. Hot flesh throbbed under his grip. It felt good. He hated that he should be so weak. He had no right to be, but couldn't help himself. These were the things he'd dedicated his life to destroying.

Now he was to become one of them.

Lilith smiled, her fine lips parting. "Suck it, Adrien. He likes a little loving before he takes a dick up his ass."

Had such words been said to him at any other time, Adrien would surely have stomped the living shit out of the offender.

Wasn't going to happen this time.

His wall of self-control crumbling, Adrien bent forward and opened his mouth. A drop of precum oozed from the tip of Sean's cock. Adrien's tongue snaked out, tasting. The blood in his head migrated toward the center of his body.

A little moan broke from Sean's throat. "Perfect."

Adrien closed his mouth over Sean's penis. Without thinking about what he was doing, his fist closed around his own erection. The rhythm between their bodies came naturally, easy. He stroked, simultaneously taking Sean's cock down his throat even as he worked his own rigid shaft.

"That feels so good," Sean moaned.

Like a conductor guiding her orchestra, Lilith shifted her position, moving behind Adrien. "You are doing well, my love," she crooned in his ear. "Take him, possess him. He is yours alone."

Adrien lifted his head. Oh, God. He could feel it inside him. And he wanted more. Everything. He had to physically restrain himself from coming right then and there.

"Let it guide you," Lilith urged.

He cupped Sean's tender ball sac, squeezing, working the mass with his fingers and thumb. "I want him," he growled. "Damn me, but I do."

Sean moaned again, enjoying the pleasure. His engorged cock bobbed, wet and shiny with saliva. "You have the best mouth," he gasped.

Lilith reached for the charm hanging around her neck, nestled snugly between her breasts. She snapped the thin chain and handed it to Adrien. "You will need this."

Adrien felt his mouth go dry as his fingers curled around the object that had tormented him in earlier days. His stomach curdled at the thought of tasting human blood. His hand trembled. Suddenly he wasn't prepared for this moment. "I can't."

Lilith shushed him with a finger across his lips. "You can. I'll go through it with you."

Puzzlement clouded his mind. "How?" He couldn't stand the delay any longer. He had to take Sean, fill the void inside, even if it killed him.

Taking his hand and Sean's, Lilith led the two men toward her bed. She slid atop its voluminous surface and opened her arms to Sean. "Come to me, love. We'll have to guide him through."

Sean slid onto the bed. His body covered Lilith's, his hips sinking between her spread thighs. She peeked over Sean's shoulder, smiling in delight. Her lips curved in a sensual smile. "The perfect position to fuck him from behind."

Adrien rubbed a hand over his face as a fresh shudder of desire shimmied down his back. Though his body felt like lead, his mind seemed to be weightless. As if he were standing outside himself watching the events of his sensual seduction unfold, an observer rather than an active participant.

Swallowing heavily, he crawled onto the bed, positioning his body between Sean and Lilith's spread legs. Sean's hips undulated gently against hers, a mesmerizing sight.

A series of small scars marked the area between Sean's spine and his crack. It was obviously a place Sean enjoyed being sucked.

Adrien pressed the tip of Lilith's charm into Sean's skin, slicing into an old scar. Blood flowed.

He leaned over and touched his mouth to Sean's warm skin. He stroked his tongue over the cut, savoring. A coppery sweet warmth filled his mouth. Not bad. The realization only heightened his need to keep exploring.

Suddenly his whole perception of the world around him changed. As the resonance of Sean's blood filled his mouth, he felt two energies merge and become one. Two energy fields began to vibrate. And then they were open to one another, Sean's life force connecting to Adrien's through the communion of blood, a series of interlocking magnetic fields binding them together on a psychic level.

Adrien lifted his head, licked his lips. It felt physically as though he were filling up, Sean's strength becoming his own.

He wanted more.

Moving more with instinct than expertise, Adrien spread Sean's ass cheeks. Nose pressing crack, he inhaled. The musky aroma enticed; rich, feral, and pungent. The smell reminded him of forbidden things. A man didn't fuck another man, but why not? He knew how he liked to be touched, what aroused him. The things he was doing to Sean. He'd admit it. He wanted them for himself. Craved the nasty forbidden the way lungs craved oxygen. To go without was to be deprived of the basic right to enjoy a sensual, sexual life.

Adrien feasted, pushing his tongue against the tightness of Sean's anus. A thin trail of blood trickled down. Damn, that tasted even better. Desire rolled through him all over again. He licked, adding his saliva to the lubrication Sean's blood would naturally provide.

Sean let out a deep moan at the same time he thrust into Lilith. "God, that makes me want to fuck all night." He raised her hips, pulled her slightly up, then impaled her again. Two bodies quivered and bucked in delight. Lilith's fingernails scratched up and down his bare back as he ground his hips savagely.

"Take him now," she urged through the moan of her own pleasure. "He is about to peak."

Adrien lost control. The beast took over his mind, shoving his thoughts aside and assuming mastery of his body. Its hunger raged through him, a terrible pain in the very fiber of his being. The dignity and humanity he'd struggled to hold on to had evaporated. He was a predator now, all instinct and self-fulfillment.

Hands settling on Sean's hips, Adrien thrust. His cock slid up Sean's ass, slowly vanishing to the hilt. Anal muscles loosened, then clenched. He discovered then he liked to see the act of penetration as he fucked.

Mmm, yes. Nice and tight.

Sean's shudder vibrated through him. The only sounds in the chamber now were those of skin slapping against skin, and the heated moans of three people indulging in lusty sex.

Adrien exhaled, pulling out slowly. Sean's asshole was tighter than any woman's cunt, gripping his cock like a hand in a velvet glove. Head tilted down, the totally erotic sight of male on male coupling aroused him all over again. His gaze lingered on the strong male back, the firm round ass he'd claimed. A man's body was even more pleasurable than he'd thought, and every bit as enticing. The sex was powerful, raw, and animalistic, very exciting and arousing.

A tingle of attraction tightened his balls. Desire spun lazily through his groin. He couldn't remember any protests he'd made earlier.

He wanted this, wanted it more than he even wanted to live or breathe. Coming together with another body had resulted in his completion, the ultimate joining of his soul to that of the collective. Each stroke of his cock seemed to pull the energy from Sean's body and deposit it straight into Adrien's veins. Three bodies moved in tandem, locked together in the pursuit of perfect bliss. Greedy gasps and convulsive shivers moved them all toward a higher plane. Ribbons of longing flickered through him, the familiar need to climax triggering within him.

His body clenched tighter. A groan vibrated through him. Adrien came, dimly aware of Sean's own orgasm triggering beneath him. He watched the man's back shudder and ripple. Anal muscles closed around his cock, milking his every last drop of semen. Beneath them, Lilith gasped and cried out.

Unable to support his weight any longer, he collapsed on top of them. He closed his eyes. The glow of the collective filled his consciousness. They were all there in his mind—incredible, enticing, amazingly sensual beings. All waiting to share the secrets of their kind with the human race.

Accept us, the voices whispered.

Closing his eyes, Adrien seemed to be wading through shimmying silver waves of mist, heading toward outstretched arms. Now he was one of them.

Kynn.

19

Cassie turned the page of the book propped in her lap, trying to concentrate on the words. She'd hoped one of the romances in the stack beside her bed would help put her to sleep. Or at least help her relax. She'd picked a historical romance, hoping the premise of a dashing knight rescuing his lady love would help drive away thoughts of the sexy man occupying the suite down the hall from hers.

No such luck.

Reading the steamy sex scenes had only served to set her nerves on edge. All she could think about was the handsome biker—and the way he'd brought her to climax in the hidden gardens. Good. But it wasn't enough. She wanted more from Adrien. More than he seemed willing to give.

As for capability . . . A small smile crossed her lips. Oh, he was more than capable. Her entire body crackled with unsatis-fied desire.

Anyone as sexy and well versed in the ways of pleasing a woman couldn't have a sexual dysfunction. Yet something held him back from indulging in full intercourse, though he clearly wanted to. At least a certain vital part of his anatomy did.

Why he wouldn't, he wouldn't say. She wondered if the scars set like stone into his skin had anything to do with his inability to let loose and enjoy sex. *Maybe he'd been abused.*

Cassie sighed and put the book aside. Concentration was negligible. She wasn't even paying attention to what the author had written. She could pick it up later, after Adrien had departed. She'd be requiring some steamy sex scenes to perk her up then. She'd definitely be putting her vibrator to good use.

Speaking of her vibrator . . .

She slid open the drawer beside her bed. She was just about to claim her favorite toy for a nice workout when an earsplitting scream cut the air.

The hair on the nape of Cassie's neck stood up in alarm. She cocked her head and frowned. "What the hell?" she said softly, breathlessly. The scream sounded like it had come up the hall. From Adrien's room.

Whether it had been a cry of pleasure or one of pain, she wasn't sure. *I intend to find out.*

Tossing aside her bedcovers, she paused only long enough to grab her robe. Not much to it, but it would cover the see-through nightie she wore. Her weakness for sexy lingerie had her going to bed in some of the sheerest creations to be found in the XXX adult catalog. Whether she slept alone or not, damn it, she intended to feel sexy!

Cassie hurried down the hall toward Adrien's room. His door was closed. He wasn't asleep, though. A thin shaft of light peeked out.

She knocked.

No answer.

Another knock. Again, no answer.

Cassie nervously nibbled her lower lip. Perhaps she should just leave him alone. She quickly rethought the notion. Adrien seemed to be having a tough time in his life. Maybe now wasn't the time to leave. Sometimes a person needed a little help in beating down the late-night demons. She'd met a few of those herself, and they weren't pleasant beasties to face all by yourself.

She took a calculated risk and opened the door.

Head in his hands, Adrien sat on the edge of the bed. By the disarray of the covers he'd obviously tossed and turned a great deal. Gisele cowered a few feet away, wide eyed and frightened.

"No," Adrien muttered to himself. "It wasn't like that. I didn't want it. I swear to God I never did." The words were coming out as if he could no longer hold them back.

"Adrien?"

His head snapped up. A morass of emotions played across his face: anguish, guilt, longing, fear. All mixed together in a jumble making for one very confused man. Straightening up, he ran his hands through his disheveled hair.

"Sorry about that," he said, obviously aware of why she'd come. "I—I must have had a nightmare. Sorry I bothered you."

"No bother." She hesitated. "You okay?"

The tension went up another notch. His gaze narrowed as some terrible thing within his mind occurred. He shook his head, fighting it away with every fiber of his being. "No," he admitted, rubbing his hands over his face. "I guess I'm not."

Her pulse picked up speed as she took in his appearance. The scent of soap and clean male skin lingered around him. He wore a pair of tight white underwear—and nothing else. His entire body was one lean rippling mass of muscle.

Resisting the urge to fan herself with a hand, Cassie silently blew out a frustrated breath. Hot and bothered before, she felt the final shreds of control threaten to slip away. Oh, how she'd love to explore every inch of him with her hands and mouth. An image of how he'd look naked and splayed across the bed sprang into her mind.

Nice. Damn nice.

Say something, she ordered herself. Anything to get her mind off his body. "I'm here if you need to talk."

He slanted her a look. "Just have a lot on my mind lately."

"Anything I can get you? A stiff shot of whiskey." She considered his red-rimmed eyes and pale moon face. "Or two, or three? Hell, the whole bottle maybe."

He shook his head. "No. I'm all right."

Looking at him, so alone and lost, Cassie decided to be honest. "You don't look all right, Adrien. You don't act all right either."

His brow furrowed. "What do I act like?"

Another shot from the hip. Armchair psychology provided by many trips to the couch herself. "Scared," she said. "Confused. Conflicted. You've got quite a mix going on inside you."

His defenses automatically rose. "What gives you that impression?"

She explained. "Scared, I can see in your face right now. Confused—you say one thing and do another. Conflicted. Definitely conflicted."

"How so?" he demanded, stung.

Cassie drew a deep breath. If she were going to be honest, it would be brutally so. "You want to make love to me, but won't let yourself do it." She eyed him. "Why, I don't know. You're a big burly guy, obviously all man from the size of that dick you're packing. One minute you're all hands, the next you pull back like desire is poison in your veins."

"I told you. I can't get involved."

"Can't?" she shot back. "Or won't?"

Anguish washed over his face. "I don't want to talk about it."

She sighed. Time to back off. He clearly wasn't ready to open up. And why should he? He didn't know her much better than any woman on the street. Fate had put them in each other's paths, though. He'd helped her. She wanted to return the favor.

She also wanted to be honest. "Sorry I gave you the third degree. I've never met a man I wanted so damn bad."

His face softened. "I've never met a woman like you either, Cassie." He half smiled. "If I could stay . . ."

She perked up. "Who says you can't?"

He shook his head. "It wouldn't work."

Exposed and just as vulnerable as he was, she could only ask, "Why not?"

His shoulders slumped. "It won't," he muttered, dismissing the idea without any thought whatsoever. "Trust me."

Too bad, she thought.

Well, she'd given it a try. And he'd shot the suggestion out of the water with his own verbal torpedo. He clearly wasn't interested in exploring the possibility.

Cassie shrugged. "If you say so." Suddenly his room wasn't the place she wanted to be. She cleared her throat. "Well, now that I know you're all right, I guess I can say good night."

Adrien leaned forward, pressing his hand to his forehead. "Cassie?" he said softly.

"Yes?"

He lifted his head and glanced around the room, his gaze slowly settling on the empty bed. "I don't want to be alone tonight."

Her pulse leapt with anticipation. She could still feel the press of his mouth on hers, his hard body close against hers. "Me either."

"Would you . . . Could you just lay here with me?"

She nodded. "I can do that." She took a deep breath and slipped off her robe.

The look on Adrien's face was one of fear warring with pure lust. Tense, he slowly rubbed the back of his neck with a hand. "Oh, man . . ."

Cassie glanced down at her sheer lingerie. "Sorry." She hauled her gown over her head and tossed it aside. Except for her skimpy panties, nothing was left to the imagination. "Better?" She stood, completely exposed. Hiding nothing, willing to give everything.

If only he'd take it.

Adrien's simmering gaze hungrily devoured her, exploring every curve. Heat flushed his pale skin. "My God," he murmured in a hoarse breath. "You're so beautiful." Tight underwear clearly outlined his growing erection.

"And getting cold." Her heart beat so fast she felt the blood threatening to tear through her veins. Her nipples were hard and distended. She stepped forward. Not too fast now, she warned herself. Don't scare him.

Doubt evaporated. His arms opened. He needed her. "I think I can help warm you up."

Cassie took an eager step forward, then another. The distance between them vanished when his strong embrace drew her in. She wasn't sure what to expect, but it didn't matter. Stepping between his spread legs, it took a tremendous amount of willpower not to put her hands on his shoulders and push him back on the bed. She wanted to rip off his shorts and impale herself on his delicious cock, fucking him until they both collapsed with exhaustion.

Adrien's big hands settled on her hips. Head tilting back, he studied her. His gaze simmered with passion. "I'm definitely conflicted now."

"Are you?" Her voice was so husky she hardly recognized it as her own.

His jaw tightened a little. "More than you could ever know." A soft groan escaped him. "I wanted you the moment I saw you, Cassie. I can't give you everything you want, but I'll give you what I can."

Her breath caught in her throat as emotion battled sexual need. "Just take it slow and easy."

"Definitely."

Adrien fell back against the mattress, dragging her with him. He immediately assumed the superior position, pinning her under his weight. His lips closed over one thrusting nipple, sucking hard.

Cassie gasped with startled pleasure. He wasn't taking it slow or easy. Her insides clenched with an aching need radiating down to her most private places. Moist liquid trickled between her legs. She relished the feel of his muscular body against hers. They seemed to fit together perfectly. It felt right, natural. His hand moved lower, coming to rest on her breast. The sensation sent blood pounding through her temples.

His gaze glittered with primitive masculine possession. "I've been thinking about this since the moment you left," he breathed, teasing her other nipple with a flick of his tongue.

She groaned and arched up against him, a silent plea for more. Tension grew, spurred on by the sensations he created inside her. "Me, too."

He traced the line of her jaw with soft fingers. "I'm sorry I'm such a jerk."

Concentrating on the fully aroused male body pressing against hers, she hardly heard him. She lifted a finger, putting it against his lips. "Don't apologize for who you are," she whispered. "Just make love to me. Any way you want."

Adrien gave her a slow, lingering kiss that sent a thrill clear to the tips of her toes. Then he nuzzled her neck, his hot breath tickling her skin. The erotic sensations traveled through her stomach, straight down into her crotch. More juices flowed between her legs, wetting her thin panties.

Cassie clenched her thighs tightly together, trying to alleviate the ache in her clit. The waves of longing crashing through her body only intensified the sweetest of pains.

Propping himself up on an elbow, he slid his palm over her flat belly. His hand slipped inside the band of her panties. Thick fingers ruffled the soft curls covering her. The tip of his index finger found her throbbing clit.

Her hand settled on top of his. "If you're going to start something, finish it. I want you to come, too."

Hearing her words, Adrien drew in an unsteady breath. "I want to," he admitted. "More than you know."

"I'm not the one holding back."

"I'm just taking things slow, Cassie," he said. "I don't want you to get hurt."

She nodded with understanding. "I don't think having full intercourse will hurt me. We've done everything but go all the way. I want you in the fullest way a woman can have a man."

Adrien groaned softly, his face full of conflict. "I want you, too. I just need to be careful." He hesitated. "I'll try not to hurt you, honey."

Cassie slipped her panties down. "You won't," she murmured. "I trust you."

His own underwear followed.

Her mouth watered. Broad shoulders, six-pack abs, and a narrow waist met her hungry gaze. He was magnificent, right down to the hard-on impressively arching against his ridged abdomen. His lips might say no, but his body definitely said yes.

She grinned. "Marvelous."

"Mmm, so are you." With thumb and forefinger, he rolled and tugged at one erect nipple.

His head dipped, and he flicked the hard tip. Cassie let out a whoosh of breath. All rational thoughts fled her mind at the return of his warm lips. All she wanted to do was feel, enjoy the sensations of pure unadulterated pleasure. The heated sensation of his mouth felt more than good.

It all felt, *oh!* so right.

Wanting to return the favor, she found his erection. Fingers wrapping around his shaft, she gently jacked up and down its length. A surge of sheer power radiated from his cock. *Definitely all man*, she thought.

Adrien's mouth captured hers again. Cassie closed her eyes, imagining his body on top of hers, his thighs between her spread legs as he positioned himself for entry.

He groaned. "Harder, honey. It's not made out of glass."

Cassie laughed low in her throat. "Any harder and I'll pull it off."

His gaze burned with delight. "Let's not get too excited." He treated her to a sexy grin. "As for the touching . . ." The easy glide of his fingers against her most sensitive flesh sent red-hot darts of flame though her every nerve ending.

She melted as long slow strokes were followed by the short teasing flicks of his fingers. "Oh, my! That feels wonderful." She spread her legs wider. Her hips bucked upward. A hint. A plea.

Adrien understood her need. He slipped two fingers inside her sex. Warm and moist muscles flexed deep inside her abdomen. He increased the tempo even as his thumb expertly worked her clit. The sensations of his digits against her softness made her crave for something harder . . . longer . . . thrusting . . . driving her over the edge into pure pleasure.

Caught on the edge of a scream, Cassie's body shuddered. Her stomach muscles clenched. She cried out, moaning like a bitch in heat as her cunt squeezed his fingers and held them.

Adrien's compelling gaze locked on hers. "I love to hear a woman enjoying herself."

"Damn you," she shot between clenched teeth. "Don't stop now."

For a reply, his fingers thrust harder. With every stroke he went deeper. Every move he made felt good, right.

Her tremors commenced in small waves and continued until they grasped her firmly in the heated convulsions of orgasm.

And still it wasn't enough. Madness engulfed her; he'd ignited a burning lust inside her, and she wasn't going to be satisfied until she felt that cock of his ramming into her. More than that, she wanted him to lose control as she had, leading him into the glorious abyss of sheer pleasure.

Adrien suddenly pulled his hand away. He sat up and slipped juice-stained fingers across her mouth. She tasted her own sweet cream mingling with her womanly fragrance an instant before his lips claimed hers.

"You taste so good." His hands moved to her breasts, cupping and squeezing them as he kissed her neck, nipping lightly with his teeth.

Cassie couldn't think, couldn't breathe. She was assaulted by sensations, overwhelmed and out of control. Her need had finally reached its peak. "Take me all the way."

Adrien's hands slid down her stomach to her hips. He gave a devilish laugh. "Not all the way. But close. I promise you. It will be good."

Gripping his penis in one hand, he stroked it a couple of times, then guided its swollen purple crown against her slit. Her body trembled as he slid it between her labia, but didn't completely enter.

Throat tight with tension and need, Cassie whimpered, wanting him penetrate her. He was holding off. She felt dizzy from her awareness of him, from her overresponsiveness to him.

To urge him on, Cassie made a soft little sound of need. "All the way," she grated. "Don't torture me, Adrien." She was completely unable to control her body's physical compulsion for intimacy with him, unable to control the soft melting sensations within her soul. Her whole body longed to melt into his, but he only tormented her.

Adrien improvised penetration. Using the tip of his penis to stimulate her clitoris, he clamped two fingers together and slid into her again. Filling her, stretching and possessing her. Tension coiled inside, sensation upon sensation building with incredible speed and intensity.

Cassie screamed as release came hot and fast, her senses exploding in a spectrum of light and stars. Gasping and breathless, she hadn't expected anything like it. Already her anticipation was building again.

She wanted more.

"Damn, I came too fast." Quivering with the aftershocks of orgasm, she ground her hips against his hand, feeling wet heat between her thighs. "Again, please . . . Make me come again. . . ."

But he wouldn't be hurried.

"Take it easy, honey. There's more where that came from." Chuckling softly, his hand undulated in a fascinating rhythm, in and out, the beginnings of a sweet, hot friction. Instead of entering her with his cock, he let the juices of her arousal create a smooth glide from her clit to belly, simulating thrusting inside her even as his fingers were doing the job most admirably. With every push she felt the ridges of his fingers creating a rasping sensation that was almost unbearable.

Her fingers dug into the sheet. "Oh, my God, that's wonderful!"

Adrien moved his free hand to her breast, squeezing, teasing the taut nipple into an erect peak.

Cassie shuddered, her lips pressed together as she struggled to make the sensations last just a moment longer. Her back arched in fierce response when he slowed his rhythm. A new game began. Just when she was about to go over the edge, he slowed his pace.

He was in control and determined to keep it. He wasn't going to let it end until he'd wrung every ounce of pleasure out of her body.

"You tease. You're tormenting me." Lifting her arms to grasp the headboard, she arched her back and moved her hips into a new position, allowing him access to the depths of her feminine core.

With every gliding motion, his fingers penetrated deeper, almost seeming to claim her in a way no other lover ever had before. It was as if her body had been created to be conquered by this man.

His gaze caught hers. She couldn't look away. "Who's the tease now, Cassie?"

No use to try and answer coherently. Words failed her, but her emotions definitely didn't. The feelings overwhelming her were sending rational thoughts right out of her head. All she wanted was to concentrate on, and enjoy, the incredible vibrations his touch produced. Somehow, this man had drawn her into the center of a whirlpool so deep and fast that she barely had time to breathe before disappearing under another crashing wave of desire.

Just when she was about to topple over the edge of the precipice and experience the most mind-blowing orgasm of her life, Adrien slowed his pace.

Cassie clenched her teeth. "Now. Both of us . . ."

For an answer, Adrien let the tension build anew, beginning a rhythm unlike any she'd ever experienced. Their bodies were coming together, parting and rejoining through thrusts that were harder, faster, and more intense than the ones before. There was no way the sensual salsa could be halted or interrupted. Without warning, his cock surged. Hot semen spurted across her belly and breasts.

Cassie clung to the wooden slats above her head even as she shook with the aftermath of her third orgasm, a powerful explosion of sensations.

She lay for a moment, utterly spent.

Adrien stretched out beside her. He nuzzled the side of her neck. "Good?"

Cassie curled into him, enjoying the warmth of his body. "Mmm. Very. That was incredible, what you did with your hands."

Adrien kissed her, a tender soul-stirring kiss expressing what he had trouble putting into words.

His hands roamed over her, boldly, freely. He stroked until her breathing grew ragged all over again. "I can do a lot more," he promised.

He made good on his promise.

20

Sitting on the branch of a tree just inside the perimeter of Cassie Wilson's property, Morgan Saint-Evanston idly swung his foot back and forth. Comfortably settled in, he was doing what he'd promised Devon: keeping an eye on Adrien.

A scrying glass about three inches around hovered in the air in front of him. Shimmers of light sparkled around the glass as scenes taking place inside the house played out.

Flask of good whiskey in one hand, cigarette in the other, Morgan was having a great time. Being omnipotent didn't get much better than watching two beautiful people make terrifically passionate love.

Through the last few days he'd watched Adrien and Cassie have sex in a variety of positions, none of which included penetration. Clever.

At his age, Morgan thought he'd learned every conceivable way to have sex. He was mistaken. On the upside, he looked forward to trying out a few of them with Julienne. She'd be in for a treat.

Cassie's, however, had come to its end.

Adrien planned to leave.

Tonight.

Not good.

Morgan took a drink. "Idiot," he muttered. "You're too damn blind to know a good thing even when you are fucking her."

Even without checking astral currents, he knew Adrien Roth planned to head to California—and Devon Carnavorn.

Keeping Adrien from reaching Rachel Carnavorn was his job. Doing that meant he'd probably have to kill Adrien.

He took a deep drag of his cigarette. "Something I don't want to do." An exhalation of clove-scented smoke trailed his words.

In this case the killing would not be justified. And if nothing else, Morgan was honorable and fair about the people he killed.

Conscience niggled. *Well, sometimes.*

He shook his head, squinting his eyes to better see the events unfolding in the glass. Good-byes were never easy.

He already felt that letting Adrien leave Cassie would be a travesty. Adrien deserved a real chance to come into the Kynn collective. If only he'd accept it.

Morgan frowned and sucked on his cigarette some more. Technically this was not his concern one way or another. Still, he felt compelled to undo some of the damage Adrien had suffered at Lilith's hands. He'd hoped having Cassie Wilson's path intersect with Adrien's would help. The two of them belonged together, damn it.

I cannot let this happen, he thought. No reason to let the stupid fool sacrifice his life because of something haunting his past.

He grimaced with memory. His own induction into the occult hadn't been easy. He, too, still wore the scars inflicted in his mortality, before he'd crossed.

The scars marking his wrists were most telling. He'd tried to kill himself.

Not once, but twice.

He grimaced. And many times thereafter.

Finding Julienne had helped temper his self-destructive tendencies quite a bit. Most days he walked upright and breathed the air of a sober man. There had been a time when he hadn't.

Tucking away his flask, he flicked his fingers toward his spy glass. It disintegrated, immediately shattering into a million tiny shards of warm light.

Ass numb from sitting, Morgan shifted his weight, careful to keep his balance. He'd already taken a tumble out of the tree once. Staying off the booze might help. A shake of his flask revealed it to be nearly empty.

Nah.

"What to do, what to do," he mused. Flicking away his ashes to the wind, he looked around. First he needed to get a message to Devon Carnavorn.

He recited the brief words of a summoning spell, then snapped his fingers.

Nothing.

Annoyance creased his forehead. "Goddamn demon messengers. Never answer when you want one." The Demon Courier Service wasn't exactly reliable nowadays. The old ways of magical communications were fading, soon to vanish.

Morgan tried the spell again, this time a little louder. Demons could be notoriously hard of hearing when they didn't feel like working. "By the powers of the north wind, I call you to carry my message afar. And by the powers of my voice, I bid you come."

Not a lot of finesse there, but it should do the trick.

The smell of pure sulpher smacked his nostrils. The air crackled and popped. Seconds later a set of beady little red eyes opened, hovering in the space his spying glass had previously occupied.

Morgan frowned. "About damn time."

A sulky voice grated. "What do you want?"

"What does anyone want when they summon a fucking demon?"

A growl. "Trouble."

Morgan shook his head, sending a curtain of dark hair straight into his eyes. You could hardly trust the DCS to show up nowadays. They were notoriously unreliable. The unofficial motto of "we'll deliver when snowballs fly in hell" often proved apt.

"We live in the twenty-first century now," the demon groused. "You could get a cell phone."

Morgan snorted. "There are some things I refuse to be committed to. Instant communication is one of them."

Red eyes narrowed in a crafty downturn. "Committed being the key word, correct?"

His patience began to fray. "Familiarity breeds contempt. I could banish you to the seventh level of hell."

"Been there, done that," the demon said without much enthusiasm.

Lighting a fresh cigarette off the stub of his first, Morgan flicked the first butt away. "You are threatening the wrong person. Do you know who I am?" He usually didn't pull rank, but this skanky little bottom feeder needed an attitude adjustment.

A menacing row of fangs appeared below the ominous eyes. "Someone who hasn't paid their bill lately."

Cheeky. Very cheeky. With a demon it was always cold hard cash.

Morgan shot a scowl at the little fucker. "Extortionist."

"Deadbeat," the demon snapped back without hesitation.

An impasse. They could sit here and argue all night. No time. Someone had to show some grace and give in.

Reaching into a pocket, Morgan fished out a gold coin. Some eighteenth-century doubloon he'd picked up on some debauchery he couldn't remember in Spain. "Enough?"

A spindly claw came out and snatched the coin. "You always were cheap."

Morgan fished out another. Demons were not above bribery.

The coin vanished into some dark recess. A flaming quill and glowing sheet of parchment appeared.

"Proceed."

21

Devon couldn't sleep. Too many thoughts were racing through his head. These last weeks had been a battle to get a little rest—one he'd been losing.

Sighing, he rolled over. For a welcome change, Rachel was sleeping peacefully. To accommodate her bulging tummy, she lay on her side. Eyes closed, her body moved in the gentle rhythm of deep sleep.

Propping himself up on one elbow, he reached out and slid his hand under her arm so that he could feel her belly. The miracle of conception and birth wasn't one he'd given much thought to in past times. Like most men, he'd found a lot of the idea unfathomable. A century ago, the men stayed firmly downstairs, smoking over a glass of brandy while the physicians attended the wives upstairs and out of earshot. Producing heirs was at the top of the list of reasons to have children, and Victorian society believed producing a son was a service a wife owed a husband and his family.

Devon had never believed he'd ever be the kind of man who

wanted a wife and children. A smile crossed his face. *I've been thoroughly hooked and reeled in.*

He gave Rachel's cheek a gentle kiss and slowly slid out of bed. He was just too damn restless to sleep.

Going downstairs, he tried to walk off the nervous energy. His children's birth day was less than three months away.

"And not a blasted thing has been resolved with Adrien." Heading into the den, he lit a few candles and poured himself a sherry. Drink in hand, he walked to the French doors and stood staring out over the gardens. Dawn wasn't even a sliver on the horizon.

He took a sip of his drink. It had been two and a half days since he'd spoken to Morgan. He had expected something to happen, but sooner.

There'd been not a word.

Problem was, he wasn't really sure what he was supposed to expect or when. He knew what had been said, what the resolution should be. What he anticipated, though, and what he might get could be two different things. If Morgan had located Adrien, surely he'd have had word by now.

"Damn it. Morgan's probably blown me off and is laid up in some French whorehouse, drunk as a lord."

Finishing his sherry, Devon had a second glass and then a third. He'd never been a heavy drinker, didn't really like the taste of hard whiskey. He hadn't eaten much, and the sweet wine went straight to his head. By the fourth glass, he was stretched out on a chaise lounge, glass tipped over on the carpet.

A visitor arrived then, in a most unusual manner.

One moment Devon was dead asleep. Suddenly, he felt a presence, a heavy weight sitting on his chest, smothering the air right out of him. His eyes flew open in panic.

On his chest sat a being: black, hunched, of no real shape. Its eyes were red, its mouth no more than a nasty slit, rows of sharp fangs. It looked down at him, head at a quizzical angle.

After a long moment, it spoke. Or at least it communicated, for it did not seem to be speaking with its mouth, but the words reverberated in his mind.

You've got mail, the imp cackled.

Shocked speechless, Devon shook his head. He didn't dare move or lift a finger. The wheels in his mind turned a mile a minute. Was he trapped in the wall of some crazy dream or was this vision indeed real? He thought he was awake. He clearly heard the grating of his own breath. Though no window was open, an almost polar breeze winnowed through the room. His body was covered in sweat. He felt the chill and shivered. The flickering flames of the candle threw strange shadows around the room, the otherworldly ballet of apparitions walking the veils between dimensions.

"I don't understand."

The imp lifted a misshapen claw. As if drawing something from an invisible pocket, a rectangular object appeared.

Devon reached out. His fingers closed around a stiff piece of parchment. The paper was old; how old he couldn't begin to guess. Its color was a dirty beige shade, as though time and the elements had taken their toll. There was no writing on its face. Folded in thirds, it was emblazoned in red wax with a strange lion's-head seal.

Barely daring to breathe, he broke the seal and unfolded the page. He was immediately enveloped in a strange greenish glow radiating from within the core of the page itself. At first, there was nothing written on the face. Then, cryptic letters began to rise to the surface. The script seemed to dance with a life of its own, each letter writhing with sensual animation.

The flaming letters of the ancient language at first made no sense to his eyes. Mouth agape, more entranced than frightened by the vision, he watched as dancing letters arranged themselves into words he could understand:

Delivery will be made at midnight.

There was no signature. One wasn't needed.

He knew exactly who it was from.

Devon blinked, eyes cutting from the page in his hand to the haunting messenger delivering it.

"Can it be so? Can I trust my eyes?"

The imp hopped off his chest, dropping to the floor. For a thing with such stubby limbs, it was amazingly graceful. An echo murmured back the words. "To trust your eyes is to know the price."

"The price was a favor," he whispered.

The imp's narrowed eyes burned into his heart, its words a hiss. "I prefer cash."

Turning, it shuffled more than walked, crossing his den, apparently heading toward a solid wall. There, it melted into the shadows, leaving no sign it had ever been present.

Devon was almost prepared to believe his wine-addled mind had invented the whole devilish scenario—except that the page remained. Before he could read it again, the paper burst into flames. In a whiff of sulphur it was gone, leaving behind only thick wisps of smoke and black ashes on the tips of his fingers.

Instead of being frightened by the experience, Devon was intrigued. He'd sought the answer to his questions, and, without provocation, without any prayer to a greater deity, it had arrived.

"Amazing," he whispered.

22

Cassie turned off the taps and stepped out of the shower. Steam billowed around her, fogging the mirrors. She breathed in the soothing heat, feeling it clear her clogged head. A headache was building behind her eyes. Seeing no way to escape it, she wrapped a thick towel around her wet body, then padded to the medicine cabinet. Opening it, she overlooked the variety of vitamins she regularly took, instead selecting a prescription painkiller. She popped two tablets into her mouth and washed the pills down with a quick drink from the faucet.

She straightened and wiped the condensation off the mirror with one hand. Her peaked reflection stared starkly back. Dark circles ringed her eyes. Her cheeks were sunken. She was losing weight despite her best efforts not to. No matter what she ate, no food appealed to her. Her appetite was dying as fast as the cells in her brain.

She sighed. The cancer was taking its toll with a vengeance. She hadn't told Adrien about her illness. He was leaving, probably for good. Why burden him?

Gisele meowed, stretching up on her hind legs to poke her with a forepaw.

Cassie reached down and picked up the cat. The Persian snuggled against her, purring with abandon. She scratched the cat behind the ears, then under the chin.

The thought of not seeing Adrien again brought a hitch to the back of her throat. "Men always leave," she whispered. She hugged the wriggling feline tighter. "We girls have to stick together, huh?"

Gisele meowed in agreement.

Adrien was a hard man to pin down. He owned almost nothing, had less interest in owning anything of value. What he did have was well worn and oft-used. He could be called thrifty. For a woman used to purchasing anything she wanted, Cassie had been dismayed by his frugal nature.

As bits of his past slipped out in conversation, she pieced together that he'd come from a poverty-ridden background. She also got the feeling he'd witnessed a lot of bad things in this world, vile things. He trusted no one, was very tight lipped about the hours he spent away on his own, and clung fiercely to his independence. The fact that he made no attempt to use her intrigued her even more; he would take nothing she offered, not even a new leather jacket. All her life, men had taken advantage of her generous nature.

Adrien seemed to want nothing more than her company.

And just as she'd decided she wanted to keep him around, he was leaving.

Cassie put the cat down, watching in amusement as Gisele splayed out on the counter, sending cosmetic and perfume bottles rolling. Cassie laughed and righted a few bottles. The cat usually crashed wherever she happened to land. She'd snooze happily for hours, have a bite to eat, then go back to her napping in a new place.

Cassie had never had a pet before. She liked the funny

scrunched face of the Persian. *Maybe I'll buy her a boyfriend. At least one of us will have someone then.*

Determined not to let her last night with Adrien be marred by sadness, Cassie combed and pinned her wet hair into place, arranging a few stray curls around her neck and face. She dusted powder across her shiny nose, then put on a little mascara and some blush for her pale cheeks. She finished with a light gloss on her lips. She'd just purchased a stunning negligee; short, sexy, and silky—just what every man should like. She slid it on, along with a matching pair of thong panties. She loved the feel of the soft fabric against her skin. She pinched her nipples so they stood out against the sheer white material.

She wanted Adrien to notice everything about her tonight.

Giving Gisele a last loving stroke, she slid on a pair of thigh-high hose, the kind that didn't need garters, and put her feet into a pair of sexy heels. "Tonight will be one he never forgets."

Opening the bathroom door, she slipped into the adjoining bedroom.

Adrien sat at the antique rolltop desk, leaning on his elbows and rubbing his temples. Though he wore his jeans and boots, he'd not yet finished dressing. He was still shirtless. Her gaze traced the solid lines of his shoulders and back. Seeing him, her stomach tightened and her head started to throb anew. Her guts churned slivers of glass. God, she didn't want to let him go.

If you love something, set it free. . . .

Cassie walked over to him and put her hands on his shoulders. She could feel the tension in his muscles, the knots under his skin. She swallowed the lump in her throat. "Something wrong, honey?" She gave the top of his head a quick kiss.

Glancing up at her, Adrien forced a smile. "No. Nothing's wrong."

Breaking away, he slid the letter he'd written into the pocket of his jacket, hung across the back of the chair. He headed for the bed and tumbled facedown, pillowing his head in his arms.

"Just taking care of a few last-minute details," he finished in a muffled voice.

Cassie drew in a breath. She knew the letter was for her. Anything good—or the final kiss-off? At least he had written her something. That was more than most men bothered with. Most just walked out and had their lawyers call hers.

Walking to the bed, Cassie climbed in beside him. She worked his shoulders a bit more, kneading his skin. She relished the feel of his flesh under her fingers. "You're tense."

He sighed and lifted his head. "Got a lot on my mind, babe. I have to leave soon. Need to get in some road time."

"So you're really going?" There. She'd said it.

Adrien rolled over. Noticing her sexy gown, his eyes showed his appreciation. He reached out and caressed her cheek. "It's something I've needed to take care of for a long time." A shadow of regret trekked across his face. "If I could take this last week back, I would. God help me, I wish I could forget what I've done."

His words brought a chilly prickle to the back of her neck. He talked like a man in trouble. "Anything I can help with?" She had the resources. If he was in some kind of mess, she wanted to help.

His fingers tracked down her throat, briefly touching the pulse under her jaw. For a moment a look of wanton desire filled his face—a look that went beyond sexual desire into something else, something akin to hunger. His tongue snaked out, and he licked his lips.

Adrien closed his eyes, as if struggling to regain a sense of control. "No. It's not about money. It's something else, something I can't control. If I stay, you'll get hurt, honey. I don't want that to happen."

She laid a hand on his bare chest. "Whatever it is, I can handle it." She let her hand trail lower to settle on his crotch. She began to rub up and down his length. Beneath his jeans his cock sprouted, burgeoning into a long, hard rod. "In fact, here's something I'd like to handle now." She lay back, spreading her legs to give him a flash of her sexy thighs and the delights that lay therein.

Adrien rolled on top of her, bracing his weight with his arms. "Damn, the things you do to me. I intend to see you well satisfied before I go."

She ran her arms up his bare arms, over his shoulders and down his back. "Oh, I'm more than satisfied." Her hands found the beltline of his jeans. She gave the material a tug. "But we haven't really made love yet."

Hearing her words, Adrien's mood abruptly shifted. He drew back, sitting up on the edge of the bed. "There's a reason we haven't." His voice was oddly taut.

She sat up, too, putting a hand on his leg. "Then not tonight, either?" Disappointment laced her words.

Adrien reached down to take her hand, squeezing her fingers. For the first time she noticed his skin was oddly chilly. "I can't make love to you the way you want. I just can't give you what you expect as a woman. I'm sorry. I haven't been honest with you. I—I haven't told you a lot of things."

Cassie searched his gaze. There was agony in his eyes, an intense, wounded misery that penetrated straight to his core. She could feel it in the tension that had risen up between them, a high wall neither could completely get around. Was it because she also had her own walls to hide behind?

Her eyes cut to the thin scars around his neck, going lower to the scars slashed into his chest and abdomen. There were more scars around his wrists, from struggling against ropes. Someone had subjected Adrien to some hardcore bondage in a not-so-distant past.

"Somebody's hurt you," she whispered, tracing a scar beside his left nipple with the soft pad of her index finger. He started but didn't pull away. "The abuse . . . was it . . . sexual?"

Adrien's brow drew down, a frown creasing his face. "Yes,"

he started to say, then shook his head. "It's not what you think." A moment of silence ensued and then he blurted, "I wasn't always the unwilling victim."

Cassie lifted her gaze to his, meeting it dead on. "Is that why you're leaving? You're going back to that life?" Her question seemed to catch him off guard. She saw him swallow, averting his eyes.

Adrien's jaw tightened. "I'm going back to end it. Once and for all. Then—maybe—I'll be free."

She lifted her chin. She was trying to keep a brave face, biting her bottom lip to keep it from trembling. "Whatever you feel you have to do, I understand." She reluctantly stood up. "If you want to come back, I'll be waiting." She didn't know why she'd said the words. She'd sworn that she wouldn't try to hold on to him.

Her words seemed to have some deep effect on him, like light penetrating a long-hidden crevasse.

Adrien's hands lifted, settling on her slender hips. He dragged her to stand between his legs. An involuntary groan escaped him. Tilting back his head, he gazed up. "Are you really willing to do that?"

Delighted by his question, she cupped his face in her hands. "Of course, I'll wait as long as I can." She bent and gave him a kiss, one that told him exactly how she felt about him. When she drew back, the sting of tears blurred her vision. She blinked and drew a breath. "I'm probably crazy to say this, but I love you."

Adrien reached up, wiping a stray tear off her cheek. "I love you, too. It's been forever since I dared to think I could love a woman."

Cassie was so thrilled that she flung her arms around his neck. "Don't forget about me while you're gone." The flutter in her stomach wasn't nerves. It was anticipation.

Tension broken, he laughed. The vulnerable expression in

his eyes was quickly replaced with a look of wanton desire. "With a body like yours, that's impossible." He took a nip at the peak of one of her breasts, which was pressing taut against her gown.

Cassie gasped and worked one thin strap off her shoulder, baring her nipple to his lips. He drew the pink tip into his mouth. She moaned and offered her other breast for suckling. He readily complied. He slid his hands under the short hem of her nightie to squeeze her firm ass cheeks. His penis blossomed anew, tight, sensitive, and definitely stretched to straining.

She gave him a playful prod with her knee. "Looks like something's come up." Before he could stop her, she slid to her knees and unbuttoned the top of his jeans. Inching down the zipper, she licked her lips. "I'll have to take care of this myself, I think." She glanced up, expecting to see pleasure etched on his features. Almost on the verge of closing his eyes and giving in, Adrien's face suddenly took on an expression of astonishment.

Cassie automatically turned her head to where his gaze was riveted, all thought of sex instantly flying out of her head. His eyes were fixed on the doorknob. It was slowly turning. A pause. Then the door eased open. A black-clad figure sidled into the room most casually.

"Hello, Adrien," an accented voice greeted.

"Goddamn you, Morgan." Adrien swore lightly under his breath. He quickly zipped his jeans. "What the hell do you want?" His voice was a frustrated growl.

Cassie scrambled on her knees to get out of the way. It was apparent by Adrien's reaction that he knew this stranger—and not in a good way. Her throat squeezed tight in panic.

"Who are you?" Feeling a chill, she belatedly remembered that her breasts were fully revealed to all who cared to look. She blushed and righted her gown.

Adrien put his hands on her shoulders and eased her back to sit on the floor. His fingers dug into her flesh. "Back off, honey.

I know him; we go back a long way," he said, words tense, eyes glaring narrowly. "He's nothing more than a damn mercenary."

The stranger seemed to take high offense. "Such harsh words coming from one who once practiced the same arts." He lifted the crossbow he carried. "Is your memory really that short?"

Both Cassie and Adrien froze.

Cassie could see the bow was loaded, and the stranger's finger was squarely on the trigger. It was aimed straight toward Adrien's heart. If he pulled it, he couldn't miss. The serrated bolt in the chamber would hit its mark. The weapon might have been long out of date, but it was still lethal.

She set aside her fear and studied him closely, trying to memorize every feature in case she needed to identify him later—that is, if either of them got out of this alive. She wondered how he could have even gotten into the house. The place was wired with the best security system money could buy. There was even a backup generator in case of power failure.

Cassie drew herself up, forcibly calming her surge of fear. "If Adrien's in some sort of trouble—if he owes any money, I'll pay it. Just give me a figure."

The stranger cocked his head. "That is a quite generous offer."

Adrien cut in. "Hush, Cassie. I told you, it's not about money. It has nothing to do with you at all, honey." He bent toward the end of the bed, reaching for his shirt. "Just a little business to settle."

Flicking back his head to clear his longish bangs out of his eyes, the man he identified by name pretended to think a minute. "Nothing against you personally, Adrien, but I have a contract to fulfill."

Adrien swore under his breath. "Nice to know which master you serve. I hope he's paying you a hell of a lot."

Morgan flung back his answer without hesitating. "Not nearly enough for the trouble." He shrugged and flashed an irreverent grin. "The sooner this ends, the sooner I can get the hell out of here."

Adrien stared at the bow. "Terribly sporting of you to kill an unarmed man. You Irish are all terrorists at heart."

Morgan's smile was almost as chilling as his unfathomable obsidian eyes. He reached into his coat.

Cassie stiffened when he withdrew a handgun. *That's it*, she thought wildly. *No worry about the cancer getting me. This sucker's going to put a bullet right in our heads.* She was surprised when he tossed the pistol on the bed.

"An Englishman would say that," came the sour remark.

Adrien reached for the weapon. By the way he handled it, he was obviously familiar with guns. His murky past grew more ominous, taking on a violent slant. Drugs? Blackmail? Murder? All possibilities ran riot in Cassie's mind, a thousand instant scenarios rising and falling in her wild imagination. Whatever Adrien had been involved in was some very bad, very dangerous shit. The man who'd come after him was a killer, plain and simple.

"Feel more secure?" Morgan indicated his own chest. "You do know if you actually have the nerve to shoot me, you are just going to piss me off."

Adrien stood up, shielding Cassie with his own body. "Maybe I'll take my chances and pull the trigger anyway. Doesn't look like I've got a choice—or much to lose. I know what you are, and I know how to kill even a beast like you." He lifted the gun. "I'll be more than glad to find out how many bullets it'll take to put you down."

Morgan pulled the trigger first.

Cassie watched in horror as the bolt punched through Adrien's shoulder. The force of the hit knocked him flat.

Clearly in agony, Adrien howled and kicked. His left hand scrabbled toward his shoulder even as the weapon he held skittered out of his hand.

Mind, nerves, and senses screaming with disbelief, Cassie scrambled to Adrien's side. "You didn't have to shoot him!" She looked helplessly at the bolt sticking out under Adrien's collarbone, between neck and shoulder. Curls of white smoke and sizzling hot blood gushed from the wound, forming a circle on the carpet. She knew what her eyes were seeing, but was too shocked for her brain to put it all into any clear order.

Adrien's words were a cry of anguish, his face twisted by the searing bolt. "Christ, that hurts!" He reached for the arrow, his hand quivering violently when he reached up and struck the butt. "It's serrated . . . push the damn thing through. . . ." The rest of his words were unintelligible. He was going into shock.

Morgan sauntered over, his face a mask of complete and utterly cold control. "It does hurt, I know." He knocked Adrien back onto the floor, at the same time casually levering a second bolt into the chamber. Lowering the bow, he leveled it right in the center of Adrien's forehead. The first wound wasn't fatal. The second one would be.

Cassie knew without doubt the stranger had killed a thousand times before and would kill a thousand times more. Adrien was just another notch on his crossbow.

Her eyes cut to the gun.

Morgan saw her. "Do not try it," he warned, his stare never leaving Adrien's face.

Cassie pulled her hands back. She held her breath, waiting for the assassin to unleash another bolt.

Adrien growled through his pain. "What fucking sorcery did you hit me with?"

"Just a bolt of consecrated ash. No magical assembly required," Morgan said offhandedly, as if imparting what should be common knowledge. "Nothing drops your kind of vampire faster. It acts as a paralyzing agent on the Kynn physiology."

Unsure if she'd heard him correctly, Cassie's ears pricked

up. She looked at the man like he'd just lost his mind. "A vampire?" she stammered. "You're crazy."

The stranger shot her a look of disapproval. "You have to be to do my job," he snapped.

"Don't pull her into this," Adrien rasped. "She's an innocent. . . . she doesn't know. . . ."

"We were all innocent at one time," Morgan countered. "Nevertheless, facts are facts. You belong to a world that does not forget or forgive easily." He prodded Adrien's forehead with the tip of the bow. "Now you be still and listen closely. The key word here is *cooperation*. Otherwise I will have to kill you, and your poor little girlfriend here will have to Hoover up your ashes." An aggrieved look crossed his face. "It would do my reputation no good to have to deliver you to Devon in a vacuum bag."

Cassie hoped he was exaggerating.

Rallying his strength, Adrien knocked the bow aside and struggled to get to his feet. He managed to raise himself only to his knees. His pupils were dilated, his stare hazy with pain and confusion. "You'd better go ahead and kill me," he gasped, pressing his wounded arm to his body. "Because if you don't, I swear I'll kill Devon." His teeth clenched fiercely, his voice finding new strength. "Then I'll take gladly a shot at you."

"Bring it on." The bow suddenly disappeared as Morgan stepped back and slung it across his shoulder. "But first, take my advice. You have everything to gain and nothing to lose if you play your cards right."

Adrien's brow wrinkled. "What do you mean?"

A crafty look crossed Morgan's face. "Perhaps I should say that I did not come for you. I came for her." With those parting words, he turned with imperious intent to eye Cassie. His brows rose in an iniquitous slant.

Scrambling to her feet, Cassie clamped her teeth against the cold nausea of dread rising in her gut. "Me?" she squeaked. She commanded her trembling legs to run, but they would not obey.

After a minute that seemed to pass like a century, Cassie managed to take one faltering step in retreat. She immediately tripped on her own high heel, falling back and landing squarely on her ass.

Morgan swept forward.

Grabbing her wrist, he wrenched her to her feet, then hefted her none too gently and quite unceremoniously over his shoulder. Wearing only a thong, her bare ass was up in the air.

Cassie squirmed rebelliously, beating her hands against her kidnapper's back. A little gasp of rage tore from her throat. "Let me go!" she cried, jostling helplessly in his tight grasp.

Morgan ignored her pleas for freedom. He gave her a firm swat on the butt. "You know where to be," he said to Adrien. "Midnight." He turned and headed from whence he had arrived.

Cassie could only watch in shocked disbelief as Adrien's form began to fragment oddly, slowly vanishing into the core of a luminous eddying mist.

With a start, she realized she and Morgan were the ones departing.

23

Devon Carnavorn was beside himself with rage.

"Have you completely lost your mind?" He pointed toward the frightened woman cowering on the chaise lounge. "That does not look like Adrien Roth to me."

Morgan Saint-Evanston ignored him and instead reached for his cigarette case. Opening it, he made a selection. "You make a mistake in underestimating me."

Clearly annoyed, he tapped his cigarette against the face of its case to tighten the tobacco. Lighting it, he ambled over to the bar and selected a decanter. He took a quick whiff of its contents. "Sherry? Is that all you have?" He grumbled something under his breath. "Have to do, I suppose." He splashed a liberal amount into a glass.

Devon threw up his hands in exasperation. He'd spent the entire day anticipating this hour, going over the words he would say to Adrien. At this moment he was utterly frustrated. He certainly hadn't expected his hired assassin to show up with some half-naked hussy. He felt as though he'd been castrated.

"You've finally gone 'round the bend and burned out every brain cell you've got in your fucking head."

Dark eyes narrowed. The sherry was downed in a single swallow. "There is method to my madness." Morgan poured a second drink, offering it to the pale woman he'd nabbed. "Take this. It will calm your nerves."

She tentatively reached out and accepted it. "Thank you." Her hand shook alarmingly when she lifted it. Wide eyes peered over the edge as she sipped, taking in every detail.

"As if your own nerves aren't already comatose," Devon snapped in a nasty aside.

Morgan recovered his glass and settled down in a nearby chair. Devon couldn't fail to notice those cigarette ashes were flying about without any clear destination.

"The lady has her place in this bourgeois drama you've set into play, Devon. She may not be Adrien Roth, but she is the next best thing: his lover." He arched a mischievous eyebrow. "Do you not think he will fly to the rescue of his lady love? If he has any sort of honor, he will not wish to see her harmed, and will therefore sacrifice his freedom to gain hers."

Devon felt his blood pressure drop a bit. The words made sense. He turned to his unexpected guest. Though she trembled, she had the good sense and presence of mind not to dissolve into hysterics. She was dressed in the sheerest of lingerie, highlighting every sexy curve. He vaguely considered offering her a robe, but decided not to. A man of hearty sexual appetites, he could appreciate the view.

"So, Adrien has a woman." Devon reached out and caught her chin. The delicate pulse in her neck jumped as she swallowed. He could feel resistance stiffening her spine, then she acquiesced and slowly tipped back her head.

His gaze searched, looking for telltale signs. To his astonishment, neither her neck nor the rise of her breasts was marked with any scar. Those were the usual places most Kynn men preferred to feed from.

"Has he never fed off you?"

Confusion crossed her face. "F-fed off m-me? What do you mean?"

Losing patience, Devon snapped, "Has Adrien ever made love to you?"

She blushed and lowered her eyes, lashes delicately brushing her cheeks. "N—no." She raised a hand to brush a few stray wisps out of her face. "At least, not in the way I'd like him to."

Devon knew exactly what she was talking about. He easily recalled his own courtship of Rachel. As badly as he wanted to take her, he'd held himself back; their lovemaking had been limited to oral sex. He wanted to ease her into his life, slowly introduce her to the world of sexual vampirism. Had Adrien been planning the same for this woman?

There was no further time to think on the matter. The peaceful interlude was short lived.

Just as the grandfather clock began to chime the midnight hour, a sudden whoosh of wind rattled the French doors. A strange mist was beginning to materialize, growing thick enough to obscure the view outside. It drifted against the windows, oddly gray and shapeless. Devon thought he saw faces—dimly, like reflections in a black pool of water—of people he vaguely recognized. Invisible claws scrabbled at the glass, attacking with a violence threatening to send shards flying in every direction.

Ariel, he thought, feeling deeply disquieted. *Lilith.* And, oh heavens, Rachel's face was there, too, etched in the depths of the mist. For a moment he was tempted to break away, rush upstairs to check on the safety of his sleeping wife. He reluctantly held his ground. Rachel was safe. A small smile crossed his lips.

Adrien could not cross the threshold unless bidden.

Through a long moment, no one moved. All eyes were riveted on the eerie display.

With a sigh, Morgan set aside his glass and climbed to his feet. He reclaimed his discarded weapon. "Get a move on, Devon. I want to get this over with and continue with my night."

Gathering his courage, strength, and the righteous anger of a man determined to protect his loved ones at any cost, Devon stalked to the doors. Unlocking them, he flung both open to the night . . . and the beast waiting outside.

Driven by a fierce, icy wind, the mist eddied into the chamber. At first a swirling mass, its motion grew slower and its core grew darker, shreds of foggy tendrils pulling together into a definite form. It took only seconds for the mist to vanish as the solid form of Adrien Roth stepped forth. He looked as though he'd dressed hastily, the shirt he'd thrown on wrinkled and crookedly buttoned.

Adrien's ferocious gaze searched the room. As his stare found and settled on his girlfriend, all hate seemed to drain out of him. He immediately passed Devon to kneel down by the lounge and gather her into his embrace.

"Cassie, darling. Are you all right?"

Cassie seemed to snap out of her shock. "Adrien," she murmured. "Is it really you?"

Adrien nodded. "Yes. I'm going to get you out of here. Nothing will happen to you, I promise."

She reached out, touching her lover's face as if to reassure herself that he was indeed solid. "It's true. You're not human." She glanced around. She didn't seem to be afraid. She was strangely, almost unnaturally, calm. "None of you are." The awe of new revelation colored her voice.

"I can't explain now," Adrien said, taking her hand. "Maybe not ever. Just know that I wanted to love you, Cassie, but I couldn't bring you into my world."

Devon stood unmoving, face rigid and unyielding at the display of tender affection. He had no pity. "Your reunion with your beloved is quite touching, but you and I have some unfinished business to settle between us."

Adrien slowly got to his feet. "You see me as the man who once judged your kind and found them unworthy to live."

Gazes locked in hostility, the two enemies stared each other down, assessing, tending, preparing.

"I see you only as a murderer, Mister Roth—a man too blind to see the truth," Devon snarled. "The Kynn have the right to exist, and my children have the right to be born."

Adrien opened the collar of his shirt to show the thin scars circling his neck. The bleakness in his eyes hardened, taking on an icy animation of their own. His lips flicked in a mirthless grin. "Did you think torture would better persuade me to see your kindred in a more favorable light?"

Devon remembered the letters that Adrien had written, outlining the perverse things Lilith had done to him. In his attempts to avenge Ariel's death, he'd acted with an impulse gone badly awry. The repercussions had created an ever-widening circle around him. "I did not intend for Lilith to take matters that far. I only wished to show you what you were killing was not wholly evil."

"You couldn't convince me," Adrien spat. "If I had the choices to make again, I would do the same exact thing." He drew himself up, squaring his shoulders. "I am one of the Amhais. We are watchers and protectors."

Devon narrowed his eyes. "If I had the choice to make again, you would die the very night we took you out of the alleys of Whitechapel."

Spreading his arms, Adrien turned his hands palm up. "That would have been my intent as well." His voice was clear and level. "You'd better not let me walk away tonight, or I will come back and kill those spawn you've bred." His hand disappeared briefly behind his back. When it came back into view, he brandished the bolt that could only have come from Morgan's crossbow. "This is all I need to take you out for good. Too bad that bastard you hired didn't do the job right when he shot me down."

Devon felt his jaw muscles tighten, along with every muscle in his body. The bolt Adrien clutched was designed to do a lot of damage. Already wounded, Adrien had all the desperation of a rabid dog backed into a corner. He had nothing to lose and would probably go to his death fighting every step of the way.

Launching toward Devon with all the fury of righteous revenge, Adrien swung the bolt in a deadly arc.

Devon felt the sting of the razor-sharp tip graze his neck, perilously close to his jugular. Staggering back, he caught his balance just as Adrien lunged in for another strike. His enemy looked bigger than a bull and was just as vicious.

Grabbing Adrien's right wrist, Devon twisted hard, letting the momentum of his own weight add to the momentum that should take Adrien to the floor.

Adrien howled, dropping the deadly bolt. He immediately countered with a twist of his body that allowed him to deliver a forward punch with his left fist. Devon dodged it as Adrien wrenched himself free.

Adrien clenched his fists, eyes taking on a glacial chill. "I'll enjoy killing you with my bare hands, you fucker," he snarled.

"I'm not dead yet," Devon snarled back. Cold prickles raced up his spine. He wasn't as equally as skilled a fighter as Adrien. Sure, he had the abnormal strength of the Kynn, but he didn't have the knowledge to back it up.

Good thing Adrien didn't know that.

Before the thought went through his mind, Adrien struck again. He came around with a smooth roundhouse kick. Right at Devon's face.

Devon barely blocked it. Somehow he finessed Adrien's kick by using his own weight as counter leverage to hit Adrien full force. Breath whooshed from Adrien's mouth as he took a direct blow to the chest. He staggered back, stunned.

"Bastard," Adrien hissed through a gasp. "You're going to pay for what you did to me." He piled the full force of his bulk at Devon, hitting like a fright train without brakes.

Together they fell, a tangle of arms and legs locked in a desperate embrace.

Hot breath scorched Devon's face. Adrien's hands were closing around his neck, strong fingers digging, squeezing. Devon felt a dizzying black cloud mushroom through his skull. He clawed desperately at the bands of steel ringing his throat.

Adrien squeezed harder and spoke through gritted teeth. "Feels oddly familiar, doesn't it?"

Devon couldn't speak. If he didn't break free soon he wouldn't last more than a few minutes. Searing fire raced through his chest in his struggle to breathe. Wave after wave of darkness began to consume him.

Time came to a halt, sliding momentarily away. Fear that Rachel might also be taken from him clenched Devon's stomach into nasty knots.

The trembling of pure fury started deep inside. He didn't even try to control it. Hardly aware his body was in motion, Devon somehow found the strength to ignore the roar of blood in his ears. Fingers clenching into his palm, he slammed his fist into Adrien's face as hard as he could.

The choking pressure immediately lessened. Adrien reared up on his knees and clawed at his busted nose. Blood dripped through his fingers. "You son-of-a-bitch."

Devon sucked in air through a great wheezing gasp. Quaking from head to foot, he wriggled from beneath Adrien's weight and dragged himself a few feet away. Somehow he found the strength to pull his aching body into a sitting position. God, he didn't want any more of this!

To his surprise Adrien apparently didn't either. His eyes were riveted to the woman Morgan had nabbed.

Devon craned his head around. Restrained by Morgan, he realized that Adrien's girlfriend had watched the whole thing play out in front of her eyes.

White and shaking, her gaze flickered down to Adrien, then back over to him. "Please," she begged softly. "Don't hurt each other any more."

Devon's chest constricted as her words echoed through him. He felt ice cold inside. He shot a glance toward his hated enemy. The expression on Adrien's face slowly changed from anger to one of shame mingled with regret.

Their gazes locked. The seconds ticked by into a painfully long minute.

Adrien slowly shook his head. Blood trickled from his nose and one corner of his mouth. He lifted his hand to his face, bringing away stained fingers. Panting heavily, he shook his head at the sight. The slightest chuckle escaped him. "I'm tired of this bullshit." His eyes narrowed, throwing an unflinching challenge. "You really want me dead, then let's get it over with."

Devon climbed to his feet. He scrubbed a shaky hand over his bruised neck. A cold, damp sweat rose on his skin, chilling him. Tension arced though him as the rhythm of his heart accelerated all over again.

Snapping out of the trance he'd fallen into, he whirled toward Morgan. "Why didn't you stop him?"

Morgan shrugged, flicking longish bangs off his forehead. "And miss the chance to watch two Englishmen beating each other senseless? Does my Irish heart good, and I rather enjoyed the sight." He smirked. "Besides, it seems to me that you had some of that coming." He stepped up and gave Devon a hearty slap on the back. "Put on that stiff upper lip, old man, and be glad you got the best of him."

Annoyance trickled through him. "You're more hindrance than help."

Morgan shrugged. "I only do what I am hired to do. No more, no less."

Fresh anger filling him, Devon whirled and pounced. "Then do it. I want the threat he brings to my family ended."

"Very well." Morgan stepped up behind the downed man. He pressed the bow to Adrien's back. "The pain will be brief."

"God, no!" Cassie screeched and covered her eyes. "Please don't!"

"Don't look, honey." Adrien glanced up over his shoulder. "You can make her forget what she's seen. Don't let her remember this."

Devon didn't feel half so generous. "The last request of a doomed man. Your feelings for her are truly touching, but I am not impressed."

Morgan cut in. "She will not remember anything. I will see to it."

"When did you get a conscience?" Devon snapped.

An ice-smooth warning came back. "Your wife could be a widow tonight."

Devon shut up, still a bit unsure as to where Morgan's allegiance lay. That crafty bastard was up to something. He just didn't know what it was—yet.

"Just pull the damn trigger."

Nothing happened.

Devon felt his mate's presence before he ever heard the fall of her footsteps. Rachel stood at the threshold. She was dressed in a robe, her hair mussed as though her head had risen from the pillow only moments before.

Barefoot, she swayed slightly as she walked, one hand pressed against her mountainous belly, as though her burden was almost too much for her to endure. Her face was drawn with discomfort and the bruise of dark circles ringed her eyes. In her other hand she held a handful of letters.

Devon felt the clutch of worry grasp at his heart. He'd thought the letters securely locked away in his desk. He'd resolved to burn them after Adrien's death. How had Rachel come to have them now?

"Stop," he said tersely.

Everyone froze.

How had Rachel known to come at this very instant? It was like providence granting Adrien a stay of execution. Hurrying to her side, Devon shelved the thought for later pondering.

"Rachel, you shouldn't be out of bed, darling." Devon tried to take the letters from her, feeling dismay and distress at her presence. He hadn't wanted her to witness such an ugly scene. He'd wanted it taken care of in a clean manner. Looking at her tired, strained face, he said, "Go back to bed. This will soon be over."

Rachel unexpectedly twisted away from her husband. "Let me go, Devon, please." She sighed with the weariness of physical fatigue but beyond her exhaustion, determination gleamed in her eyes. She'd come to have her say. Her searching gaze fixed on Adrien. She walked over to him, her stride hampered by her size. When she came to a stop, she stood unmoving; beautiful, proud, and angry.

Devon stood riveted, part of him poised for action, part of him paralyzed with dismay. Why had Rachel come? What did she wish to say? Didn't she realize the danger she was in?

Eyes filled with gentle compassion, Rachel held out her hand. "You're the man who wrote these horrible letters."

Adrien's face was grim. The silence was so thick a knife could slice it. "Yes."

"Is it true, the things you wrote about Lilith and my husband?"

"Yes." Adrien looked uncomfortable. "I was sired against

my will into this damnation." He held up his bloodstained fingers. "I fall to their hungers even as I despise myself."

Rachel let the letters drop, a scattering of pages around her feet. "If these things are true, then it is my husband who should be down on his knees, asking your forgiveness."

"Rubbish!" Devon said, and began to say more.

His wife stopped him from imparting anything further. "Devon, contain yourself."

Devon stared in blank dismay. Finally, he blurted, "Rachel, please; it isn't your place to do this." His voice struggled with the rage and pain he was feeling.

Rachel shook her head stubbornly. Her face was drawn with anguish. "It *is* my place. What you did was wrong; that can't be denied."

Hands spread helplessly, Devon had no argument.

Rachel looked down at Adrien, placing one hand on her belly, the other on his head as if she were attempting to make a connection with the man who'd threatened her. "I understand your need for vengeance, but my children are innocents, unknowing of what they will be born into. With every fiber of my being, I believe they've been conceived for a reason and I was chosen to give birth to them. If murder must be committed to protect their lives"—she paused, drawing in a deep breath— "then the order will come from the lips of their mother."

Devon rushed to his wife, pressing a quick kiss into her hair. "You didn't let me down," he whispered in her ear.

Exhausted, Rachel's head dropped heavily for a moment against him, and she sighed then, fighting to corral her strength. She raised her head. "I want this nightmare over," she said quite clearly.

Devon motioned to Morgan. "Do it. Now."

Adrien closed his eyes and crossed his body. "May God have mercy on all your souls. And may He grant mercy on mine."

24

With a small fragmentary thought, Cassie wondered if she weren't in the midst of some strange dream. Without really willing it, the thought tangled through her mind that the cancer had somehow overtaken her; that she was really lying comatose in some hospital room with an IV in her arm, her brain the victim of some twisted, wishful nightmare.

Vampires . . . Assassins . . . a lover who walked on the wind . . . Could any mind, however invaded by illness, dream up such a strange brew? For an instant, she would have believed herself utterly and completely unconscious, except that she felt the soft silk of her spare gown against her skin, felt the chill of goose bumps rising. On another level, even clearer, she was aware she was awake and what was happening was all too real. Something profound had come into her life. She felt a strange prickle go up and down her spine. She'd be a fool not to grab at it with both hands.

I have nothing to lose.

Breaking past Devon and Rachel, Cassie joined her lover. "If you're going to kill him, then kill me, too." When only shocked stares met her announcement, she cleared her voice and stated, "It's not like I have anything to live for."

Still on his knees, Adrien looked up at her. "Don't be foolish. This isn't a game." He sent a glare over his shoulder. "This wasn't anything you should have been involved in."

Cassie wet her lips. Her mouth was bone dry, nerves all a-tremble. She forced herself to appear calm when she addressed Devon and Rachel. "My life is nothing, soon to end." She clenched her hands into fists, gathering her courage. "I'll trade my life for his."

Devon Carnavorn gathered his scattered composure. "Why would you wish to give your life for that of this man?"

Cassie made a faint gesture of negation. "I'm dying."

Rachel broke free of her husband's hold. Taking Cassie's hands, Rachel led her to sit down on the chaise. The inquiry in her gaze made Cassie feel wholly exposed. Cassie, in turn, noticed Devon's wife looked wearied and haggard. Her pregnancy had taken its toll. The woman had no business being up and about. She should be in bed resting.

"Is what you say true?"

Cassie had never discussed her cancer to anyone other than her physicians. Even her own mother didn't know the truth about her health. She bit her lip, struggling to force the answer through the barrier of self-denial. Her eyes were level and tearless, but inside her heart was breaking.

"Yes," she said, keeping her voice even with effort. The tears escaped then. She didn't let them fall, blinking and flicking them away with the tips of her fingers.

Devon's smooth brow was wrinkled with a frown. He turned to her kidnapper. "You can read certain—things—about people, can't you?"

After a moment of hesitation, Morgan nodded. "I can."

"Is she telling the truth?"

Adrien rose swiftly to his feet. "It's just a trick," he said, cutting Morgan's passage short. "She's just trying to save my life." He hurried to Cassie's side, pulling her to her feet, away from Rachel.

Looking into his eyes, she could see that his mind was working, racing for an answer that would offer them both a shot at freedom. Cassie knew he could depart with ease; she'd witnessed his entrance. A flash of insight told her he couldn't easily spirit her away. He wasn't as practiced and powerful as the other two beings.

"Good try, honey, but there's no use in offering your life for mine."

Cassie countered, very simply and honestly, "I'm not lying. I have a couple of years at the most, if that long."

Before Adrien could stop her, she stepped toward Morgan. He was the most intimidating of the three, and not simply because he held the most weapons. There was something even more otherworldly about him than Devon, Adrien, and Rachel combined. She remembered what he'd said to Adrien before they'd departed her bedroom: *you have everything to gain if you play your cards right.*

Well, Adrien was deliberately tossing away all the good cards. She wasn't willing to let him throw away his life, or hers. Something wonderful was in her grasp. She wanted it with all her might. This was her only chance, and it was now or never.

A look passed between Cassie and Morgan.

Morgan had the twinkle of a rogue in his eyes, and the slightest of smiles turned up one corner of his fine mouth. Cassie entertained the odd notion that he was carefully putting each of them into place like a chess master. He knew exactly how the strings should be pulled and he was doing just that. She didn't know why she trusted him, but she did.

"Tell them." She forced herself to relax, deliberately quieting her breathing. This was not going to be easy.

Tossing the crossbow to Devon, Morgan lifted his left hand toward her body, palm out, all five fingers splayed. He briefly passed his hand over the level of her chest. A look of puzzlement crossed his face. He shook his head as though searching for his concentration. His hand rose, toward her head, passing in front of her face. His eyes burned with a fierce intensity. Then, very lightly, his hand came to rest, his middle finger pressing at her temple, thumb at her jaw. He pressed harder.

Staring into his eyes, Cassie felt a jolt go through her mind, passing from the physical into the molecular level. She tried to focus on the beat and rhythm his touch introduced. For an instant her vision dimmed, and in a second of psi-awareness, she merged with the pulsing of blood cells in her veins, the beat of her heart. And then her third eye moved into her skull and she saw the hungry gray beast feasting on the tender pink cells of her brain.

In an instant the link was broken.

Cassie trembled, knees going weak. For a second she felt herself struggle at the edge of a great abyss, heard herself gasp, near to retching. A nausea that wasn't even definite enough to be relieved by vomiting attacked her, accompanied by a strange sensation crawling through her bowels. The physical side effects of being psychically invaded were like the effects of a strong poison. Lights flashed behind her eyes, as if emitted from inside her own skull. She stayed still, eyes closed, until the swaying sickness in her stomach retreated a little. Her own hands pressed against her forehead.

Morgan announced, "She has a cancer in her mind." He turned away, giving a slight shake of his head. "I need a cigarette." Flinging himself back into the chair he'd earlier occupied, he lit up, then drank down the remainder of his sherry. Lowering his empty glass, he said, "This is getting tedious and boring. If you have the nerve, kill Adrien now or let him go."

Devon slowly shook his head and laid the crossbow aside.

Rachel smiled softly and nodded, reaching for her husband's hand. "No one will die tonight."

Adrien wrapped his arms around Cassie's slender waist, drawing her close. His forehead touched hers. "Why didn't you tell me?"

She swallowed, choked a little, then said, "How could I? Would you want to be held to a dying woman? What's happened tonight has opened my eyes to so many things—wonderful things."

"How can you call this hell wonderful?" Adrien asked, incredulous.

"I'm not blind. I know everything I've seen tonight and it's incredible. You people have been granted an amazing gift, a lifetime free of old age, pain—or sickness...." She paused, swallowing the lump at the back of her throat.

"You're looking through rose-colored glasses," Adrien said softly. "Eternity is not what you believe it to be."

Cassie placed a single finger across his lips, silencing him. "Eternity *is* everything when you have no future. You have one, Adrien, yet you'd willingly throw it away. You may not have chosen such an existence, but *it* chose you." She searched his eyes. "If you love me as you say, then choose me. Please, share your gift with me."

Adrien gave a bitter grimace. "You don't know what you're asking, Cassie."

Seeing faint surprise and hesitation in his gaze, she insisted, "I do know what I'm reaching for. I don't want to die. What's waiting for me is more brutal than anything that could happen to me now."

Adrien raised his eyebrows. "It's not that easy...." he started to say. "Are you—certain—it's what you would want?"

Once the thought came into her mind, it would not be dispelled. "Spending more time with you," she answered with a sigh, "would be heaven."

By the look on Adrien's face, she could see he was warring with his emotions. His doubts and prejudices were holding fast, not so easily chased away. She said nothing more, afraid that he would resent her if she tried to sway him to accept something against his will.

After the longest moment had passed, Adrien slowly bent and gathered the letters he'd written, letters Rachel had cast back.

"All my hate is here, in these pages," he confessed. "I wore my need for revenge like blinders, never seeing anything else in this world, for I always felt my world had been taken from me. I—I never realized it was not stolen away. Lilith may have taken my mortal life, but I am the one who refused to accept my own as one of the Kynn." He cast the pages into the fireplace. In an instant, only ashes remained.

Cassie nodded in silent encouragement when Adrien looked at her.

Adrien then looked at Devon. "Can my threats ever be forgiven?"

Devon slid an arm around Rachel. "I can forgive Ariel's death. That past must be lain aside. With my wife, I treasure the new chances I myself have been given. It is only fair I give you that second chance."

A shy, tentative manner seemed to overtake Adrien. "Would the making of a new Kynn woman be permissible?"

Devon inclined his head. "A new member is always welcome." He looked troubled as he continued, "It is to my eternal regret that I left you in Lilith's hands. She twisted the joy you could have experienced." In a bold move, he stepped up and held out his hand. "Many blessings to your new she-shaey, Adrien. May your days together be happy ones."

A suspicious look crossed Adrien's face, which he quickly squelched. He tentatively took Devon's hand. "Many blessings on your wife and children to be."

Relieved and delighted that peace had been attained, Cassie placed her hands atop those of the men. She couldn't help smiling. "Thank you both."

She glanced back at Rachel, who nodded and patted her bulging belly—a gesture of hope Cassie dare not dream of just yet.

Whatever turns lie in the road ahead, we will face them together.

Devon stepped back, clearing his throat. "You are both free to go."

Rachel tugged gently at her husband's sleeve. "The lady is hardly dressed to go out into the night. Shouldn't we offer the hospitality of our home? I am sure she and Adrien would like to be alone. It will take time while she, ah, adjusts."

Her husband quickly caught the gist behind her words. "Of course," he said, sharing a knowing glance with his wife. "You two must do us the honor of staying the night. I have just the perfect rooms available."

Cassie looked at Adrien. Though he looked as nervous as a schoolboy before the headmaster, he tentatively nodded.

"Thank you," she answered for both of them, sliding her hand into her lover's. "We'd be delighted to stay."

25

Cassie sat down on the king-sized bed. She gave the comforter a light stroke, enjoying the feel of the material under her hand. This was nice, better than anything she had.

It'll be luxurious to lie on, she thought. A small smile crossed her lips. *Even nicer to make love on.*

She watched Adrien close the door and lock it. Instead of turning on the overhead lights and filling the room with illumination, he turned on only one small lamp beside the table. He seemed to need the darkness.

He immediately turned to her. His features were strangely taut. "I don't know if I can do this."

She felt her stomach clench. "What do you mean?"

Adrien sat down on the bed beside her, his face half in shadow, half in light. He looked very mysterious, very otherworldly. "I mean, I don't know if I can make you one of the Kynn."

She inclined her head. "Is that what you're called?" She mulled the word. "Kynn. I like it." She wanted him to come to her, crush her in his strong embrace and cover her with kisses, but something in him—a faint sense of hesitation—kept him away. She felt his tension, his discomfort. He did not have to say a word. His body was tense, hands clenched, jaw rigid.

Cassie slid off the bed. She went to the window, pushing aside the heavy drapes and sliding up the glass to let in the night air. She leaned against the sill, looking out to the gardens. Under the wisps of moonlight, they had a surreal, frozen cast. It was as though all breath but her own had ceased in this world. "This isn't something you want. I can feel it in you."

Behind her, Adrien left the bed.

She heard his soft footsteps as he walked up. His hands slid around her waist and she laid her head back on his shoulder. Their bodies swayed together gently. Neither said a word, simply enjoying each other's touch.

"If only you knew how much I wanted to tell you," he finally said, breaking the silence. "Every time I pulled you into my arms, the words were on my lips." He nuzzled the nape of her neck, nipping gently. "The need to take you"—he licked her skin, leaving a moist trail—"to taste you, almost drove me insane."

She closed her eyes for a moment, trying to collect her thoughts, which scattered at each touch from this man. "I wanted you to. Why didn't you?"

"All my life, I was taught to hate and fear the occultic beings, and to hunt them. I destroyed without knowing the truth." He drew a deep breath. "My hate of Lilith kept me alone, locked in my own shell. I thought myself unworthy, tainted by their evil kiss. I never believed I'd find a woman who could so willingly accept me." He held her tighter. "I want to be with you, Cassie. Now and forever."

Before she sank into sweet oblivion, she said, "Do you really want forever? I can feel hesitation in you." Her gut was telling her that if he didn't take her tonight, this very hour, he'd walk out of her life forever. She hadn't waited this long to find her soul mate, only to discover that the barriers between their worlds couldn't be bridged. She realized with sudden clarity that it was his own fear holding him back from taking her completely.

Adrien drew back, turning her around to face him. With a hand that wasn't quite steady, he drew off his shirt, baring his chest. A strange charm she'd never seen before hung around his neck from a sturdy silver chain; a triangle of three sharp eyelets. The edges looked razor sharp. Dried blood clung to his skin, flaking off in patches around the injury he'd earlier suffered. Amazingly, it'd healed; a puckered white scar was in the place of what should be a fresh, ugly wound. "The Kynn are predators," he said simply. "These scars are the marks of Lilith's feeding off me before she made me."

Cassie reached out, touching the freshest addition to his flesh. He flinched, but did not draw back. It'd always seemed to her eyes that the cuts were not the product of accident, but deliberation. Now she knew.

"Would you have to do that to me?" The thought did not disturb her. Quite the opposite. It excited her.

Adrien nodded. "We make the cuts to feed." He paused, then hurried to say, "But blood is only a small part of the hunger. We only drink it to make a connection, to tap into other energies your body emits."

Her brow wrinkled. "Other energies?"

"Sexual energy, the energy of creation." He took her hand. Turning up her palm, he made small circles on her skin. "When the Kynn make love to a person, we take those energies into our own bodies. Afterward, the victim is left feeling weakened, literally drained. It feels like the flu. A healthy person can recover in a day or two."

She laughed lightly with comprehension. "Ah, so that's why you wouldn't make love to me?"

"Yes. I'd be feeding off you." He cast his gaze to the floor.

"You were more to me than just another source." His eyes came up. "I've taken hundreds of women, nameless, faceless women to feed my hunger. You would have to do that, too. Make love to strange men to sate your needs."

She considered the implications of his words; this situation was more complicated than she'd thought. "I won't be making love to them. I'll be having sex. That's what you do. You have sex with those women, right? They mean nothing to you, like eating another meal."

"I think of it that way."

"But you can still make love to me?"

"Two Kynn cannot draw off each other. We'd be safe, yes."

"How does it happen? This change?"

Adrien paled noticeably. Cassie saw unhappiness cover his gaze.

Adrien cleared his throat, finally saying, "It's in the blood."

Cassie nodded, waiting for him to continue.

His eyes darkened, his mouth thinned. "When introduced into a healthy body, it seems to act as a sort of virus, overwhelming and rearranging human DNA into an entirely new structure. The night Lilith 'made' me, I died—part of the self-induced asphyxiation of my body killing itself. My heart ceased beating, my lungs drawing air. Lilith's breath revived me."

She flinched at the barely disguised anger in his tone. "But she brought you back."

Adrien's jaw tightened. "Yes, she did." He forced himself to put aside anger, taking her hands into his. His fingers were warm, strong, reassuring when they linked with hers. A reluctant smile tugged his lips. "Do you still want to cross?" He almost spoke the words as if he were afraid she'd be the one to change her mind.

Throat dry, heart pounding, Cassie closed her eyes and inhaled a deep breath. "I want to share this life with you, make love to you and with you." A single tear slid down her cheek.

"Do you want the same thing? If not, speak your piece now. I won't try to hold you. Ever. It has to be your decision, too."

Cradling her cheek, Adrien swiped her tear away with the pad of his thumb. "I want this. I want you. I don't want to live with lies and deceptions anymore."

"Really?"

He nodded. "Yes."

"Me, too." Cassie drew back, sniffling a little, wiping her face with her hands. By some miracle this man had come into her life, changing everything. Whatever happened from here on out, he would always be beside her, supporting her, loving her. Nothing would part them, not even death.

Adrien touched his mouth to hers softly. "Don't be afraid," he whispered. "I'll never leave you." He stroked his tongue between her lips, savoring.

With a soft moan, Cassie captured a handful of his hair. Searching, tasting, teasing, the heat his touch stoked turned into an inferno.

Slowly, he eased his lips from hers. Senses strung tight, his body trembled. "Wow."

Quivering with the aftershock, Cassie touched her lips, tracing with a finger the path his tongue had etched. The simple beauty of his kiss was stunning. "I agree. Wow." With that thought, a slew of nervous butterflies took flight in her stomach. She realized she was afraid, feeling so much more than she'd ever thought she could for a man. "What happens next?"

Adrien smiled, a slow curving of the lips that sent moist warmth trickling between the juncture of her thighs. "We take a shower."

Tremors coursed through her, hot and pulsing. Cassie squeezed her thighs together, temporarily sating her pulsing clit. She was so wet her panties clung to her satiny skin. "A bath?"

A wicked gleam sparked in his eyes. "I want the chance to

touch you all over, and I'm not exactly the nicest smelling guy in the world right now."

Slow, sexy grin spreading, Adrien stepped back. Sitting down on the bed, he pulled off his boots. Setting them aside, he stood up, stripping away the rest of his clothing with painstaking slowness, lingering over each button in his shirt and jeans, drawing out her anticipation.

Cassie devoured the sight with appreciation, his broad shoulders and chiseled abs feeding her hungry gaze. Oh, damn. . . . It was definitely about to get hot in here. She'd experienced attraction before, but never on a level like this. This desire almost completely debilitated her.

Giving her a sultry smile, Adrien continued his stripping. Hesitating a second to draw out the tease, he finally pushed down his jeans, fingertips skimming his thickly muscled thighs, a sight that simply melted a woman's senses. Nestled amid a downy thatch of soft brown hair, his magnificent cock was far from flaccid.

Cassie flushed hotly, her imagination conjuring all kinds of X-rated images. Without hesitation, she shed her sheer lingerie.

Ten minutes later, they were in the shower. There was nothing but the water between them and yearnings of the most primitive kind.

Slicked with soap, Adrien's hands made slow, slippery circles across her skin. She felt a strange prickle go up her spine when he started to knead her firm ass cheeks. Drawing her buttocks apart, he slid his cock along the crevice even as he trailed his lips along her neck. She could feel the hard wall of his thighs against hers, felt the steely strength of him coiled like a cobra ready to strike.

"I've needed you, Cassie." He bent his head to nibble at the sensitive flesh beneath her right ear. Hips positioned between his commanding hands, he pressed his erection harder against her, the beginning of a slow, gentle rhythm. His teeth nipped at the soft slope between her shoulder and neck.

Bracing her hands against the wall of the shower, Cassie bit down on her lower lip to keep from crying out for him to take her. She pressed back against him and the motion dragged a long, fevered groan from him. When the friction became too intense to be borne any longer, Adrien dug his fingers into her hips. In one ferocious movement, his forceful body tensed.

They stood under the water, the steam billowing around them in a gentle cloud. When he'd regained his composure, Adrien guided her around to face him, giving the tip of her nose a quick kiss.

"Thank you. I had to do that. Holding out, waiting to have you, is driving me crazy."

"I hope you don't have to wait much longer."

"Your energies have to be at the peak for the crossing." He circled one nipple with the tip of his finger. The little nub tightened and Cassie stiffened as fresh desire knifed through her. All her reason was beginning to fade, as lost as a wraith in the fog. Fingers digging into his shoulders, she dragged in a ragged breath when he bent to taste one of her nipples. Flicking his tongue lightly over the tip, he teased her a minute before closing his lips over the distended bud. He pinched the other nipple, twisting it lightly until she cried out.

"What's the matter?"

"Your touch. It's like no other; you touch my skin and I feel you so deep inside. . . ." The need of him was a pounding ache, penetrating to a place she could not physically reach. But he could.

Adrien chuckled. "Oh, you'll feel me deep inside, all right." His hand slid down over her flat belly. He parted her legs with his hand. Finding her clit, he caressed until she was warm, wet, and twisting. He was hitting all the right spots, hands and lips following well-traveled and well-explored paths. He'd memorized every inch of her, knew how she liked to be fondled and stroked.

Just as she was about to hit her peak, Adrien drew back, giving her a long, slow kiss. "Don't come yet."

"Awful hard not to when you're doing what you're doing," she breathed, gritting her teeth against that ache deep in her loins. Her clit was afire. The need to climax—and soon—was building inside her, threatening to erupt like a volcano disgorging a rush of hot lava.

Turning off the water, Adrien grabbed a thick towel. He dried her body with long, loving strokes, missing not an inch of her. As squeaky and clean as a virgin on Sunday morning, she felt pure, cleansed.

Cassie was ready when Adrien took her hand in his and led her back into the bedroom.

26

Cassie pressed a hand to her stomach. Nerves and nausea clashed. Now that the time was so close, the jitters were beginning to hit her hard. "How do we do this? How does one become Kynn?"

Adrien drew an unsteady breath. "I have to kill you. . . . Your human life must be shed."

She imagined wriggling out of her life the way a snake wriggled out of its skin. "How do I come back?"

His features were oddly stark in the half-light. "My blood will take your life. My breath will bring you back." He shook his head. "But I've never tried it, never made one be like me. I've only had it done . . . to me."

Cassie reached up to stroke his cheek. "Then whatever was done to you, do it to me." She thought she saw a blush darken his cheeks.

He seemed to think a moment, then nodded. "It won't be easy on you, but I'll do my best to try. I'll need to tie you up so you won't injure yourself during the crossing. It can get violent."

"Sounds kinky."

Cassie looked around the room, considering the bed, then a nearby chair. The bed was a canopied one, with four sturdy posts to the front and rear. She walked over to it, stretching her arms across the two rear posts to test the width. Pressing both her wrists against the hard wood, she found the perfect spot. "Here. Tie me to these posts."

"Standing or sitting?"

"Sitting. Facing you."

"All right." Adrien started to reach for his belt, but realized that would not be enough to securely lash both hands.

"My stockings," Cassie suggested, nodding toward their discarded clothing.

Adrien retrieved the stockings. Stretching them taut, he bound her wrists to the posts. The mattress was level with the back of her knees, not uncomfortable at all. She tugged at the ties and found she could not free her hands. She bounced on the bed, testing the comfort of the mattress on her bare ass. A nervous laugh escaped her. "I think we're a go." The way she was trussed gave him perfect access to every bit of her body.

His gaze grew serious. "I can stop, anytime you say. If you get scared or change your mind, just tell me."

She shook her head. "I'm going all the way." The enormity of what she was about to do was a weight around her neck. She was grasping at straws, hoping against hope that the decision she'd made was the right one. She thought again about what she'd seen and heard. How to distinguish reality from fantasy when there was a malicious tumor growing in her brain. Was her desperation and fear of death leading her to believe in things that weren't true at all?

It's a chance I have to take. Would dying now really make much difference? As with the hairs on her head, her days were numbered. Each day that passed was one less to look forward to. The grave would be cold and dark, and she'd be alone. That thought frightened her more than the idea of perishing at the hands of a madman. At least she'd die reaching for hope.

"I want to do this right," he said, seeming more than a little nervous himself.

Cassie watched him move in the shadows. Naked, he was magnificent, tall and lean. When he looked at her, there was a new fire in his eyes, a look she recognized. He'd wanted her before, but had not dared take her. Now he was free to do just that, and the inner animal inside him was unleashed and ready to feast. His member was again half-erect in anticipation. The shadows were his only clothing, his eyes touching her as surely as his hands soon would.

Still, there was resistance in the set of his jaw. It was as though she was drawing him to her against his will.

"Cassie," he said, a hoarse whisper conveying both his need and his hunger.

She said nothing. She simply waited.

After what seemed an eternity, Adrien came to her. A desperate, angry moan broke from deep in his throat. Falling to his knees, his hands slipped around her slender waist and drew her body to his, claiming her lips in a single long kiss of pent-up desire. Her lips parted willingly for the searing invasion of his tongue. Her back arched as one of his hands sought, then closed over, her breast. The tips of her nipples were hard, pulsing buttons.

Cassie groaned with her need. Between her legs she felt the moistness of her desire all over again. Her entire being was focused on the undeniable need to be taken by Adrien, fucked until she screamed in pleasure.

"Please. . . . Take me all the way. Nothing else matters."

Adrien's eyes flashed with violent passion. "There's no stopping now."

His hands closed over her full breasts. Kneading them gently, his fingers chafed the pink rosebuds until they throbbed.

Then, as a tease, he drew his fingertips over her rib cage, down to her belly, then back up again. With a wicked grin, he dipped his head and traced the circumference of one rosy nipple. Beams of intense pleasure radiated through her body. She gasped aloud.

Adrien only laughed low in his throat. His lips closed over the aching button again and he suckled as if taking in long-denied nourishment. He pulled away briefly to kiss the valley between her breasts, then turned his attention to her other nipple. As he nipped at the bud, Cassie flexed her fingers, arms pulling to escape the tight binds. She longed to run her fingers through his hair, hold him close.

A low moan of frustration escaped her. She shivered.

"Cold?" His hands settled possessively on the supple flesh rounding her hips. The sensation was spellbinding, sending a new flood of warmth through her loins.

"Far from it," she breathed, voice filled with the wondrous fury of desire.

Adrien's mouth seared Cassie's flesh as he nibbled at the vulnerable skin above the line of her Venus mound. Her head fell back in utter surrender when his hand slid up between her thighs to caress the rosebud hidden between silken nether lips. Making her widen her legs, his searching fingers found her pulsing clit. He rubbed back and forth against the little nub, using her own cream to heighten her sensitivity to his touch.

"Let me know when you're nearing climax," he said, fighting to keep his own control. "That's when your energies will be at their strongest. That's when I will start your change."

"Mmm . . . don't keep me hanging." She groaned with helpless abandon when he added the warm pressure of his mouth. He slid two fingers deep.

Head thrashing from side to side in delirium, Cassie ground her cunt shamelessly against his face. Her arms ached from being bound up at the level of her head, but she did not care.

That pain only added to the exquisite torment Adrien was so expertly inflicting on her body. Her back arched. The pressure of pleasure was too great, so much so that she almost couldn't bear it. Her orgasm was building.

Adrien suddenly reared back. His hand flew to his neck, jerking the charm hanging there loose. His eyes glowed from the depths of his skull, blazing with a hunger that went beyond the physical. "I'll only have this one chance to know you as a human woman," he breathed. With one edge of the charm, he made a tiny cut at the hollow of her throat. A brief agony lanced through her before he leaned forward, pressing his lips to it as blood welled. She could feel his tongue rasping against her sensitive skin, soothing away the dull ache.

Hands cupping her ass, he half pulled her off the bed so that she was sitting on his lap, her knees on either side of his hips. He pressed the tip of his cock to her sex, hesitated, then plunged in.

Cassie whimpered, filled with the need for a thing she could not even begin to imagine or define. Adrien pumped with a rhythmic ferocity that made his skin deliciously slick with sweat. She felt her core ripple around him, grasping at him, drawing him deeper.

Then, as though some beast were latching onto her, she felt an unfamiliar ice-laced darkness flow through her. Out of the maelstrom came the bubbling whirl of uncountable, dark, twisted shapes: menacing half-seen faces with gnashing teeth. The teeth bit hard and deep, thousands of tongues beginning to suck away the essences of the sexual energy Adrien aroused in her. Her flesh seemed to crawl with a strange animation.

Bleeding. Freezing. Withering. "You're taking too much from me. . . ." She gasped painfully, twisting her arms against her bindings, feeling—relishing—the gratifying burn at her wrists.

Giving a strangled cry of frustrated desire, Adrien pulled

out of her. Climbing to his feet, he used the charm on himself, slashing just above his navel. Catching a handful of her hair, he pushed her forward and forced her mouth to the wound.

"Drink of me, Cassie," he grunted, eyes glittering with an otherworldly fire. "Drink of me and live."

She tasted his blood, a saccharine nectar sliding like liquid fire down her throat. Immediately a burn like acid settled in the pit of her stomach and her heart raced with comprehension. Her body felt like it was shriveling, as some dark creature latched onto and began to slurp away the very blood in her veins. Sucking so hard the very marrow would seep from her bones. Pain was her master and it lashed at her again and again, going past the physical to her core. Her body convulsed in a series of violent spasms. Fear overcame her and she began to recede into unconsciousness. Adrien had betrayed her. She was going to die.

Oh, God, she thought wildly. *What's happening to me?* Her eyes fluttered shut, her soul aching with intense fear.

All of a sudden, the pain ceased, blinking out the way an overheated lightbulb would. In another instant a dazzling light abruptly smacked her full in the face, as her soul seemed to take flight on the wings of some unknown force. She cringed at first, but something about its warmth welcomed her into its infinite embrace. She sensed rather than physically felt the relaxing of her muscles as her body lost breath and went limp. For an instant, she heard the beating of her heart. Then there was nothing except an ever-expanding pool of silence.

Eyes beyond the physical opened and focused. Consciousness bloomed afresh. When she could think again, she saw that she was looking down at her own body. Her physical shell did not move, not even to breathe. For all intents and purposes she was dead, yet all too aware of the fact.

With a brief tingling shock, she realized that she was no more than a wraith, floating dreamily over the room. With a certain ironic detachment, she stared down on her slumped form. She moved, gliding around the room, visiting it from various angles. She felt stronger, filled with an energy no human mind could ever imagine or comprehend. The freedom of being formless and shapeless was amazing. She was tempted to follow the white pulsing light hovering at the edges of the room. It called like a siren song, urging her to join it, merge with it.

The light was death. Instinct told her to stay away, stay focused on her physical form. There was still a very thin thread attaching her to it. Break that, and she'd be lost.

Detached from her physical self, Cassie watched Adrien untie her wrists. He caught her limp form before it crumpled to the floor. Lifting her naked body, he laid her gently out on the bed. Hope stirred in her when he sat down beside her, gently stroking her pale cheek.

"Come back to me, Cassie." She did not hear so much as sense the words. He bent, pressing his mouth to hers, sharing his breath, pushing air into her paralyzed lungs.

Cassie's free-floating spirit was immediately dragged back into her physical body. A dreamy liquid ecstasy began to flow through her; an unearthly and incredible power was going inside her, filling her to the brim with the energy it had earlier sucked away. She felt a consciousness merge with her own, a thing not quite human, yet wholly sacred. She embraced it and welcomed it, and in return it gave her resurrection.

Eyelids fluttering open, awareness returned in a soft glow of satisfaction. She'd walked through the clutch of the Reaper and emerged on the other side, unscathed. She remembered being one with Adrien, but now she was a separate entity; whole, healed, and surging with strength.

His face a mask of worry, Adrien pressed his cool fingers to her throat, and his warm mouth claimed hers. "Welcome back, beloved," he whispered against her lips, brushing damp curls off her forehead. "How do you feel?"

"Mmm . . . tired. But a good tired."

"That will pass soon, I promise." Stretching out beside her, Adrien's hand drew soft circles on her bare belly. "You're mine forever now."

Cassie groped, placing a hand on his bare chest. "Adrien," she murmured sleepily. She swam in an extraordinary harmonious inertia, relaxed and rejuvenated.

"Yes, darling?" His hand slid down to find her most private place. He began a slow, teasing stroke against her clit. Pleasure made her cry out softly when he slid two fingers into her velvety depths.

Eyes closing in delight, Cassie moved her hand lower, finding the crux of his thighs. Her fingers curled around his cock and he shuddered at her touch.

"Just as soon as I get my strength back, we're going to finish what you started . . ."

Epilogue

His guests ensconced in their own suite and his wife safely tucked away in her own bed, Devon Carnavorn returned to see after the comfort of his last visitor.

As he walked downstairs, he replayed the night's events in his mind. Things had not quite progressed as he'd imagined they would. It was odd the way events had meshed so perfectly together. In fact, everything almost seemed, well, arranged.

There was one who knew the truth.

Morgan Saint-Evanston stood out on the verandah, quietly smoking. He appeared to be considering the night and its mysteries. The dawn was still a while away. For him, the night was still young.

Pouring two glasses of sherry, Devon sidled up. Morgan accepted a glass without comment, sipping the smooth wine.

"Just out of curiosity," Devon opened conversationally, "how long did it take you to find Adrien?"

Morgan flicked ashes away. "I found him the first night I went out."

"That was almost three nights ago."

A shrug. "He needed a little time."

"How long have he and the girl been together?"

"Three days."

Devon nodded. "So she was 'the one.' How did you know?"

A wry smirk of self congratulation crossed Morgan's face. "I have a knack for these things."

"Ah, I see." Devon swirled the burgundy liquid. More pieces of the puzzle came into place. In his mind he was thinking of a certain demonic delivery.

"I wonder," he mused aloud, "how Adrien's letters happened to fall into my wife's hands. She knew nothing of our, ah, meeting, yet still she showed up as if on cue. Could you clue me in on how letters locked in my desk at work came to be so conveniently in her possession?"

Morgan lifted his drink, affecting the vapid gambit he often assumed when he did not want anyone to think he had a thought in his head beyond his next carnal excursion. "Ask her," he mumbled into his glass. "I have not a clue."

Devon narrowed his eyes. "I think you do. In fact, I think you maneuvered this whole thing around to suit yourself."

Glass lowering, Morgan drew his shoulders back as if readying for an argument. Surprisingly, none arose.

Instead he took a long draw off his cigarette. "Then you give me no choice," he said though a rush of smoke. "I shall have to call in my favor. I must insist that you make no further inquiry."

Devon was stunned by the simplicity of the request. Delight filled him. It was a relief to be let off the hook so easily. "Done. I shall not ask again." Tickled to the core, he waited a moment, then asked, "Anything else, or am I now absolutely debt free?"

More gray ashes fed the night-scented wind. "I have asked. You have given. I am satisfied."

Devon couldn't resist one final prod. After all, this was a being who regularly cast death's shadow. "You crafty thing.

Getting sentimental in your old age, aren't you? I thought you didn't believe in happy endings."

The assassin gave him a sidelong glance. "There are no happy endings in this world." A touch of irony graced his lips in a thin smile. "But there are second chances."

And with that, Morgan Saint-Evanston was gone, vanishing back into the night and the dimensions that had birthed him. Only the scent of cloves remained, a cloying fragrance floating like a dream on the chilly breeze.

Devon Carnavorn stood a moment longer. Then, he went inside, shutting and locking the doors behind him.

Here's a preview of
EXPOSING CASEY!

On sale now from Aphrodisia!

1

I watched in silence as Connor Grant moved across the large open gallery space that dominated the first floor. He'd never told me he loved me or even that he liked being with me, for that matter. He'd told a million lies with his actions and his body. How could a man give a woman so much pleasure and also give nothing? I knew he was from Great Britain and that both of his parents were dead. He had a law-enforcement background that he could not talk about and no siblings. That was it; and I'd gotten that from his personnel file.

It had been my rule for years not to get involved with a man I worked with. I'd broken that rule with him and I was paying the price. Every time I saw the bastard, my knees got a little weak with the memory of him. As a lover, he'd been the perfect combination of demanding and giving; it was just too bad that he was a motherfucker in the vertical position.

He was moving toward me, smiling and weaving his way through the crowd of people I'd put between us. After dumping his ass, I'd taken a two-week vacation. Fourteen days in the U.S. Virgin Islands had given me new sense of self and a fantastic tan. I took a drink from my glass and pursed my lips as he came to a stop in front of me.

"Casey."

"Mr. Grant." I tried to keep my voice cool and neutral.

I watched shock and then anger drift across his face in equal measure. "Back to that, are we?"

"Seems like we never really left it." I glanced around the room for a way to escape.

"I'd like to talk to you."

"I'd like to forget you exist." I tried to move past him but he took my arm to stop me. His grip was firm but not painful. "Let go, Connor. You've made it abundantly clear what you can offer me and what you never will. Frankly, I can buy a dick in a store."

"We have a good thing."

"No, we had an empty and physical thing. Now, we have nothing." I looked to his hand. "Let me go."

His hand fell away and he sighed. "I'd hoped you'd be over this by now."

"You just hoped I'd still fuck you," I murmured softly and cleared my throat. "We're way past that."

At least, I was damn positive we were past that. Connor was attractive in a truly British kind of way. He'd worked for the Holman Gallery for over a year and had been the head of security for nearly four months. We'd been fucking for just over five months when I realized through no admission of his own that he never wanted anything serious with me or any other woman. It's true that he'd never made promises to me. He'd also never told me how much the idea of marriage or even a committed relationship freaked him out. If he'd had his druthers, I still wouldn't know.

He caught up with me in the staff hall that led to the administrative area. I stopped, turned around, and glared at him. "What?"

"You can't just dismiss what we are to each other."

EXPOSING CASEY / 261

"No, but I'm very capable of realizing what I'll never be to you." I pushed my finger against his chest. "I deserve more."

"I can't argue with that." He grabbed my hand and pulled me to him. "Case, I've missed you."

I stilled myself against the small thrill it gave me to hear him say it. But, I knew deep down he really didn't mean it. "You miss putting your dick in me."

He slid one hand around me, pressed against the small of my back until I was flush against him. "True. I miss talking to you, hearing about your day. Where have you been?"

"I went on vacation. That's no secret."

"Three months early and you didn't tell anyone where you were going."

"I'm a grown woman." I pulled briefly but sighed when his grip tightened. "I'm entitled to a private life."

"I thought I was a part of that private life."

"You don't want to be." I shoved at his chest and sighed at how weak I was about it.

The truth was, being in his arms felt great and just about as right as I could imagine. A year ago, he'd walked into the gallery and I'd spent the day in damp panties. His cool blue eyes, dark brown hair, and tight body had put more than one woman in the gallery on the edge of orgasm.

My body was already a jangle of raw nerves and I winced as my nipples started to tighten against his chest. "Just let go."

"And if I can't?"

"You don't have a choice," I snapped. "Go find another woman; it won't be hard."

"You can't tell me that you don't want me."

He covered my mouth with his and I responded before I could think better of it. Parting my lips to his questing tongue was as easy as breathing. His big hands slid down my back and pulled me closer. My body was screaming, "hell, yes," but my mind wasn't having it.

I fisted my hands in the lapels of his jacket and jerked my mouth from his. "Don't."

"Case."

I sucked in a deep breath and closed my eyes against the sudden tears. "I can't do this."

"Do what?"

I met his gaze and tears slid down my cheeks. "I can't be your fuck. I can't be that woman you call in the middle of the night when your bed is cold or you can't sleep. I need something you can't give me and I'm begging you to leave me alone."

He released me and took a step back; concern softened his eyes but his own displeasure was still very evident. Connor wasn't used to women dumping him. He'd been furious two weeks ago when I'd left his apartment and that fury still lingered.

"I don't make it a habit to hurt women."

Well, I doubted seriously he set out to do it, but I was confident I was the most recent in a line of women who didn't get what they wanted from him.

"You never made promises to me." I wiped at the tears and sucked in a deep breath to steady myself. "And I realized that they were never coming. I'm just disappointed. I'll get over it."

"You mean you'll get over me," he muttered.

"You never let me get close enough to get attached. I'm not one of those women who confuse sex and love." I crossed my arms over my breasts and shook my head. "Look, the others will speculate but they won't ask questions. In a few months, they won't even care about what happened between us."

And maybe in a few months I could look at him and not be angry. I turned and walked quickly to the end of the hall and pulled open the door to the office area. At my desk, I pushed off the high-heeled shoes I'd donned for the party and stared at the blank screen of my computer. It had been just a little over a year since I'd taken the promotion that'd pulled me off the sales floor and into the administration area.

Jane Tilwell, my boss and mentor, had thrown a lot in my lap from the very start, but I was confident that I'd proven myself.

The door opened and the click of high heels on the floor told me that one of the women from the party had followed along to see how I was. I glanced up and smiled softly for Mercy Rothell-Montgomery. She was the director of the gallery and one of my favorite people on earth. Gloriously redheaded, strong-minded, and very pregnant, she looked a little out of sorts.

"What did he do to you?"

My mouth dropped open briefly but I shut it quickly. "What? Nothing."

"Don't give me that. You're sitting at your desk, crying in the dark. He did something." She crossed her arms and glared.

I wiped at my damp face, startled that I was still crying. "We just don't work, that's all. He didn't do anything *to* me." I glanced toward the door as it opened again and Jane came through it. Great, I had my doubts about being able to fend them both off. "I'm all right."

Jane came to a stop beside Mercy, took off her shoes, and pursed her lips. "He's at the bar with a scotch neat, and you're in here in the dark. Sounds like you're both just doing great. He looks so miserable I couldn't even lecture him for drinking on duty."

There were plenty of security guards at the party; in fact, Connor hadn't planned to work it at all. However, I'd never known him ever to shirk his duty.

Jane waved at me with her shoes as she continued. "Are you crying?"

"No." I glared at Mercy when she started to speak. "I wouldn't cry over a man." I reached down to pick up my own shoes and shook my head. "Look, you guys, I'm fine. If you two don't go back to the party, your men will come looking for you, and, frankly, if I wanted to be on display I would have stayed at the party."

"The party is over and the men know better." She pointed toward her office. "In there, right now."

Sighing, I stood up and stomped toward her office. "Fine, but I'm not talking about him."

Being made a liar really sucks. I snuggled down in the over-stuffed chair in Jane's office and sighed. The two of them had spent the last hour listening to me bitch about Connor's commitment issues, but I hadn't even skimmed the surface of my real problem.

Jane was on the couch and Mercy was in a chair that matched the one I'd claimed. They both looked irritated, but were at a loss as to what to say to make me feel better. I looked at Mercy's swollen belly and bit my lip.

"I'm thirty years old."